Lucy Morris lives in Esse[x]
two young children and tw[o ...]
massively sweet tooth and [...]
and Irn-Bru. She's a member of the UK Romantic
Novelists' Association, and was delighted when
Mills & Boon accepted her manuscript after she'd
submitted her story to the Warriors Wanted! blitz for
Viking, Medieval and Highlander romances. Writing
for Mills & Boon Historical is a dream come true
for her, and she hopes you enjoy her books!

Also by Lucy Morris

*The Viking Chief's Marriage Alliance
A Nun for the Viking Warrior
The Viking She Loves to Hate
Snowed In with the Viking
'Her Bought Viking Husband'
in Convenient Vows with a Viking
How the Wallflower Wins a Duke
Wedding Night with Her Viking Enemy*

Shieldmaiden Sisters miniseries

*The Viking She Would Have Married
Tempted by Her Outcast Viking
Beguiling Her Enemy Warrior*

Discover more at millsandboon.co.uk.

THE LORD'S MADDENING MISS

Lucy Morris

MILLS & BOON

All rights reserved including the right of reproduction in whole or in part in any form. This edition is published by arrangement with Harlequin Enterprises ULC.

This is a work of fiction. Names, characters, places, locations and incidents are purely fictional and bear no relationship to any real life individuals, living or dead, or to any actual places, business establishments, locations, events or incidents. Any resemblance is entirely coincidental.

This book is sold subject to the condition that it shall not, by way of trade or otherwise, be lent, resold, hired out or otherwise circulated without the prior consent of the publisher in any form of binding or cover other than that in which it is published and without a similar condition including this condition being imposed on the subsequent purchaser.

® and TM are trademarks owned and used by the trademark owner and/or its licensee. Trademarks marked with ® are registered with the United Kingdom Patent Office and/or the Office for Harmonisation in the Internal Market and in other countries.

First published in Great Britain 2025
by Mills & Boon, an imprint of HarperCollins*Publishers* Ltd,
1 London Bridge Street, London, SE1 9GF

www.harpercollins.co.uk

HarperCollins*Publishers*, Macken House, 39/40 Mayor Street Upper, Dublin 1, D01 C9W8, Ireland

The Lord's Maddening Miss © 2025 Lucy Morris

ISBN: 978-0-263-34518-6

05/25

This book contains FSC™ certified paper and other controlled sources to ensure responsible forest management.

For more information visit www.harpercollins.co.uk/green.

Printed and Bound in the UK using 100% Renewable Electricity at CPI Group (UK) Ltd, Croydon, CR0 4YY

For Sue, aka Virginia Heath.
I am eternally grateful for the friendship,
advice and laughs you have given me!
Cheers! x

Prologue

Oxford University,
May 1809

Hawk's head was about to explode, and the steady thumping of the blood in his ears and the constant churning of his stomach were clear indicators that things had taken a debauched turn last night. Which wasn't unexpected, considering they'd been celebrating the end of their time at Oxford.

They had waved goodbye to their youth and were now facing adulthood. He didn't feel like a grown man at this moment with his guts in turmoil.

Hawk gingerly raised himself onto an elbow, his muscles screaming in protest from his long night on the floor.

Why was he on the floor?

A beam of piercing light shot like a bullet through his brain, only adding to his pain and discomfort.

Squinting, he quickly realised that he wasn't in his own room, but Ezra's.

'Ezra?' he croaked, crawling up into a sitting position and gripping the small bed's leg as if it were flotsam in a storm. The sunshine streaming in from the open window seemed determined to blind him, and he shrank away from it with a bad-tempered snarl.

Why on earth hadn't he gone back to his own room?

A grunt was the only answer from the bed, and he slapped Ezra's foot as it twitched beside his neck, tickling it.

Ash was slumped in one of the two chairs, his head dropped on the table and the bottle of cognac still in his hand. Adam was sprawled in the other chair, the back of his head propped precariously on Ezra's bookshelf as he slept.

Would he miss Oxford?

No.

But he would miss these men.

Three long years of studying ancient history, and the only thing he valued were the friends he had made here. But he knew he would do it again in a heartbeat. Anything to avoid the sombre misery of home.

Except, soon they would be parted, to begin their lives and careers… *Wouldn't they?*

A sudden memory of him quoting Shakespeare last night while balancing on a stool popped into his mind. 'Once more unto the breach, dear friends, once more!'

he had roared, waving someone's umbrella in the air as if it were a sabre.

What an idiot!

The vague memory chimed against something else in his muddled brain, but no matter how much he sifted through the thought, he couldn't quite put his finger on it. All he could remember was lots of cheering. Which made sense, as they had been celebrating their graduation and the end of an era.

Hawk sighed miserably at the thought.

He'd learned to laugh here. To relax amongst friends who accepted him for who he was, and not for the role he would eventually play...as a baron and peer. Enjoying brotherly rough-and-tumble japes, drinks and laughs with his friends. The sort of things he could never enjoy with his own brother, the current baron—the Right Honourable Lord Archibald Hawksmere.

He wished he could, but it was impossible.

Archie was too sick, too fragile. He was the head of the family, but his weak heart meant he already had one foot in the grave. Archie loved him, but mostly valued Hawk as his heir, reminding him constantly not to waste his good health and live his life to the full—because one day, Archie would be gone.

His sister Cleo was no comfort. She was too wrapped up in the love of her fiancé Charles and in the planning of their expensive wedding. She was almost gleeful in her desire to escape the role of mother that had been thrust upon her by their parents' untimely deaths.

Archie and Cleo were twins, with a good nine years between themselves and Hawk. They did not feel like his siblings, and instead were more like benevolent guardians. He barely remembered his parents, who had died when he was very young. Which according to Cleo was *probably for the best.* So he had never felt at home anywhere, until he'd met Ash, Adam and Ezra. Now he couldn't imagine a day without them.

With a groan, Hawk stumbled to his feet and valiantly headed towards the jug of water by the wash basin—his salvation.

As he passed Ash, he heard him mumble something like, 'Sweet Amelia, will you do me the honour...' Hawk gave a derisive snort at his friend's rambling.

He needs to propose to that girl quickly before it's too late!

Another chime went off in Hawk's head, but the reason for his thoughts was as elusive as a ghost.

Water. I need water.

He grabbed the jug and drank deeply. It was stale and a little dusty, but beggars couldn't be choosers.

After drinking his fill, he wiped his mouth and belched, grimacing as he tasted smoke and brandy at the back of his throat. He leaned against the wash basin to gather his strength, and then looked around the room with a frown.

He was missing something... But he never missed anything!

It was why he was called Hawk, not only as a nod to his family name, but also because his friends often joked that he never failed to spot a problem.

But what problem was it this time?

They all seemed to have survived the night without any broken bones...even the fiery-tempered Ezra had ended the night without any evidence of a fight or scuffle on his knuckles. His hand still clutched his cravat, the black silk pouring down to the floor from the bed.

A memory flashed in his mind like lightning. All four of them, arm in arm, striding down the street and waving their cravats over their heads. *'For king and country!'*

Hawk swayed towards the table, feeling dizzy as another grim chime rang inside his head.

Ash's white cravat was piled in the centre of the table, along with his blue one and Adam's red.

Red, white and blue.

'Oh, God!' Hawk gasped, bracing his arms against the table and feeling as if he was about to throw up.

Adam woke, rubbing his eyes with a weary sigh and sitting more upright in his seat, wincing at the awkward way his neck had been tilted. 'What time is it? When do we need to go?'

Hawk groaned, his chin dropping to his chest and

wishing he had a chair to sit in; his knees felt weak. 'Did we really...?'

Adam grinned back at him, looking far too spritely for Hawk's comfort. 'Did we...decide to buy ourselves a commission in the cavalry, fight Napoleon and more importantly, piss off my father by not joining the clergy? Well, then yes, we really did decide to do that. No getting out of it now. A promise is a promise.' The final words were said with mock sternness and a wag of his finger. No doubt similar to the way his overbearing father might have done to him.

Hawk gave a grim nod and swallowed the rock in his throat.

'For king and country!' Adam bellowed cheerfully, causing Ezra and Ash to wake up with a jerk.

Ezra fell off the bed, and Ash lifted his head enough to weakly respond with a mumbled, 'For king and country!' before dropping his head back down on the table with a thud. From the floor, Ezra lifted his cravat with a limp wrist and waved it valiantly, repeating in a slightly slurred tone, 'For king and country...' He then grabbed the blankets from the bed and covered his head with them as he grumbled, 'Oh, God! Why is it so bright in here?'

Adam slapped Hawk's arm, which as usual did nothing considering the size of Hawk. 'Look at you. You were born for this!'

Hawk nodded, accepting his fate. There was no

point in denying it. Where his brothers led, he would follow—to watch their backs and keep them safe.

They were his family, and he would protect them. After all, there was nothing he could do for his brother and sister now, except wait. A prospect that turned his stomach far more than even the idea of warfare, because he *couldn't* stay. Not if it was just to watch his brother slowly fade away until he needed *replacing*. Even if it was inevitable, Hawk could not face it. Watching Archie die would be unbearable. He knew his brother well; he would spend the time he had left *preparing* Hawk for his new role. No, he'd rather not face that…not yet.

One last adventure with his friends seemed fitting. *Still… Why did it have to be the cavalry?*

'I bloody *hate* horses,' he grumbled.

Chapter One

Lady Bulphan's ball,
May 1816

Seven years of fighting in the bloodiest of campaigns, and for what? So that he could stand in Lady Bulphan's ballroom and be bored out of his mind?

The twirling silks and feathers were such a strange sight after all the blood and gore he'd witnessed over the years, that it almost hurt to look at the oblivious ton parading around in their gaudy finery.

Flexing his fists, he tried to remind his body that there was nothing to fear or feel anxious about; he was home. But his body couldn't seem to shake the memories of battle. The loud music and bustling crowd made his head spin, and he frowned darkly at the dancers as he reminded himself that he was no longer in danger...that *this* was normal.

But it didn't feel normal. More than anything he

wanted to go home. Read a book with a glass of whisky in hand and enjoy some peace and quiet.

But a wager was a wager, and he had lost. Something he very rarely did, and which always irritated him. But just as he had followed his friends into battle, he would follow them into the mouth of the ton—if he had to. Although, as another bejewelled mama craned her neck to catch his eye, he thought he might actually *prefer* a battlefield.

He swept his gaze away, ignoring her completely and praying she would move on to the next poor fellow. Thankfully, she did, her feathers bristling like a peacock as she huffed past him with obvious annoyance.

Where were the others? He'd met up with Adam and the others early on, and then promptly lost them again, not long after he'd arrived.

Ash, he could understand leaving early, and although he'd tried to deny it, seeing Amelia again must have stung. He had never confessed his feelings to her, and she'd married someone else with a heavier purse in the intervening years that he'd been away at war. Now she was a rich and merry widow by all accounts. Such a thing would leave a bitter taste in any man's mouth.

If he'd left...could Hawk leave, too?

But then he saw Ash waltzing with the very woman he should have avoided—Amelia.

Well, that won't end well!

But where was Ezra? The man was harder to catch than smoke. He'd not seen him since their initial greeting, although he was probably on a similar mission to Adam's. Searching for a pretty chit to hang off his arm—something to take their minds off their other troubles.

Hawk worried about all of his friends, but currently Adam concerned him the most.

Adam's constant bravado was a mask, and he could tell his best friend was struggling. His brother's decline in health and soaring debts were taking their toll on his friend. Hawk understood the burden and grief of a dying brother all too well, and despite Adam's charming smiles and flirtatious distractions, he knew he was deeply troubled about the future.

Unfortunately, there was only one *legal* solution open to him—a profitable marriage. If Adam was ever going to train in the law, he needed funds to do so.

Although, Hawk wasn't sure if Adam had accepted his fate yet. Had he gone searching for a distraction, or a bride amongst the dazzling array of women on offer?

Either way, Hawk pitied him.

Out of all his friends, Hawk suspected he was the only one *not* looking for a marriage partner. Ezra needed a bride to please the viscount, while Adam's and Ash's needs were far more…financial.

They all had their reasons. But Hawk was lucky—

he wasn't affluent by any means, but as the Baron Hawksmere, he was a man with a small amount of land and some income. Surely, he could respectfully maintain himself and his sister Cleo until he sorted out her finances properly, something he was determined to do.

Hawk would never marry; a couple of dalliances here and there with courtesans or discreet widows possibly. But he had no intention of fathering a family of his own. His nephews could be his heirs…

After all, there were enough of them!

His brother-in-law Charles had done *something* right before he died, even if it was only begetting more mouths to feed. Frankly, he didn't care about his hereditary title and would happily let it fall into oblivion, as long as his sister and nephews were comfortable.

No, he was content to manage his personal affairs and avoid society altogether. Except for Wednesday at White's with his friends… *That* was sacrosanct!

A young miss waved her fan alluringly at him, and he had to sharply look away to avoid encouraging her.

He *really* shouldn't be here. *This was a complete waste of time!*

He hated social events at the best of times; he always felt so awkward. He didn't have the slim, elegant figure of a dandy. He looked like a great hulking bear compared to the men around him, and he didn't have

Adam's charm, Ezra's good looks or Ash's friendly manner, either. He just...didn't fit in.

Besides, Lady Bulphan's ball was a marriage market and he was most definitely *not* buying. Women only caused problems, and Cleo was hard enough to deal with at present. He should be checking through the accounts, finding out where all that damn money had gone.

But instead, he was stuck here, like a classical statue watching the chaos unfold around him. He needed a drink. But he'd given his whisky flask to Adam.

Damn! But it was a fine whisky, too—nothing like the usual tongue-stripping moonshine that came illicitly down from the Highlands; it was far smoother and richer than anything he'd ever tasted before, and had an amber glow to it. He'd discovered it at White's and been quietly informed that it was smuggled in with the Scottish beer from Sunshine Brewery.

As he was entertaining himself by reminiscing on the fine quality of his favourite tipple, a feminine fragrance of peach and blossom tickled his nose.

He heard her before he saw her.

A rich and husky Scottish accent that seemed to have been conjured up by his thoughts of Highland whisky. Except her tone was distinctly sharp and laced with disapproval. 'Are you Lord Hawksmere? I have a bone to pick with you, *my lord*!'

There was so much contempt in her tone he doubted

the nod to his title was sincere; she'd said it as if she were scraping something off her shoe.

'I am Lord Hawksmere.' He turned and looked down at her. Surprised at the great distance between them considering her imperious tone.

Staring up at him was a short, plump and rather pretty redhead. If her lilting brogue wasn't enough of a giveaway, the plaid overdress to her gown announced her heritage in a tapestry of blues and greens. Her hands were firmly planted on her ample hips as if she was about to scold him.

This was no simpering debutante; this was a woman in her prime who had the courage of a lion.

'And you are, madam?' he asked dryly, unsure of what he could have possibly done to enrage her. He'd never seen her before in his life, and he would surely remember her, with her startlingly direct pansy-blue eyes.

Her scowl deepened. 'My name is *Miss* Maggie Mackenzie, and I am your sister's neighbour!' Shockingly, she followed this by poking him firmly in the chest with her finger. 'You would know that if you ever cared to visit!'

Maggie was seething, which was unusual for her, but Lord Hawksmere had managed the impossible. He was an arrogant, imposing, miserable English lord—

everything she hated in a man. It also didn't help that he'd treated her friend Cleo terribly.

She had been in two minds whether to come tonight, and had only agreed because her uncle had insisted she accompany him, *To help keep the debutantes away!* he'd joked. But he wasn't entirely wrong; the ton hated that William was wealthy and still unmarried. But she knew he mainly wanted to go out to cheer her up.

Since arriving in London for the season, they'd both been shocked by the decline in Cleo's home and appearance.

In Maggie's opinion, Cleo's brother was a miserly, cold-hearted man who cared nothing for anyone but himself. Since returning from war, he'd abandoned his widowed sister and her four young bairns to fend for themselves. Where was this man's sense of duty, his love for his family? His care and compassion?

It was non-existent!

Last year Cleo had buried her twin brother and her husband within a couple of months of each other. No wonder she was so broken, and what was her youngest sibling doing to help? Drinking and sneering at all the guests at Lady Bulphan's ball!

As if he were so far above them! Which, granted, he was...physically at least.

The man was a giant, as well as a brute!

She'd seen him from across the room and realised the family resemblance immediately. Black hair and dark eyes, handsome features—although, he lacked the elegance of his older siblings and appeared far more...robust. He had a thick, square jaw and a twisted nose that suggested it had been broken at one time. She'd asked a few of her friends and sure enough, he was indeed Baron Hawksmere...or she supposed she should say The Right Honourable Lord Hawksmere...or perhaps she should use his military title, Colonel Hawksmere?

No, that didn't seem right.

It was all so confusing!

She wasn't familiar with the English rules—and had never cared to learn them, as she didn't speak to the aristocracy of the ton often, and Archie had always been...well, just... *Archie*, at least to her, and not *my lord* or *Baron Hawksmere*. What was his Christian name? Archie and Cleo always called him *Hawk*.

Surely, he wasn't Hawk Hawksmere? It seemed daft, but plausible... The English were odd.

When she had imagined Cleo and Archie's younger brother, she had pictured someone very much like them in appearance. There was even a family portrait of them in their townhouse. Willowy, elegant Cleo and Archie, with a slightly rotund and much smaller little brother standing next to them, a bad-tempered scowl on his chubby little face. She'd always imagined him to grow up much the same as his siblings... despite the bulky start.

Except he hadn't. He was a bear of a man. The well-tailored cut of his dark blue tailcoat accentuated his thick, muscular chest and broad shoulders. Cleo had said he was a cavalry man and she could well imagine it, with his thick thighs and impossibly long legs. She guessed he would be terrifying in battle, charging across a field, his sabre raised.

But Maggie was a Scot and she refused to be intimidated by some Sassenach lord. She would gladly give him a piece of her mind, regardless of his scowls! And so she had...loudly.

'Perhaps you should lower your voice, miss, before you cause a scene,' Lord Hawksmere said curtly, his tone low and menacing as he backed her up into the alcove, out of sight from prying eyes.

'Is that all you care about, appearances?' she hissed. 'Well, my lord, perhaps you should care a little more about your sister and nephews' appearances! Or should I say the lack of! They barely leave that mausoleum of a house according to Mrs Wimple—she's the housekeeper in case you didn't know. The boys are bouncing off the walls, while your sister spends most of her days in bed! What little allowance you send them is barely enough to cover their daily food and candle expenses. They are on the edge of ruin!

I am sure your brother Archie would be horrified by the state they are in!'

A flush crept up Lord Hawksmere's neck, but she suspected it wasn't due to embarrassment. His eyes were dark pools of obsidian and they narrowed on her as he snapped, 'You have no idea what you are talking about, Miss Mackenzie!'

'And you do?' She gave him a bitter laugh. 'When was the last time you visited Cleo and the boys? Mrs Wimple tells me you've only called on them once since returning to England! Once, in what? Six months!'

He blinked, and she could tell she had finally struck a chord in him. 'I have seen her several times.'

'Oh, yes! At the tea rooms or the solicitor's office. How gracious of you! Perhaps you should come and see her at home. See the truth of it for yourself! Four boys do not survive on fresh air alone, my lord!'

She was about to spin away, triumphant in her dressing down of him, when her uncle chose that unfortunate moment to barrel over to them. Completely oblivious to the tension between them, and more than a little merry from the champagne—his accent as thick as a highland fog—he said, 'Ah, Maggie! I have been searching high and low for ye! Will you not introduce me to yer friend?' William gave her an unsubtle wink, and she wished at that moment that she hadn't been quite so courageous in confronting Lord Hawksmere.

Her inebriated uncle would see Lord Hawksmere as a potential suitor, and that made her nervous. Her uncle was not subtle in wanting to find her a match—unfortunately, in a moment of weakness, she had once confessed that she only wanted to marry for love. William had vowed to help her find it—even if he was a little indelicate in *helping* her at times. Usually, she laughed it off, but she doubted she could do that this time!

Crisply, she replied, 'This is Cleo's brother, *Lord Hawksmere*. My lord, this is my uncle, Mr William Mackenzie.' She hoped she'd put enough venom in his name to convey her disapproval—and she'd mentioned her bad impression of Cleo's brother a hundred times before, so surely, he would take the hint and they could make their excuses and leave…

Sadly, he did not.

With her uncle's usual cheerfulness, he cried, 'Ah, yes, a pleasure to meet you, Lord Hawksmere! Did you also get in touch with us about investing in Sunshine Brewery? I had to admit I was surprised when I saw your name on the letter of interest. We have been friends of your family for many years—but I'm sure you were too busy fighting Napoleon to remember our names being mentioned by your sister or brother. I wanted to arrange a proper meeting with you. How fortunate we have crossed paths tonight!'

Both Lord Hawksmere and Maggie blinked in surprise.

Was he interested in her family's company?

Lord Hawksmere recovered first. 'You're the owner of Sunshine Brewery?'

'Part owner. My brother and I own the company together. Affordable, delicious beer for Scotland and beyond...*amongst other things*.' Uncle William gave a very unsubtle wink that made her eyes roll—he really needed to be more careful in the future, especially about her own little illicit venture. 'We like to experiment,' her uncle added with a proud smile in Maggie's direction. 'Did you know Maggie is our company's namesake? She's our Miss Sunshine, helping to ensure each brew is as delicious as the last.'

'Is that so?' said Lord Hawksmere. The dry smile on his lips suggested he thought her anything but a *Miss Sunshine*.

'Indeed, she was born not long after we'd produced our first successful brew!' explained her uncle enthusiastically, oblivious to the baron's tone. 'She's lived up to it, too. Everybody loves her. She is witty, clever and the kindest soul you could ever care to meet! Heaven only knows why she's not married yet, when all of her silly sisters are. Honestly, it is beyond me! Granted, she doesn't have much in way of a dowry—but I'm sure you ken a good investment when you see it.'

'Uncle!' Maggie gasped in horror. This was far

worse than she could have *ever* imagined. Her uncle blushed, realising his mistake by the rebuke in her tone. Taking a deep breath, she added, 'Perhaps I should get you a glass of water, Uncle?' Not waiting for a reply, she turned to stride away.

Unfortunately, she still managed to hear Lord Hawksmere's stern reply, because the waltz happened to end at that very moment, and his words felt like a shout in the sudden quiet of the ballroom. 'Mr Mackenzie, believe me, I have *no interest* in anything other than your business.'

Chapter Two

'What an *odious, mutton-heided lout*!' Maggie grumbled as she slathered a generous dollop of jam on her morning roll. She needed the sweetness to take away the bitter sting of Lord Hawksmere's outrageous snub last night.

He had ruined her night at one of the highlights of the London season. Lady Bulphan's ball was always exceptionally fun and attended by all. But last night she'd left early, too embarrassed to remain after his callous words. Anyone with half a brain would have realised he was talking about her. From past experience, she knew the best thing to do was run and hide. She'd practically dragged her poor uncle out by his elbow.

At least she knew that people would quickly forget or lose interest, especially if she pretended ignorance. However, she still resented the rudeness of the man and had decided to avoid reading the gossip columns, in case it had been mentioned.

'Are you still raging about Lord Hawksmere?' Her uncle sighed, looking over the rim of his coffee cup with one auburn brow raised. 'I checked the papers. It only mentions that Lord Hawksmere has declared he will remain a bachelor "much to some people's disappointment." Nothing about you at all, and I imagine you weren't the only one snubbed by him that night… Och, Maggie, it's not like you to mither over something so silly as a young man's approval.'

She bristled, making her own coffee strong with a heavy dose of sugar. 'Approval? *You* practically offered me to him on a plate. It was humiliating! Who is to say that *I* would ever consider him, either? Pompous, numpty-headed…*odious man*!' Her final insults ended in a growl.

'I said I was sorry, lass. I thought you were getting on well. You were so close to one another…in the *shadows*,' her uncle teased, and she scowled back at him, not quite ready to forgive his part in it. She loved her uncle dearly and was very close to him—he wasn't far off in age from her with only eleven years between them, and most people said they were alike in both colouring and temperament. Which was a kind way of saying they were both friendly redheads with a *sturdy* figure.

'We were not *in the shadows*! It was an alcove—of sorts, and I was giving him a piece of my mind!' Maggie said defensively.

But she quickly blushed, realising she *had* stood a little too close to Lord Hawksmere and had even poked him in the chest with her finger. She squirmed at the memory; she had expected soft flesh to meet her finger, but had been met by hard muscle instead. She fumbled with her coffee cup as she stirred it. 'You must agree that he has treated Cleo terribly.'

William looked out of the breakfast room and into the garden, avoiding her eyes and appearing to find great interest in the pretty blossom and flowers outside the large windows. 'You are a loyal friend, Maggie. But I suspect Cleo hasn't been entirely honest with you or even herself…especially when it comes to Charles.'

Uncle William had always disliked Cleo's husband, Charles. Maggie couldn't understand why as the man had always been charming and friendly with her.

Thoughtfully, she asked, 'I don't suppose *you* feel anything…more for Cleo. Beyond friendly affection?'

Her uncle visibly flinched in his seat before answering with a deep sigh. 'Do not get yourself unnecessarily excited over fanciful notions, my dear. Cleo needs friends not admirers at this difficult time. Besides, she would never consider me.'

Maggie was not convinced by his answer, and in fact, it gave her hope. 'But you *have* considered her? And why wouldn't she consider you? You are of a similar age, enjoy spending time together… And she has been a widow now for over a year. It would be perfectly acceptable if you were to show an interest in her. It might even help her out of this melancholy.'

'Maggie...' he warned. 'I know how you love to see romance everywhere and encourage matchmaking wherever you go, but you must not interfere in this regard.'

'But wouldn't it be wonderful for my two closest friends to fall in love and marry?'

'Cleo is still grieving her husband and brother. *That* was clear when we arrived.'

That put a damp blanket over her plans. 'Yes, I must concede that she is very much still in mourning.' She shook her head. 'You are right. We must be sensitive of her situation. She has lost a beloved husband and the father of her children, as well as her twin brother in the same year. We must support her in every way that we can.'

And if something were to happen naturally between Cleo and William...then all the better! Maggie thought with a smile.

It broke her heart to think of sweet Cleo alone for the rest of her days. Especially as William would make a wonderful partner and stepfather to her children. The boys already adored him.

Before she could ponder that thought any further, William said, 'I had a letter yesterday...from yer mother. She wants to be kept informed of your progress this season, as she's unable to join us this year.'

Maggie lived most of the year in Scotland with her family. But when the marriage market of Edinburgh had offered her family little hope for her, her mother had insisted she attend the London season instead, praying that the current fashion and *novelty* as a Scot would help her fare better with suitors. *It hadn't.*

Despite the sweetness of her coffee, it still tasted bitter on her tongue. 'What *progress* does she expect? I have plenty of friends and enjoy my time here, but I've never once been courted. The marriage ship has most definitely sailed, and *without* me on it, thank heavens!'

He frowned. 'You don't mean that.'

She didn't. Maggie loved love and wanted nothing more than to experience it. But she would gladly die on the rack before admitting it.

No, it was much better to help others; at least then there was a chance she would succeed.

'What is the point of wishing for something that is so unlikely to happen? Tell my mother to stop fretting! And…do be more careful about what you say in public. I thought you were about to let slip about our other *little venture*. It will do us no good to have that snuffed out before it's even begun.'

'But he's a lord! He might have influence in government and help us to end these ridiculous taxes.'

'He may…' She paused for effect. 'Or he may get us

sent to the old bailey. Let's try to get help from people we know and *trust* first.'

Maggie's small whisky distillery and smuggling business was a little hobby of theirs, which would seem like madness to most people, but the Mackenzies took a perverse pleasure in flouting English laws. Her uncle was also using his influence in London circles to help guide future whisky licensing and laws—so it wasn't completely deranged. They hoped that Maggie's little distillery would grow into a reputable business one day and be ahead of its time in both quality and production because of her illicit work now.

'Sorry, lass, it won't happen again. I'd had too much to drink and forgot myself,' William conceded. 'I will also let your mother know all is well.'

All is well. A coded message of reassurance to her mother. It basically said that Uncle William would be taking Maggie to all the great balls and entertainments that London had to offer. That he would be placing her in the best possible situations to secure her a match. But that, as usual, there were no suitors on the horizon to speak of.

Her mother was English, so she probably thought prospects would be better down south. A mistake, but a well-meaning one.

Still, it always depressed Maggie to know that she was disappointing her mother, even with nearly four hundred miles between them. But nothing could change the fact that she was an old hen in a coop full of sprightly young things. Some London families had more than one daughter out this season, and after the war there was definitely a shortage of young men. Maggie had no hope of a match this season, which never normally bothered her, but having it pointed out so plainly to someone like Lord Hawksmere had made her feel more undesirable than ever.

She needed to cheer herself up.

Perhaps playing with Cleo's boys would help?

After breakfast, Maggie made her way out into the garden, not bothering with a shawl because she had no intention of staying outside for long. She carried a small bag of gifts in her hand.

Their garden was only a narrow patch of land with the mews behind it—nothing like the sprawling country estate back home. But it was south-facing, full of light and it always made her feel brighter in spirit. When visiting Cleo, she always preferred this route; it saved her having to put on her spencer jacket for propriety's sake or bother Mrs Wimple, who was already overstretched as it was, due to Cleo's lack of servants.

Mrs Wimple was both cook and housekeeper, while her husband, Mr Wimple, was the coachman and butler. Their daughter Daisy was both scullery maid and nanny; their son Robert both groom and footman. It was a ridiculous situation considering Archie had previously employed eight servants in total to run the house. But the others had all left for better paid positions, or at least positions that *actually* paid.

Maggie made her way down the patio steps and through her landscaped garden with its carefully sculpted hedges, pergolas and pristine flower beds. The bees flitting merrily around the roses and marigolds without a care in the world. She walked past the stone benches, and then squeezed through the gap in the wall that separated them from their neighbours and the mews.

It was reasonably easy to get through, and her dress barely snagged on the climbing clematis and honeysuckle as she wiggled through the gap. She sighed a little when she saw the state of Cleo's garden in comparison to her own. It was definitely much worse than it had been last season, and she hadn't walked through the garden when they first arrived a couple of days ago, as Uncle William had wanted a more formal greeting.

That had been a grim affair, Cleo a mere shell of a woman still wearing black despite the time for mourning clothes having already passed. Before they left, Maggie had grilled Mrs Wimple about it. But Mrs Wimple had only worried her further, explaining that since Charles's death, things had only gone from bad to worse.

The cupboards were stripped of all luxuries, and Cleo had only been visited by her husband's solicitor and her brother once; she had refused all other callers until no one bothered to visit anymore.

She had moved her family into her brother's home two years ago to help care for him. But it seemed she had no intention of returning to her old home—perhaps the memories were too difficult to bear since her husband's death?

Maggie wished she'd come down sooner to help her through the grief of Charles. But her sister Anne's child had been unwell, and Maggie had felt torn between consoling her friend and helping her family.

Guilt gnawed at her belly as she looked at the miserable garden... She'd never imagined it would get this bad.

Had Cleo let her gardener go? Maggie wondered how she might sneak her own gardener in to do some tidying up. She knew that there would be no point in offering it. Cleo was proud to a fault, and Maggie would have to suggest some day out with the boys to manage it. Perhaps they could take a trip to the pleasure gardens? Or, better yet, go for some tea and ices at Gunter's in Berkely Square. Something inexpensive and *reasonably* quiet, or Cleo would make some excuse not to go. She'd never been very sociable *before* her husband's death, so Maggie imagined it would be much worse now.

As she walked through the overgrown tangle of bushes and weeds, she noted that the boys' tree swing looked as if it had seen better days, the rope dangerously threadbare. There were balls and croquet sets scattered in the overgrown lawn that were a hazard underfoot, and Maggie almost tripped over one of the hoops.

Yes, it was definitely worse. The problem was that she and Uncle William weren't here most of the time. Only coming to London for the social season, and then returning to Scotland for the rest of the year. William to his Edinburgh townhouse, and Maggie to her family's country estate with its old distillery.

A team of twelve servants managed the upkeep of their London townhouse in their absence, or whenever her extended family decided they wanted a change of scene. Which meant it was rarely left unattended for long.

The Mackenzie clan was a large and sprawling one, after all. The Mackenzie brewery kept them affluent and well looked after, but there were so many of them, all working within the same company, that her father often joked that they were far richer on paper than in pennies. However, they were still far better off than poor Cleo by the looks of it, which proved her father wrong.

She took the servant steps down to the basement kitchen. As usual, the door was unlocked, but Mrs Wimple was nowhere to be seen. She put her little bag of gifts on the table, where Mrs Wimple would easily find it, and made her way towards the sounds of thunder that could only be the boys causing mischief upstairs.

They were in the music room, or what would have been the music room, but currently looked more like a battlefield. Peter, the eldest, had created a fort out of an old bed sheet and draped it over the pianoforte, poking his head out from beneath it, a battalion of tin soldiers laid out in squares in front of him. While the twins, Francis and Thomas, were rolling billiard balls at them with paper bicorn hats on their heads, shouting, 'Die, English dogs!' in an insultingly bad French accent.

'Gracious!' declared Maggie, announcing her presence just as one billiard ball smacked into the leg of the pianoforte and ricocheted back, flying past her skirts into the hall.

'Maggie!' the boys shouted in unison, dashing away from their positions to swarm her in sticky fingers and hugs. She embraced them back, dropping a little to gather them close, realising miserably that they were all so much taller than the last time she had seen them.

'Where's baby Matthew?'

'Daisy's taken him for his nap. He can walk now... just about,' said Peter.

Well, that explained why they were alone and causing mischief.

'Where's your mother?' she asked lightly, hoping that they wouldn't say *in bed*.

Peter pulled away first, a serious look on his face that was far too wise for his six years. 'She got dressed today. Our uncle is here.'

'Lord Hawksmere?' she gasped.

Had he actually listened to her? Was that why he was visiting now?

Francis and Thomas both nodded, speaking over each other.

'She's crying again.'

'Uncle makes her cry.'

Maggie stiffened. 'Well, we shall see about that! You boys keep playing—although be gentle with the billiard balls!'

They nodded, Peter adding, 'They are in the drawing room.'

Maggie gave them another quick hug and then left.

It wasn't long before she heard a raised masculine voice from the direction of the drawing room. She quickened her pace and gave a little knock as she heard Lord Hawksmere thunder, 'What did you expect, Cleo? *He lied to you!* Why can you not understand that? He lied!'

She heard a loud sob from inside the room, and it was too much for Maggie to ignore so she stepped inside without invitation or announcement, not caring for the consequences.

Chapter Three

Hawk glared at the unwelcome intrusion. He'd sent Mrs Wimple out to get more supplies, as the cupboards were bare. But he'd told the boys not to bother them unless it was urgent, so he was more than a little surprised when an unexpected copper-headed guest waltzed into the room as if she owned it.

'Good morning, Cleo!' Miss Mackenzie gave Hawk a sharp look as if he was as welcome as a drunk lech in a nunnery. *'Lord Hawksmere.'*

Why did he feel as if he was in trouble? Damn and blast it! He owned this house!

Taking a moment to calm himself, he put the sheaf of papers he'd been holding on the mantelpiece and tucked them behind the clock and an odd arrangement of pebbles and rocks, probably curated by the children. The amount of clutter on every surface of this house constantly astounded him. After years with very few personal possessions, he found it uncomfortable to be surrounded by so much *useless* stuff.

He took a deep breath to calm the building frustration with Cleo that had caused him to raise his voice. He didn't like to shout at her, but he didn't know how else he was going to make her realise the magnitude of the situation.

The worst part of it all were the lies. He'd known about some of the debt; had thought he'd paid it off. But apparently, there was more that Cleo was hiding from him—foolishly hoping to sort it out herself without his knowledge. Until he knew the situation fully, he couldn't move forward with any of his plans of investing...*or even know if he had enough money to invest at all.*

The interfering neighbour from next door was the least of his worries, but he resented her presence because politeness dictated he welcome her—even when she'd flouted all rules of society herself by entering unannounced.

'Did the boys let you in, Miss Mackenzie? I am sorry we didn't hear the bell ring...'

Had the little band of hellions scurried out, leaving the front door open behind them?

He wouldn't put it past them. Glancing towards the window he noticed the outside street was thankfully empty—so they hadn't escaped. There seemed to be no order or discipline in the house or children, and certainly not enough staff to manage either properly.

Miss Mackenzie gave him a haughty look as she

said mildly, 'I would be surprised if you could hear anything at all. You seemed rather *animated*. But as it happens, I came in my usual way.'

What did that mean...her usual way? Had she leapt over the wall? Climbed in through a window? What on earth was this daft woman talking about?

Cleo seemed to know because she gave her a beaming smile and rushed to welcome her, taking her hand and leading her towards the low sofa. 'I am so glad you are here, Maggie. As soon as Mrs Wimple is back, I shall order us some tea.'

They were conspiring against him. With a deep and resigned sigh, Hawk took the opposite chaise longue. To his alarm he sank deeply in the seat, his knees almost in line with his shoulders. He dreaded to think what he must look like, his bottom sunk to the floor.

'Oh, I should have said! The boys broke it the other day.' Cleo gasped, but to his annoyance, Miss *Sunshine* giggled.

Miss Mackenzie, *or Maggie*, as his sister called her, pointed to the end of the tattered piece of furniture. 'It is a little more...*firm* at that end.'

Groaning with discomfort and a large measure of annoyance, Hawk managed to rally the strength in his knees to rise up from his sunken seat and stood. It was like trying to mount a horse from a ditch and he grunted a little with the effort.

'I hope you don't mind,' Maggie spoke to Cleo,

thankfully turning away from his indignity to clutch his sister's hands. 'But in your letter you mentioned having to dye some of your dresses to become mourning dresses, and so I brought some greys and lavenders with me—for the transition back into society. I thought you might appreciate a few different styles... when you are ready, of course. I don't mean to rush you...just thought I'd give you some options.'

Hawk bristled at the implication they were too poor to buy mourning clothes, which, to be fair, might not be far off the truth. At least until he sorted the truth of their accounts—something he was hoping to do with Cleo today, except they'd been interrupted.

He took one of the chairs from the side of the room and thudded it down beside the useless chaise longue. 'I am sure nothing you own will fit my sister, Miss Mackenzie.' Before sitting down, he glanced meaningfully at her small curvy figure. She was half the height of Cleo's long, thin frame. 'Although, we thank you for the kindness.'

Hopefully, she would get the hint and leave.

Miss Mackenzie stiffened, her blue pansy eyes narrowing sharply on him. 'I never said they were mine. They are my aunt's, and are much more suited to Cleo's elegant frame.' She turned back to Cleo with a haughty sniff before squeezing her hand gently. 'I shall send them round to you. Take whatever you wish.'

Cleo nodded with thanks, but she seemed distant, distracted even. Her eyes not quite focused on anything at all. In contrast, Miss Mackenzie was as vibrant as a marigold, the mop of red ringlets bouncing at the nape of her neck with each movement she made. The emerald green of her gown highlighting the contrasting colour of her hair beautifully. She really was a striking woman, the kind one couldn't ignore, even if one wanted to. However, she had no such problem with him, pointedly ignoring Hawk and turning away as if dismissing *him* from the room.

Had he somehow offended Miss Mackenzie? Was it the comment about their different shapes? But why would that trouble her? Of course, she was a different shape to Cleo, who was as thin as a stick at the best of times, and so much worse since the deaths of her husband and brother. He had to admit he'd been deeply worried about the decline in her appearance when he'd first seen her, and his return hadn't seemed to have helped matters, either.

The black mourning gown—which she still wore despite it being over a year since Charles's death—only seemed to highlight the paleness of her skin and the dark circles beneath her eyes. After not seeing her for years, he'd been shocked by the change in his sister; she was little more than a skeleton, devoid of colour and life.

Perhaps it was for the best that Miss Mackenzie had

interrupted them... He had let his frustration with her get the better of him. Perhaps he should be gentler with Cleo, more understanding...like Miss Mackenzie, he realised, although he hated to admit it.

A clatter from the entrance announced Mrs Wimple's return, and she entered the room after a polite tap, still wearing her bonnet and jacket, and looking flushed in the cheeks from her trip. She only seemed mildly surprised by the presence of Miss Mackenzie, which was telling in itself.

'My lord, I did as you asked. All the deliveries will arrive later today.'

'Thank you, Mrs Wimple,' he replied, pausing a little before asking, 'Are you able to serve some tea for the ladies?' He hoped there was enough in the stores to manage such a task. 'Or perhaps you have somewhere to be, Miss Mackenzie?' *Like your own home.*

Miss Mackenzie shook her head briskly. 'Nowhere at all, my lord. I actually brought some gifts from Edinburgh with me, Mrs Wimple. You will find them in the kitchen. Perhaps you could serve them? I think the boys will appreciate the shortbread.'

To Hawk's surprise, Mrs Wimple beamed at Miss Mackenzie as if she were a Scottish saint bestowing a miracle of biscuits upon the world. 'They will, indeed, Miss Mackenzie! I'll be back shortly with the tea.' With a respectful dip she hurried from the room, looking far more jubilant than before.

Not thinking he could bear any more pleasantries—or uncomfortable seats—he rose, startling both women with his sudden movement. 'Excuse me, ladies. I will leave you to your tea. I have some matters to attend to. Cleo, once your guest has left, we can discuss our matters further, yes?' Before he left, he took the papers from the mantelpiece, looking meaningfully at his sister to indicate that their discussion was not over.

As he closed the door behind him, he heard Miss Mackenzie ask, 'Shall I stay forever?'

He frowned as he heard Cleo giggle in response. 'Yes, please!'

Oddly, the lack of respect didn't bother him. Mainly because it was the first time he had heard Cleo laugh since he'd returned from war.

Perhaps Miss Mackenzie wasn't so bad after all?

'Sadly, I think it will be permanent,' said Cleo with a miserable sigh as she sipped her cup of tea, ignoring the biscuit on her plate. 'He plans to move in next week and let his rooms go at The Albany.'

It was a short time after Lord Hawksmere had left. The tea had arrived and they were now able to speak more freely, safe in the knowledge that his study door was firmly closed. Maggie was hoping she could get some shortbread into her friend, something to fatten her up, but unfortunately, Cleo hadn't eaten a crumb.

Maggie frowned, sympathising with her poor friend's circumstances. 'I suppose it is his home, too... But what about *your* old house?'

Cleo had only moved in to help with her ailing brother. Maggie had thought it a little strange that she'd not moved back home after Archie's death, but had presumed Cleo found comfort in her childhood home after the loss of her brother, and Charles had said they needed to do some renovations.

Cleo's bottom lip wobbled. 'Apparently, it is already gone. Sold away. Hawk—my brother—that's what he insists we call him...' She took another deep breath. 'Well, he says that Charles sold it... But...that can't be right. He was living there and overseeing the renovations...right up until...'

Maggie knew what she was going to say before the sob strangled her friend. She hurried to take her hand to comfort her. 'All will be well, sweetheart, I swear it.'

'No,' cried Cleo, shaking her head firmly. 'Nothing will ever be right ever again. It's all my fault, Maggie.'

'How could it be your fault? Charles died because of an accident. It was no one's fault.'

Well, that wasn't entirely true.

Charles had been an overly confident rider, often to the point of recklessness. She'd seen him racing curricles in the park, and he'd had a thoroughbred he could barely handle. She hadn't been surprised when she'd heard he'd fallen from his curricle and broken his neck.

But Cleo seemed determined to take the blame for it as she wiped her eyes and said, 'It *was* my fault. I kept pestering him to come and stay with us. He was always racing back and forth between the two houses.'

'You were grieving the loss of Archie. Of course, you wanted your husband by your side. It was just unfortunate about the woodworm…' Maggie frowned, wondering how true the story of the woodworm was, or if her uncle was right and Charles had been keeping secrets from Cleo. Now that she thought about it, Charles had been very vague about the renovations, always insisting that Cleo stay away as the floors were dangerous.

Strangely, Cleo seemed to take comfort in the mention of the woodworm. 'Yes, and that must be why Charles had to sell the house! We couldn't live there anymore, and woodworm is such a terrible pest—it gets in everywhere. Better to sell up and buy somewhere new.'

Confused, Maggie asked, 'So, you *did* know about the house being sold?'

Cleo stiffened, reaching for the teapot as she poured them another cup, despite them being barely half-empty.

'Cleo?'

She shrugged, not meeting her eyes. 'Charles would

never lie to me about anything...' She shook her head firmly, her dark eyes full of emotion. 'He must have told me and I simply forgot—or I wasn't paying attention. That must be it. I was just so busy dealing with Archie's funeral. He *must* have told me.'

Maggie wasn't sure what to believe. The only thing for certain was that her friend was deeply troubled.

'What about your allowance—has Lord Hawksmere increased it?'

Cleo stiffened, and then began to pour more tea. 'It was silly of me to try to live on so little. I just... Hawk is my little brother. I was embarrassed.'

That, Maggie could believe. Cleo had refused any offer of help from her; the only things she would accept were gifts for the children or second-hand clothes.

'I think you should get some fresh air,' Maggie said decisively, after they chatted for a long time about everything and nothing, hoping to distract Cleo from her woes. 'Or, we could go get ices?'

'Oh, I don't think I can... I'm still in mourning,' Cleo said half-heartedly, and it wasn't the first time she'd heard such excuses. Cleo was never keen to leave the comfort of her home.

Maggie tried to cajole her gently. 'No one would judge you, Cleo. It's been over a year since Charles's and Archie's passing. I understand it must be difficult for you. But people will expect to see you back in society soon.'

'They can expect whatever they please!' She bristled, this time with a stubborn tilt to her jaw. 'I will not forget my husband so easily! You cannot expect me to go *dancing* like a merry widow!'

'Not dancing... Just out of the house.' Maggie tried a different approach. 'Surely, the boys must be desperate to stretch their legs...'

'They have the garden, and Mrs Wimple or Daisy sometimes takes them out.'

Maggie took a deep breath. 'But a trip to the pleasure gardens or the park with you would be far more enjoyable for them, and surely it would tire them out more than the garden, which may help you all, in fact, especially where sleep is concerned...'

'Perhaps...the park—for the boys,' said Cleo thoughtfully, and Maggie felt as if she had won a substantial victory.

'Tomorrow?'

'No, that's too soon. I need to prepare for Hawk's arrival. The rooms are in a bit of a state.' She winced and Maggie laughed. She could well imagine the chaos of four boys; she'd had a similar chaotic household growing up.

'This day next week, then? Let's say eleven,' Maggie said briskly, rising before Cleo could argue any further. 'I should get going. I still haven't fully unpacked! And, don't worry, I will see myself out.'

She left the drawing room feeling much better about

her progress, and even stopped by the boys to tell them about their upcoming trip. It was an underhanded thing to do, as she knew the boys' excitement would also ensure Cleo went through with it. But it was for the good of the family so Maggie saw no issue with it.

It also meant she could greet Daisy and baby Matthew, who had awoken from his nap and was now playing Napoleon while being bounced on Daisy's knee. Maggie was startled by how much the young baby had grown, and ended up playing a few games with the children before leaving.

There were no more raised voices or crying coming from Lord Hawksmere's study as she passed it, so Maggie was relieved that whatever *talk* he'd had with Cleo couldn't have been so bad. Either that or Cleo had gone to her room and avoided the conversation altogether, which would not have surprised Maggie.

Mrs Wimple was busy in the kitchen preparing dinner, and Maggie asked her if there was anything else they needed urgently.

'No, miss, but that's very kind of you. Thank heavens for the young lord's return—that's all I'll say on the matter.'

Mrs Wimple said that last phrase a lot, but she did, in fact, always have more to say on most matters. It was why Maggie liked her so much. Her words surprised her, though. She was hoping for an ally against Lord Hawksmere. 'But I thought part of the issue was that his allowances were too strict. Has he increased them, then?'

'Ahh, that's what we all thought…but there seems to have been a *misunderstanding* about what the money was for.' Mrs Wimple wouldn't meet her eye as she went back to her chores. 'I think the mistress gets confused about the money—who's been paid, who hasn't—and she tried to sort it out herself… But I am sure things will be a lot easier to manage now that he has moved in. Thanks to him, the grocer and butcher will start deliveries again, and he's promised me more help! We'll have his valet joining us next week. So, that's one more person to help already, and the lord has promised us more as soon as he can arrange it. So, hopefully we'll be back to how things should be soon.'

'That's wonderful,' Maggie said, relieved at the improvements already taking place, 'but are you sure there's nothing else you need? Please do say if there is. We can keep it between the two of us.' She gave her a wink. Over the years she had developed a rapport with the servants in both their houses, but she liked the Wimples most of all.

Mrs Wimple chuckled with a shake of her head. 'No, miss, but thank you. I bought enough to manage for now. Everything else will arrive tomorrow or later today.'

Maggie smiled, relieved to hear it. 'Oh, and before I forget! I've managed to convince Cleo to take the children to the park this time next week. But I can provide the picnic for that—so don't worry about it.'

'Oh, that's a wonderful idea, miss!' Her voice lowered conspiratorially. 'She never goes out these days... it's such a pity. Hopefully, that will improve, too, now that you're here for the season.'

'I am sure it will.' Maggie nodded, satisfied with her plan.

After saying her goodbyes, she practically skipped out the back door and up the servant steps, feeling as if the day was much brighter and more hopeful than before. She strolled across the overgrown lawn back towards the wall, pondering all the contradictions she had heard this morning in regard to Lord Hawksmere.

She was halfway down the garden when a loud masculine voice called out to her. 'Miss Mackenzie!'

She turned to see Lord Hawksmere at the patio door—she'd forgotten Archie's study overlooked the garden—*actually, it was his study now*, she corrected.

Lord Hawksmere strode towards her, his long legs eating up the space between them with frightening speed.

'My lord, you may want to—'

'Miss Mackenzie,' he interrupted her before she could warn him of the danger. His brow was deeply marred by a scowl as he approached. 'I must insist you use the front—'

His sentence was cut off as his foot was caught on

a hidden hoop in the long grass, and he stumbled towards her with wide, horrified eyes. The matter was made even worse when a croquet mallet sprung up from nowhere, catching him in the lower thigh of his other leg. If he'd been unbalanced before, he was truly done for now!

Lord Hawksmere, and his broad body of well over six feet, came flying towards her, eclipsing the sun and the rest of the world from view with his huge frame.

There was a moment that seemed to stretch forever when they both stared into each other's wide eyes. Equally horrified by the inevitable fall from grace that they would both suffer in the next breath.

'Lord Hawk—' she managed to gasp before it was entirely too late. And despite a valiant effort to try to brace both hands either side of her, it wasn't enough to stop the weight of his large torso as it knocked her to the ground and crushed the air from her lungs.

They landed…hard, with him on top of her in the most intimate of positions.

Maggie was flattened by the sheer weight of Lord Hawksmere's chest. Her face pressed into the linen of his shirt and silk waistcoat. But it was the thick wall of muscle that knocked the wind out of her.

She had often daydreamed what it would be like to be held tightly in a handsome man's embrace. Now she could say she knew it intimately…if she ever dared to admit it.

But she wasn't sure if she'd ever be able to breathe again, let alone confess it.

Chapter Four

Hawk was mortified.

For a moment he wondered if he should pretend he were actually dead—death would be a kindness.

His face was damp from being pressed into the long grass, but even worse was the knowledge that a young woman lay flattened beneath him, her soft, curvy flesh pinned intimately under his body. But worst of all was the strangled groan she made, which finally caused him to gather his wits enough to fly off her as quickly as possible.

He stumbled backwards as he got to his feet, and then realised belatedly that the poor woman was still sprawled on the ground. Her skirts up by her knees, displaying shapely calves wrapped in white stockings and tied with a tartan ribbon, as well as a scandalous sliver of bare thigh that made him distinctly uncomfortable. Her previously artfully curled hair had lost several pins and was now a lopsided mop. Her pretty face flushed with a blush so bright she looked as if she was about to faint.

Good God, what had he done?

'Forgive me, Miss Mackenzie!' He offered her his hand, but she ignored it; she was still gasping for air like a fish out of water, and she grabbed his arm as she struggled to sit upright.

If he had insulted her before, it was painfully clear that she would hate him forever after this, and rightly so.

She made a choked wheezing sound and he fell back to his knees, reaching around to pat her back gently, desperate to help, but also aware that she might not want his help. It took him a moment to realise what she'd said.

'Maggie!' she croaked again, seemingly getting her breath back enough to say grimly, 'I think...we are well enough acquainted...for first names, don't you?'

Her breasts were rising and falling with each gasped breath, and he found himself momentarily distracted by the swell of her bosom. She looked like a luscious strumpet who'd been thoroughly tumbled, and it made him a little dizzy to realise he wanted her. He really shouldn't be lusting after a woman, especially after knocking her down like a house of cards.

She tugged at her skirts and he realised he was kneeling on the fabric, stopping her from being able to cover herself. He leapt to his feet and then reached for her arm, tugging her up quickly, a little too quickly because she went flying up so fast that she thumped into his chest for a second time. She used her hand against his chest to press away from him while making another alarming wheezing sound that he realised belatedly was a choked laugh. She had a far better sense of humour than he did at this moment.

'Forgive me! I…tripped… I… It was an accident…' He paused, taking a deep breath. 'Are you well… *Maggie?*'

She smiled, and even though she was still flushed it was a brilliant sight to see. 'I am fine. It will take a bigger bear than you to flatten me… And, what should I call you anyway?'

'Hawk,' he said, feeling a little odd that she had just described him as a far less than complimentary animal.

She laughed, brushing down her skirts as she stared up at him with mischievous eyes. 'I can't call you that! It is a nickname, isn't it? Archie used to joke that you refused to answer to anything else…but surely…'

'I prefer Hawk,' he grumbled—*he hated his real name.*

'As you wish.' She then wagged a finger at him. 'But I want to know it anyway. I am a curious creature by nature.'

'I think you should sit down first. You've had enough of a shock as it is.'

She giggled at his joke as he led her by the elbow to one of the stone benches, and for some strange reason the sound made his stomach tighten, as well as other much lower parts of him. He sat down with her, taking a moment to brush the dirt from his knees, and decided to change the subject. 'What I was going to say...before our accident—'

'*Your* accident,' she reminded him firmly, waving a hand in front of her face, as if to cool the heat in her cheeks.

'My accident,' he admitted. What with the chaise longue incident and this fall, she must think him an unbearably clumsy fellow—which he was. He took a deep breath, bracing himself. 'I wanted to ask you to please use the front door in the future.'

'Cleo doesn't mind me coming in through the garden.'

'But I mind,' he said firmly. He didn't want to be constantly on guard in his own home. He felt unsettled as it was; a complete stranger strolling around would only disturb him further. Especially one he found so...attractive. He flinched at the realisation. He couldn't be distracted by her! She was a respectable *miss*, a woman who deserved to be married to a handsome man of means—who could provide for her in the way that she was accustomed.

Who frankly didn't knock her down as if he were playing skittles, or embarrass her in public with his cold manners and clumsy behaviour! Besides, he had to focus on looking after his own family first; he couldn't add to his burden any further, and he certainly could never make her happy. She obviously found him ridiculous, and in the end, he would only disappoint her.

Maggie seemed oblivious to the rudeness of her intrusion, however, and asked, 'Why?'

'Because…well, this garden is dangerous to walk in at the moment,' he said, struggling to find an excuse.

'My gardener could help you tidy it up a bit. In fact, I was going to suggest my gardener do that tomorrow.' At his huff of annoyance, she quickly added, 'There is so little for him to do in our garden, he may as well help Cleo with hers.'

'It is *my* garden now, and I will employ a gardener.'

'Just a little tidy…cut the grass—remove the hoops and mallets.' She added the last with a teasing smile that made his heart race although whether it was still from annoyance or something more *carnal*, he wasn't entirely sure. At his look of warning, she shrugged. 'It has only been dangerous for you. I was making my way through perfectly fine until you came along…'

'It is also…*unseemly*,' he added, hoping she would eventually see sense.

She sighed. 'It is quicker and causes less effort for Mrs Wimple.'

'Again, I will ensure there are enough staff for that no longer to be an issue.'

She frowned, as if he'd said something troubling, and she looked back at the house with a worried expression. 'Cleo hasn't been entirely honest with me, has she?'

Should he lie? Pretend all was well, as Cleo seemed determined to do? 'What did she tell you?'

Maggie turned to face him. *Damn, she was pretty!* With her hair curling around her shoulders—it begged to be further unravelled. 'She told me that you gave her a very strict allowance. So much so that she's had to reduce her staff. She said she was still waiting on her inheritance from Charles...that there were *issues* with it... But I'm beginning to think...'

'There is no inheritance from Charles, and I've no idea why— She should have lots from the sale of her house at least.' Startled by his runaway mouth, he added after a pause, 'I shouldn't be telling you this, I barely know you, and anyway, you shouldn't concern yourself over our family matters. I will sort it out eventually.'

Maggie seemed unworried by his concern as she waved a hand dismissively. 'I am a close friend to your family, and would never break your confidence. But... Did Charles really sell it? Perhaps there is a misunderstanding?'

'Yes—there are already new owners living there.'

'So much for *woodworm*, then! William was right, Charles was a liar after all.' She sighed, and he could well imagine why, but she explained it anyway. 'At first, Cleo said she knew nothing about him selling the house. But now she says she always knew it was a possibility, because of the woodworm, and that perhaps she just *forgot* about it... I suspect she's lying to herself to protect his memory. Honestly, I don't know what to believe anymore.'

Hawk sighed and joined her in staring up at his childhood home. 'Neither do I.'

'Was Charles...in *debt*?' She whispered that last word as if it were scandalous. He wondered if she had any idea how much of a cad Charles had been. He doubted it. For all her brazen behaviour, she seemed a sweet and kind person at heart. The type not to suspect bad in anyone...unlike him, who always imagined the worst.

'I'm not sure... I don't understand where all the money went from the house sale. There were plenty of debtors. But I just need to find them all and work out where it went. It also appears that Cleo has borrowed money herself, and she's been trying to pay it back from her allowance without telling me about it. I wasn't being unnecessarily strict, believe me.'

Maggie gasped and turned to face him. 'But that makes no sense! Cleo barely leaves the house. How could she run up debts?'

'I know, there is a lot to sort out—and more debtors seem to turn up each day,' he said grimly, not sure why he trusted her with this, but finding himself unable to stop himself from telling her the truth. 'At the very worst, I will have to rent out or sell our house in the country to pay it all off. This will leave us with some money to invest and live on... More, if I can find out what happened to the money from her house sale.'

Her expression softened. 'I am sorry—for criticising you before... I didn't know the full story.'

He shrugged. 'That is understandable. I do not understand it fully myself.'

Maggie nodded thoughtfully. 'She can be...rather contradictory...sometimes.'

An understatement! But there was something else he was keen to know. 'Were you here last year, Miss Mackenzie? When my brother passed away.'

Maggie's eyes rounded and then softened with sympathy; it was as if she could see past his words to the hurt beneath. 'I was.'

He cleared his throat. 'How was it?' he asked, unsure of how to word the painful question.

'He died in his sleep, after a short period of decline. I believe it would have been peaceful.'

His jaw tightened as if it were made of stone. He nodded briskly. 'I couldn't be here for Archie, or when Charles died. Cleo resents me for it.'

Maggie nodded and touched his arm. 'You were

away at war. She will understand in time. I *know* Archie did.'

He blinked in surprise. 'You were friends with Archie?'

She nodded, her hand trailing away from his arm to rest in her lap, making him feel somehow bereft. 'Archie was so proud of you. He used to read the papers religiously and always kept the reports that mentioned the Thirteenth Light Dragoons—I shall show you the scrapbook he made next time I visit.'

How did this woman, whom he had never met until recently, know so much about his family?

'Thank you…for telling me that. And forgive me. I said at the ball last night that you knew nothing…but it appears I was wrong in that regard.'

She gave him a radiant smile and then nudged him with her elbow. 'Archie would not like either of you to mope around. I think it is time for Cleo to end her mourning, don't you? For the good of the family. She was always shy before, but she did enjoy socialising. I think it would help her recovery if she went out in the world again.'

He nodded, bewildered at why he was agreeing with her.

'Grand! Then I can rely on your help next week!'

'Next week?' He felt as if he were on a runaway horse, unable to control his fate.

'Yes! We are all going to the park. Uncle William,

the boys and Cleo included. Afterwards, I will help you look for the sale papers, or any information regarding this mystery. Charles used Archie's study a lot of the time. There must be something!'

He nodded thoughtfully. 'That explains the mess in the study and why I can't find the deeds to the country house, either.'

A worrying thought clouded his mind... *What if Charles had tried to sell more than his own house?* Except the country house was owned by the Hawksmeres; there was no way he could sell it without his permission...surely?

As if reading his mind, Maggie's hand returned to his arm to pat it gently once more. 'All will be well, just give it time.'

He drowned in the soft blue of her eyes for a moment and then forced himself to look away. 'Shall I escort you home?'

'Only if you help me through the wall...because I am not going out front!'

He sighed, resolved to his fate. 'Fine, show me how you got in... That way I can ensure it is closed up for good.'

She laughed—even though he'd not been joking, and they both rose, picking their way carefully along the grass until they reached the gap in the wall at the end of the garden, which she squeezed through, warning him as she did so, 'I much prefer it this way.

It means I don't have to follow the usual rules of etiquette and can see my friends and the boys whenever I wish.'

'It isn't...' He paused, struggling to find the politest way of explaining himself. 'Surely, you understand that your reputation as an unmarried woman—'

She snorted, *actually* snorted! As if his concerns were ridiculous. 'I am a spinster! No one cares about my reputation anymore, and I haven't had a chaperone for years!'

He wasn't sure what else to say. She didn't look like a spinster; she looked vibrant and lush. Now that he was standing beside her, guiding her through the gap with her hand in his, he could smell the scent of jasmine and peaches on her skin, ripe and floral.

'Please,' she implored, her blue eyes sparkling in the spring sunshine. 'I promise not to be a nuisance.'

He frowned—more because of the effect she had on him than anything else, and he was unable to outright refuse her a second time. 'I have business to attend to, but I think you understand my feelings on the matter. Good day, *Maggie*.'

He allowed himself that one small intimacy—it would have seemed churlish not to after their earlier conversation. He had spoken more about his own thoughts and feelings in the past ten minutes than he'd ever spoken to anyone else, with the possible exception of his friends.

She nodded, her bodice lightly scraping against the wall and flowers as she sidestepped into her property. He looked away, shocked by his lustful gaze.

Once she was through, she gave a cheerful curtsy that seemed almost mocking. 'Good day… Oh!' Her eyes widened. 'You never told me your name—'

'Goodbye, Maggie,' he said firmly, walking away before she could question him any further.

There was a merry giggle from behind the wall, followed by a cheerful, 'Mark my words. I *will* find it out eventually!'

He didn't doubt her.

Chapter Five

A week later two carriages rolled into Hyde Park, and all but one person tumbled out with a sigh of relief. Cleo being the notable exception as she lingered inside, unwilling to leave.

It had been a cramped journey, but thankfully reasonably short. The older boys were full of excitement, and they leapt from the carriages before the wheels had come to a full stop. Of course, Cleo was the last to disembark, her hand gripping the door tightly as if she were afraid to leave it.

'Come along, Cleo. We want to find a good spot,' Maggie called out as she stepped down from her own carriage with Uncle William, Daisy and baby Matthew. With all the best will in the world, there was no way all four boys and Daisy would have fit in Cleo's carriage along with Cleo and Lord Hawksmere, so they'd all had to muddle together. Not that Maggie cared; she was used to travelling in large groups with her family.

'It looks like rain,' said Cleo, frowning up at the three wispy clouds in the sky. Mithering and fussing about the bad weather had been Cleo's favourite pastime in the lead-up to their trip. But to Maggie's delight, the sun had finally shone on the day of their planned outing.

'Not at all. It's a fine day. Let's go sit beneath that oak over there and have our picnic,' said Maggie, already nodding to the footmen to unload the baskets. She hoped it would encourage her friend to take the final step—Cleo looked as if she might bolt at any moment.

Hawk reached up and offered his sister his arm, speaking in a surprisingly gentle tone as he said, 'We'll keep the carriages nearby so we can leave at the first sign of rain.'

Cleo bit her lip with apprehension, but eventually took his arm to climb down. When her black slipper finally touched the ground, Maggie sighed with relief.

It had taken long enough to get them out of the house as it was. It was now *fashionable hour* in the park—the busiest time, where all the finely dressed ladies and gentlemen promenaded or took carriage rides, wanting to be seen and admired by the ton. Not exactly ideal for Cleo's first proper outing, but they'd managed to get her to leave the house at least, although she was still resolute in her wearing of black from head to toe, despite the array of grey and lavender gowns she'd been offered. But Maggie took her victories wherever she could find them, and *this* was most definitely a victory.

As expected, Cleo hadn't been feeling well this morning, and had tried to insist they go on without her. Of course, Maggie wasn't going to accept that, and so she had spent over an hour insisting that fresh air would do her a world of good, while subtly getting her ready to leave at the same time.

Hawk—for what else was she to call him after he'd refused to tell her his name—had become an unlikely ally in her plan. Even helping to load the carriage when he realised there weren't nearly enough footmen to do the job quickly enough to get going before Cleo thought up another excuse to stay home.

They made their way over to the majestic oak, and William sighed happily as he flopped down on the spread-out blanket, propping his back against the trunk. 'Isn't it grand to have some sunshine at last? I feel as if it has rained all year!'

'It's not terribly warm, though, is it?' said Cleo, and she shivered, pulling her shawl closer around her. 'I hope the children don't catch a cold.'

William laughed. 'They'll be fine. Compared to Edinburgh this is a perfect day!' He leaned back, fumbling in the inside of his coat and removing a flask. 'But here, have a sip of whisky to keep away the chill. We call it *uisge beatha*, water of life.'

Cleo recoiled away from the flask as if he'd offered her a venomous snake. 'No, thank you,' she said, and after a moment of hesitation they both laughed.

Maggie's heart skipped a beat with excitement as she realised once again how well suited her uncle and Cleo were for each other. William could be too bold and mischievous at times, but Cleo was a calming presence for him, and he in turn gave her the confidence to shine.

She examined them both closely; they were about the same age. William had the characteristic colouring and sturdy frame of a Mackenzie, while Cleo was slim and dark. They were opposites, but she realised her uncle had a charm and easy manner that suited Cleo's quietness, and he was handsome in a roguish sort of way, with only a few streaks of white in his dark auburn hair.

'Suit yourself.' William grinned, taking a sip and then hissing between his teeth as he sucked in a sharp breath. 'It's a good one, lass. Best yet!' He winked at Maggie for good measure, and she was sure she saw Hawk give her a curious look as he took the offered flask from her uncle and gave it a sip.

She held her breath as she waited for his opinion, and was secretly delighted when he tilted his head with a nod of appreciation. 'It is good, smoother than most. Where did you get it?'

Before Uncle William could open his big mouth, she

quickly interjected, 'Uncle William gets his whisky from a distillery not far from us. They follow what a Mr Usher has started to do with his whisky…aging it in used sherry casks. It's a very new technique, but it's already started having some wonderful results on the taste, sweetening it and adding an oaky smoke to the flavour…' She stopped speaking, worried she'd revealed too much—and by the incredulous look on everyone's faces she was sure she had. 'I was told about it at a dinner party,' she finished lamely. She'd deliberately not said whether it was a legal distillery or one of the many illegal ones. She didn't dare say that it was her own unlicenced batch—one that she'd spent the past four years perfecting.

When Hawk offered her the flask next, she declined with a shake of her head. 'No, thank you,' she said, not wanting to fan the flames of suspicion.

The problem with Uncle William was that he was far too confident in his own position. So much so that he regularly forgot the severity of their crime. In Scotland, he hosted parties for magistrates, and the local excise men regularly received a fat goose for turning a blind eye to their shipments. It was fine at home, where they knew everyone—but in London…they should be more cautious.

Maggie had a momentary pang of guilt, however, when she realised that she had expected Hawk to tell her his secrets and yet, she still did not feel comfortable sharing her own…

What did that say about her?

In the end, she decided it would be safer to change the conversation entirely, and she called out to the children. 'Boys! Would you like to eat first or play?' she asked them with a teasing smile, already knowing the answer by their bouncing feet.

'Play!' they shouted in unison, already grabbing croquet mallets, hoops and two balls from the game's basket. According to Daisy, Lord Hawksmere had spent most of his first week at home pulling the hoops and mallets out of his lawn and generally tidying the garden. She had to admit she'd spotted him out her bedroom window a few times, working hard in only his shirt and breeches. It seemed he preferred to do the manual work himself; either that or he was too impatient to wait for a gardener.

For a fleeting moment she had wondered if he'd done it because he was worried about her safety; but then she quickly dismissed that as fanciful and decided he was probably just an orderly man by nature, and wanted to avoid another fall himself. Today his cravat was well starched and tied elegantly at his neck. She doubted he approved of mess.

'Is your friend Adam really getting married next week?' Cleo asked Hawk conversationally as she began to unpack the picnic.

'Yes,' muttered Hawk with a frown, glancing at Maggie and William as if he wished they hadn't heard them speaking about his friend.

'Who's this? Don't tell me we've had our first casualty of the season!' teased William.

Hawk's grim expression didn't lighten at the joke. 'My close friend, Major Adam Mayhew, will be marrying a Miss Gwendolyn Trym later next week. It will be a small, intimate ceremony with only close friends and family attending.'

'Trym…' Maggie said thoughtfully. 'Is she connected with Trym's Furniture? I have some of their pieces in our London house, very fine quality.'

'Yes, she's the Trym's heiress.'

William frowned. 'Don't think we've ever met her, have we, Maggie?'

Maggie shook her head. She'd heard of some scandal connected with the name a few years ago. But she didn't like to judge a person without at least meeting them first, and that included spreading gossip.

Hawk didn't elaborate further, saying only, 'I'd be grateful if you didn't mention it to anyone until after they have announced it officially.'

Cleo only waved a hand dismissively. 'William and Maggie won't say anything. You can trust them. But why are they getting married so quickly? And with a special licence at that. It's bound to cause rumours!'

'Nothing untoward has taken place. They wish

only to marry quickly.' Hawk shrugged before adding weakly, 'They're in...*love*.'

Maggie didn't fully believe him. When he'd mentioned love, he'd not seemed in the least bit sincere. But she guessed he was protecting his friend's privacy, and she couldn't argue with that.

'Well, I suppose Adam has always been a reckless sort! The type to act before he thinks, I can understand that. Sometimes your emotions just get the better of you...' Cleo said thoughtfully, and Maggie wondered if she was thinking of her own whirlwind romance with Charles. They'd also married quickly.

'Well, I think it all sounds very romantic. I wish them the very best of luck!' said Maggie with a smile, and William raised his flask in a silent toast.

Hawk didn't seem to agree, but said nothing and avoided her gaze.

The boys played a couple of rounds of croquet, arguing constantly until eventually every adult was begging them to return to the blanket to eat—if only to enjoy some silence. Baby Matthew was already chewing happily through a block of cheese, when the three boys flopped onto the blanket and began to feast on the picnic.

'Meals are so much better now that you've come to live with us, Uncle Hawk,' said Peter cheerfully, demolishing a meat pie within seconds.

Maggie caught the stiffening of Cleo's spine right before Hawk answered, 'You have Miss Mackenzie to thank for today's meal—apparently she insisted.' He gave her a deeply disapproving scowl that she obviously ignored.

'Well, it was my idea to come out. It seemed only fair that I provide the refreshments.'

'We will have to repay the favour by having you both over to dinner, perhaps one night this week?' asked Cleo, and everyone nodded with agreement.

A large group of ladies and gentlemen on fine thoroughbred horses trotted past and the children watched them with interest, talking amongst themselves to decide which of the beautiful horses they liked best.

Francis prodded Hawk thoughtfully. 'I bet you had a very big horse when you were in the cavalry. Did you ever fall off?'

Cleo looked to her hands and an awkward silence descended, as everyone realised the implication of the question. Francis was probably thinking of their father's death, as he had fallen from a curricle.

Hawk smiled down at him with a kind expression. 'I did. Many times, but I was lucky enough never to be badly hurt—they were very good horses, you see, well trained. I rode lots of different horses, but I can safely say that they were better trained than I ever was.'

'Which one was your favourite?' asked Thomas.

'A chestnut Arabian mare called Fatima. She was

an excellent horse, fearless in battle. She would bite and stamp on the enemy whenever they tried to get close.'

'What happened to her?' asked a wide-eyed Peter.

There was a moment, fleeting though it was, where a sadness seemed to wash over Hawk's expression. But it was gone in an instant when he replied cheerfully, 'She's growing fat on hay and apples at a stud farm I believe, enjoying her well-earned retirement from the military.'

'Shame you couldn't keep her.'

'Indeed. I would have accepted her in a heartbeat.'

Maggie didn't believe him for the second time that day, and when she caught his eye, he gave a slight tilt of his head as if acknowledging the fact that he had lied to the children. She expected it was to save them from a bitter truth, one they did not need after so much loss suffered already.

'I am sure she is enjoying the peace and quiet after battle,' Maggie said cheerfully. 'Perhaps you would like to go horse racing today on the Scottish Red Devil?' She looked meaningfully at her uncle.

William groaned heavily and patted his stomach. 'Och! I think the Scottish Red Devil is a little full after lunch.'

'Oh, I am sure a little canter will do him good!' laughed Maggie, and the boys all agreed, pulling desperately on William's tailcoat.

Hawk looked between them, confused at their behaviour, until her uncle gave a loud neigh and shook his head dramatically as he rose from his seat. The squeals of delight from the children were enough to make her uncle grin, and he began to jump a little and paw at the ground with his boots, his two arms bent at the elbows in front of him in true horsey fashion.

Cleo and Maggie sank against each other in a fit of giggles at her uncle's silly display, and Hawk looked more than a little horrified by it, until he saw the excitement in his nephews' faces, and then his expression softened considerably.

'Who's first?' asked William with a horse-like rumble of his throat.

'Me! Me! Me!' cried all the children in unison, and Maggie rose to her feet, knowing that she would have to manage this chaos if anyone was going to end the day without a tantrum.

'Alphabetical order today,' she said firmly.

Francis looked as if he were about to cry, right up until the moment he mumbled through the alphabet and realised he was first. At which point he punched his arm in the air with a loud cheer.

William dipped his body a little, and Maggie helped Francis onto his back. 'Perhaps we should add some jumps…to make it interesting,' she said to the other boys, wanting to give them something to do.

Her uncle gave her a bad-tempered look as the children all yelled with agreement and began to gather mallets and baskets to create a course for them. Through gritted teeth he said, 'Perhaps the Red Witch should join the race, too?'

Maggie sighed. 'Sadly, I think the Red Witch is unable to ride today. Bad hay...or so I've heard.'

'Please, Maggie!' shouted the boys, and Maggie began to regret her earlier teasing of her uncle. The boys were so much bigger than last year, and there were quite a few passers-by—she'd end up the talk of the ton!

'The Black Stallion will take part in the race,' said Hawk firmly, rising to his feet and striding over as if he were accepting a duel.

Maggie gave him a grateful smile. Hawk was so tall he had to practically get on his knees to be low enough for Peter to climb onto his back. But Hawk didn't grumble.

'That's not fair! Matthew was before Peter!' declared Thomas bad-temperedly.

'Matthew is a little too young to ride. But that does mean it's your turn next, Thomas.' She could see the argument brewing in the boy's mind, and so she added, 'Each race we'll swap out one of the riders. Three races, so that you'll have two rides each. That's fair.'

'Just two rides?' sighed Thomas.

'Well, four rides. If the horses have the strength for six races...'

The two men exchanged a look of dismay.

Hiding her smile, she handed Thomas a handkerchief. 'The flag for the start of the race. You can wave it.'

Thomas nodded, solemnly taking the handkerchief and the responsibility with a serious expression. 'You should judge the winner,' he said, pointing to the end of the track, and obediently Maggie went to stand a few steps after the last hurdle. Which was a mallet balanced about a foot off the ground by two empty cordial bottles.

'Ready?' bellowed Thomas, and the two men stepped up to the stick marking their starting position. Uncle William began to huff loudly and paw at the ground, not caring at the stylish people who walked past giving him curious looks.

Hawk looked a little awkward at first, but when he saw Cleo laugh and heard Francis giggle, he was soon jostling Peter and making his own dramatic neighing sounds.

The boys were already in hysterical giggles before Thomas waved the starting flag. But when he did so, the men suddenly became far more competitive than anyone could have imagined.

Uncle William bounded forward, bouncing the much lighter Francis easily over the jumps.

But Hawk was longer in the leg and had seen battle; he ran forward with long, sure-footed strides and sailed over the hurdles, Peter yelling encouragement in his ear as he quickly overtook her uncle.

Hawk easily won the first race, and by the end of the final race—the sixth—a small crowd had gathered to watch and cheer them on. Maggie was certain Hawk had fumbled a couple of races, deliberately losing to ensure the boys had an equal number of wins. It was a sweet gesture and made for a much easier end to the game.

His eyes were bright, his face flushed, and the carefully tied cravat had been pulled loose to show off his Adam's apple and throat; a light sheen covered his skin that she found oddly distracting. He really was a handsome devil, even more so now that she knew he had a soft spot for his nephews and was protective of his friends.

She envied Miss Trym, with her handsome major desperate to marry her. It sounded wonderfully romantic. Even if the speed of their marriage was due to a secret scandal…she still wished it could happen to her. To be swept off her feet and married within weeks, her lover unable to bear being parted from her. And, if Major Mayhew was anything like Hawk, he'd make a wonderful husband and father.

Maggie flinched at her wayward thoughts.

Who was she kidding?

The most romantic thing that had ever happened to her was when Hawk had knocked her off her feet by accident in the garden... And she could hardly call that romance!

Even if she did find herself thinking of it often...

Chapter Six

Despite the boys' pleading, the horses were finally done for.

'I beg mercy! This horse needs to be put out to pasture!' cried her uncle loudly, and the crowd booed and laughed with equal measure before dispersing.

However, the boys were not done, and they continued to race and jump through their makeshift course, this time without their trusty steeds.

Uncle William collapsed onto the blanket with a heavy sigh. 'I swear those boys are eating rocks. They never used to be that heavy!'

Maggie chuckled as she poured him some fruit cordial and handed it to him. 'Don't be so dramatic.'

'Easy for you to say. You weren't the one giving piggyback rides!'

Hawk lowered himself carefully onto the blanket as if he was worried about knocking something over, his dark hair dropping forward into an adorable curl that he swept back with a brush of his hand. 'I don't know what you're talking about, William. I could have gone another six races.'

'Nonsense!' declared her uncle between gulps of his drink.

'Thank you for joining in—the boys loved it! And there was no way I could have managed it. William's right. They are so much bigger this year.' Maggie offered Hawk a glass of the cordial and he took it, their hands brushing against one another, causing tingles to shoot up her arm. Her eyes caught his and she could have sworn there was fire within them, golden sparks inside the brown that she'd never noticed until now.

Or perhaps...it was just wishful thinking?

'My pleasure,' he said quietly, the sound rolling across her skin like a rush of heat from an open kiln.

'I want to go home.' The crisp, frigid voice of Cleo cut through the air like a knife, turning the mood from jubilant to glum with the utterance of only five words.

Maggie turned to face her friend, shocked by her tone. 'Oh, are you not feeling well?'

'No, I am not,' Cleo replied curtly, gathering her shawl closer around her. Maggie noticed that Daisy also looked a little subdued, her eyes deliberately focused on Matthew as she bounced the grizzling baby in her lap. 'Not that any of you noticed,' Cleo added sourly.

They glanced around each other guiltily, and William sat upright with obvious concern. 'I'm sorry,

Cleo. The races did take rather a long time. Is there anything I can get you?'

'If you could ready the carriages, please,' she answered tartly. 'It looks as if it will rain at any moment, and Matthew is very grouchy from missing his nap.'

They all frowned up at the sky and realised it did look a little grey overhead. They'd not realised because they were having so much fun, and Maggie felt terrible that they'd pretty much ignored Cleo entirely. Even if Cleo *could* have easily joined them... Still, it was her first outing, and Maggie was surely being impatient and unkind to expect more from her.

William said tactfully, 'I think you're right. But don't worry. I'll speak to the coachmen—we'll be away in no time at all.' With a quick nod, her uncle rushed away in the direction of the carriages.

'I'm so sorry, Cleo. I was a little distracted with the races. I should have rejoined you. I apologise. But...' Maggie paused, desperate for Cleo not to return to her earlier melancholy. She realised she had spent far too much time admiring Lord Hawksmere—of all people—when she should have been looking after Cleo. 'You must agree. It was good to take the boys out. They've had such a lovely day.'

Cleo's eyes narrowed in a way she had never seen before. There was so much anger and bitterness in her expression. 'I know what is best for *my* boys.'

Maggie felt as if she'd been slapped and she stared

down at her hands, hoping not to cry. 'Of course, I apologise…'

Hawk's calm voice intervened. 'Cleo, that is unfair. Maggie didn't mean—'

'*Maggie?*' snapped Cleo with venom. 'You are that well acquainted, then? After only a single day of knowing one another? Does she know your real name? *H—*'

Hawk was quick to interrupt. 'Hawk is the name I answer to. You know that.'

Cleo gave a derisive snort before charging on. 'How quickly things change! You say I must break my mourning and sit in parks playing silly games when my husband and twin brother lie dead in the earth. How easily you both forget them when I cannot. But you know *best*, don't you? For both myself and my children, it seems. *However*, I will remind you—' she stabbed a finger at Maggie '—that *you* were not here after Charles died…and…' Her finger and gaze jerked towards Hawk in accusation. 'And *you* were *never* here! So you do not get to control our lives, or tell me what to do now! If I wish to stay home, *I will*!'

Cleo stood, brushing down her skirts angrily. 'As you enjoy my children's company so much, *brother*, then you can ride back with Miss Mackenzie and her uncle. I wish to finally spend some time *alone* with my children without either of you interfering for a change!'

Cleo strode away, leaving both of them reeling from the harsh dressing down they'd received.

'I'll go gather the children, my lord,' said Daisy quietly, perching Matthew on her hip as she swiftly made her exit.

'She didn't mean it,' he said quietly, drawing Maggie's attention back to him and his kind expression. 'She's angry at me and the harsh truths I've had to tell her recently.'

'I'm sorry but perhaps she's right... I shouldn't have left her alone for so long.'

He shook his head. 'She's just angry. Grief does that. It makes you lash out, especially at the people you care about.' That sad expression washed over his face for a second time, and she remembered Archie once telling her that Hawk had been a *handful* as a child.

'You speak as if from experience.'

Hawk gave a grim nod. 'I gave them a hard time growing up. I disobeyed and resented them. I didn't understand that they were just doing their best, that they didn't know how to be a parent to me because they were still so young themselves. And from what I have heard about my parents...they were not particularly affectionate people. It was no wonder we butted heads with one another. It must be hard for Cleo to have me as the head of the family now when she dealt with all my nonsense before, not to mention being forced to be a mother to me—when she was so young herself.'

Maggie nodded, trying to remind herself that Cleo's outburst was uncharacteristic and merely a reflection of her own grief. How many times had she resented being the eldest to her own clan of siblings? It was understandable that Cleo would find the change of her circumstances difficult.

At least Cleo had a brother who was kind and understanding, who was patient with her and protective of their family.

'What happened to Fatima?' she asked softly.

He blinked as if surprised by the change in conversation, although in her mind they flowed smoothly from one to the other. He had opened a door into his past, and she knew from watching him with the boys and Cleo that there were many things he kept hidden—for the good of those around him.

'My horse?' he asked and at her nod, he looked away from her to frown into the distance. 'She was badly hurt... I put her out of her misery.'

'I'm sorry,' Maggie said, reaching over the short distance between them to rest her hand on his sleeve. 'For what Cleo said to you and for what happened to your horse. Neither of them were fair.'

He shrugged off her touch, getting to his feet and offering her his hand. 'No, but it seems I have an ally in you. We will help Cleo out of this ditch, whether she likes it or not.'

She smiled, taking his hand as she got to her feet. 'Agreed! Although, perhaps we should be a little gentler and more considerate in the future?'

'Agreed.' Hawk looked over to Cleo, who was firmly ushering the children into her carriage. 'Your uncle... He's about the same age as Cleo, isn't he?'

Maggie nodded. 'Yes.'

He appeared thoughtful. 'She doesn't do well alone...never has.'

'I have wondered the same,' she said with a knowing smile and when he turned back to her, she explained, 'But... William doesn't believe there is any hope for them.'

Hawk disappointed her by nodding in agreement. 'Perhaps he is right. She does not seem keen to move on.'

Maggie tried a different tack. 'But he does care for her... I am sure of it. Personally, I think they would make a good match. If she ever stops mourning Charles, maybe we could encourage them?'

He frowned. 'Charles doesn't deserve her tears.'

Maggie took a step closer, lowering her voice. 'Have you learned something?'

Hawk shook his head. 'It's bad. And I suspect there's even more secrets to uncover.'

Maggie was about to ask more but William was

waving at them, urging them to get into the carriage. So she said quickly, 'Don't speak of it in front of my uncle. He's terrible at keeping secrets.'

A smile twitched at the corner of Hawk's mouth. 'I gathered as much.'

'And if he knows our plans regarding the two of them… Well, he won't approve of it. He thinks I'm a meddler and a hopeless romantic, and I imagine we won't see Cleo for dust if she gets wind of it.'

'Then we shall have to work in secret,' said Hawk with a sensual look that caused her toes to curl within her silk slippers.

'Indeed…' She tried to shrug away the warmth of his look. He probably couldn't help being this charming… It didn't mean anything, and she shouldn't read anything more into it. 'Now, speaking of secrets… Your name.'

Hawk groaned. 'Please don't. I cannot even stomach hearing it, let alone saying it.'

'Is it truly that bad?'

He grimaced as an answer, and she tried to hide her smile.

'Then let me guess at it. From what Cleo said earlier, I at least know it starts with the letter *H*.'

Hawk rolled his eyes.

'Henry?'

'No.'

'Heath?'

'No.'

'Hugo?'

'No!'

'Harry? Harold? Hans? Horatio?'

Hawk shook his head at each suggestion. 'You will be here all day if that is your method.'

'I've got it! Herbert!' She gasped, but not because her guess was right. Hawk had still shaken his head in response. It was the sudden splatter of rain falling on their heads that had made Maggie flinch.

'We have to go! From now on you only get one guess per day!' His hand grabbed hers and they began to run towards the coaches as the rain started to pour. Maggie tried her best to hold her skirts up enough to run while Hawk used his hat to try to cover her hair from the downpour.

As they reached the coach and she clambered into the carriage, she belatedly realised their ungloved hands were interlocked. She stared down at her hand in his, his skin darker than hers and covered in little scars and roughened callouses from years of riding and battle. She thought it lovely and beautiful, and she was reluctant to let it go.

But her uncle reached out to help her climb inside and Hawk offered him her hand, his fingers slipping from hers into a more gentle hold, behaving like the perfect gentleman.

He would probably think nothing of the touch, but

Maggie knew she would obsess over it tonight as she'd done after their stumble in the garden. She couldn't seem to shake him from her thoughts, and even though she knew it was foolish, her romantic heart fluttered as she took her seat and pretended not to care.

Chapter Seven

Two days later the Mackenzies joined them for dinner. Hawk had been relieved when Cleo sent the invitation, and the evening had progressed far better than he'd expected.

For a start, Maggie had arrived through the front door this time, looking bright and lovely as always in a turquoise evening gown. The silk rustled as she moved—proving she could not be silent even when she wasn't speaking. She seemed to always draw his attention no matter what. Even turning at one point during their greeting to whisper at him, 'Is it Hansel?'

'Absolutely not!' he'd hissed back at her, trying hard not to smile himself. She could have easily asked Cleo to tell her but, he supposed, where was the fun in that?

Cleo must have immediately felt repentant about her harsh words at the park, or she wouldn't have sent the invitation for dinner so quickly. She greeted her guests with a cautious friendliness that he was sure his sister meant as an apology in her odd brittle way. In turn, the Mackenzies were far more gracious and kinder than they needed to be, going along with the pretence that all was well between them.

Hawk did not mind what Cleo had said to him—after all, it was true; he was an unwelcome guest—but her condemnation of Maggie was completely unwarranted. He'd been ready to point it out to her after she'd calmed down, but had decided against it after hearing Cleo weeping in her room for most of the night after they'd returned. He was sure she regretted her harsh words and wanted to make peace, but Cleo had always found dealing with her emotions difficult, and he suspected she was waiting for the right moment to apologise.

This was confirmed at dinner when Cleo leaned in close to Maggie and whispered, 'I am sorry…about the other day.'

With an understanding smile Maggie patted her hand affectionately. 'There is nothing to forgive. I am sorry for being so distracted, both that day and before. I returned to Scotland after Archie because Anne's bairn was ill, but I should have written to you more regularly.'

Cleo sighed, a deep sadness entering her expression. 'No, do not blame yourself for that. After all, how were you to know that I… I wasn't—' she struggled to find the words, her cheeks and nose flushing with emotion that she fought to control '—myself... I'm still not. I find myself becoming irritable for no reason, angry at everyone and everything. I think seeing you all playing with the boys the other day only reminded me that Charles and Archie... Well, that they're no longer here, and that they'll never be able to play with the boys again. I wanted to join you, but for some reason, I couldn't. It felt like a betrayal. And I was so bitter and angry about it. Does that make any sense?'

'I understand,' said Maggie quietly.

Cleo gave her a sad smile. 'How could you? I don't even understand it myself.'

William gave them both a warm smile. 'You can always shout at me. I do not mind, and I am usually to blame anyway.'

Cleo shook her head emphatically. 'Oh, no, William, I could never blame you for anything.'

Maggie glanced at Hawk with a raised brow as if to say, *See, they are meant for each other!* Hawk merely shrugged. If anything, Cleo's words had made him realise that she still wasn't ready to move on. She was still very much in the throes of grief.

Hawk happened to notice the Mackenzie ribbon in her hair at that moment. A tiny little bow of tartan, and he wondered if she did it on purpose, wearing her clan colours in some way at all times. Her uncle certainly did, as he always wore Highland dress, tartan trews, or at the very least a tartan waistcoat, as he did tonight. Maggie had worn a Mackenzie tartan spencer jacket to the park, and the tartan overdress at the ball. So she must also deliberately wear it at all times. There was something very rebellious about it, even though the wearing of tartan had not been illegal for years.

Strangely, the sight of the little bow nestled amongst her coppery pile of curls made his stomach tighten. Because Hawk couldn't help but remember the last time he'd seen the Mackenzie ribbon...wrapped around her shapely legs to hold her stockings up.

He squirmed a little at the erotic memory and was grateful when William interrupted his wicked thoughts by asking, 'So, Maggie, what are your plans this London season?'

Maggie laughed. 'Apart from disappointing my mother?'

That made Hawk curious in a way that made his heart beat a little faster, as if she were proposing something scandalous. 'Why would you disappoint your mother?' he asked mildly, although a wicked part of him wanted to ask, *how and with whom?*

'Oh, I always do!' declared Maggie with a brightness that seemed somehow forced. 'Every year when I return home unmarried.'

William gave her a reproachful look. 'She only wants to see you happy.'

'I am happy!' Maggie said firmly, taking another large sip of her wine. 'I have wonderful friends and family who care for me dearly. As well as other interests...'

'Ah yes, your brewing,' said Cleo. 'How did your latest batch turn out? I remember you saying you were nervous about it.'

'Much better than I had hoped. But I still think there is room for improvement.' Maggie smiled, but there was something secretive and naughty about it and it made him wonder again about her family's business.

'Well, I would love to try it someday. You must bring some down with you next time.'

Maggie shrugged. 'When it is absolutely perfect, I will.'

'So other than ignoring your mother's requests to find a soul mate, what balls and soirees have you set your sights on?' asked William again.

Maggie paused thoughtfully before answering, 'Oh...*all* of them.'

William chuckled. 'Then I shall prepare myself.'

Maggie dazzled in the candlelight as she lowered her chin and said with mock gravity. 'Thank you, Uncle. I know how much society and entertainments task you. Next week will be particularly gruelling as Lady Flemming is hosting a games night at her home on Tuesday, and I would also like to go to the British Museum and the Opera. There is also the Renshaw

Ball, and, of course, The Wrexham's Ball at the end of the season—which I always adore. Oh! And I believe there's also a benefit ball soon at Artington Hall. Honestly, it will be a struggle to fit it all in!' She then turned a little in her seat towards Cleo. 'I don't suppose I can beg you to join us for any or all of these outings? It always takes me a couple of weeks to reacquaint myself with the ton.'

Hawk blinked. Maggie really was a social butterfly, and he almost felt sorry for William...although, he suspected he enjoyed it just as much as she did. Hawk, on the other hand, couldn't think of anything worse. He hated balls.

Cleo glanced towards Hawk. 'Artington Hall, isn't that...?'

Hawk nodded with a sigh. 'Yes, that's my friend Ezra's estate. It seems he's taken a young *emigre* and her brother under his wing. Their house was burned down in a recent attack.'

'Oh, how awful!'

'The benefit is to help support people like them who have lost everything in the revolution. Unfortunately, as his friend, I will have to attend *that* ball at least,' said Hawk grimly. When one of his friends needed him, he was always duty bound to help...even if it was a tedious ball.

'Then let us all go!' declared Maggie, looking hopefully at Cleo.

Cleo was already shaking her head. 'No, I don't feel up to it…it's too soon. But go ahead without me.' Then she seemed to rethink for a moment because she said quietly as if afraid to admit it to the world, 'I would quite like to go to Lord and Lady Wrexham's ball, though. Hopefully, I will feel up to attending social events by the end of the season. And I would like to reacquaint myself with them. Lady Wrexham is an old friend of mine.'

Maggie grinned with pleasure. 'Then we shall definitely all go to that—if you're able, and this benefit sounds fun, too. What do you think, William?'

William nodded with an easy smile. 'Of course.'

After dinner the men flouted convention to take their brandy with the ladies in the drawing room. William and Cleo walked ahead of them, as they were deep in conversation about their mutual acquaintances, Lord and Lady Wrexham.

As they walked down the hallway from the dining room to the drawing room, Maggie asked him, 'Did you find the papers you were looking for?'

'I haven't had a chance to look properly. I've been a little busy…' He frowned up at the ceiling as the patter of little feet went running over their heads, followed not long after by a muffled reprimand that sounded as if Daisy had her work cut out for her tonight. They seemed to be awake all day and night…it was exhausting. 'Perhaps a boarding school or the military *would* be better for the boys?'

Maggie giggled as if he'd made a great jest. But at his guilty expression her smile quickly fell into a scowl. 'You cannot be serious!'

He sighed. 'I may have...contemplated it for a moment. But Cleo refused to consider it.'

'Of course she did! Why on earth would you think that a good idea? They've lost their father and uncle in one fell swoop. You can't send them away from their mother!' She hissed the last sentence quietly, her eyes flitting nervously to the open drawing room door that William and Cleo had just gone through. Then with a loud voice, she called out, 'I will help you look for those papers. We'll join you in a moment!'

She then grabbed his arm and ushered him into the study as if he were a rude child deserving of a dressing down. For some reason he didn't argue it, and she easily pulled him into the dim light of the study.

She left the door slightly ajar, for propriety's sake, but rounded on him with a glare.

Lifting his hands up in surrender, he said, 'I did not say I was *going* to do it! Only that I contemplated it for a brief moment...about the same time the boys knocked over my brother's prize Chinese vase. *And*...' he added, infuriated that he felt the need to defend himself in her eyes. 'I am well aware of their loss. Both of Charles and Archie. So believe me, I know how painfully long and lonely those childhood years can be. But finding friends and interacting with one's peers is essential to happiness and growth. For example, without my university friends, I would not have become the man I am today.'

Her lips were still tightly pursed, but her shoulders relaxed a little. 'They are still bairns, and I am sure you relied on your relationship with your own siblings to help you through those tough times...didn't you?' she asked hesitantly, a shadow of worry crossing over her face.

'I do not remember my parents well, as I suspect the boys—with the exception of Peter—will barely remember Charles or Archie, either. I remember it irritated Cleo that I could forget them so easily. Perhaps that is why she struggles to put aside her mourning now? But I concede your point. They are too young to be away from Cleo. However, they cannot continue to run riot in this household, unchecked and uneducated. They require a tutor, like other young boys their age. Except... I have found finding one surprisingly difficult. I have had no response from my advertisement—apart from a gentleman who took one look at their antics and ran for the hills.'

It seemed as if his speech had softened Maggie's heart to his plight, because she was quick to offer her assistance in that bossy way of hers. 'I will ask around for some recommendations from the ladies of the ton.

There may be some tutors and governesses who are preparing to leave their current positions. There have been a lot of debutantes this year, and some families may cancel their employment sooner than expected.'

He was surprised by her offer, and almost defensively rejected it, but then realised that he *did* need her. 'That would be most helpful of you, thank you.'

He should take help where he could get it, and he *was* grateful for the offer, even though he hated to admit it. He went on to explain, drawing her by the elbow farther into the room so that Cleo would not overhear. 'Part of the reason Cleo hasn't been able to employ anyone is because she seems to have lost touch with many of her friends and acquaintances who could have helped her. I suspect she had become somewhat of a recluse even before Charles's death. Would you say that was accurate?'

Maggie nodded with a sad expression. 'Yes, at first, I thought it was because Archie was so unwell. But now I suspect that might have been an excuse. After having Matthew…she seemed less inclined to go out in society…and…' She bit her plump lower lip as if unsure whether to say any more.

His eyes seemed unable to look away from that captured morsel of flesh, and his chest tightened. 'Go on,' he urged, clearing his throat roughly when he heard the husky tone of his voice.

'And…' She glanced at the doorway, and they

heard Cleo begin to play the pianoforte in the drawing room—a soft and romantic song. 'Charles encouraged it. He complained often of her overspending on the boys. Although, I never saw anything of the sort… and yet, I hear he was seen at gambling dens and clubs—Uncle William saw him often at White's…'

Guilt churned in Hawk's stomach. 'Then my own absence after my return did not help. I thought that by giving her space to grieve…' His words failed him as he had failed Cleo. 'It is obvious now that I have been utterly useless, and that I am, at least, partly to blame for the mess Cleo has got herself into. For example, one unscrupulous debtor was harassing her for the repayment of Charles's debts, despite the fact that I had already cleared it with him. He used our lack of communication to his advantage. I have since dealt with him.'

The memory of teaching that scoundrel a lesson made his hand involuntarily flex into a fist at his side, and her gaze dropped down to the movement, her clever eyes always so observant.

She was not horrified at the slight scuffs to his knuckles as another lady might have been. She even stepped closer towards him, the scent of jasmine and peaches filling his nose with a sweet nectar that made his mouth water.

'Hawk,' she said softly, his name like a caress on her tongue, followed by the much brisker reprimand that followed, 'They need you. Not just to pay off the debts and to sort out their finances. But to help them to grieve and grow. Especially the boys. They need someone to look up to, to be a guiding hand in their life.'

Amusement teased the corners of his mouth at her concern. 'I have already accepted that fate. I realised not long after you approached me at Lady Bulphan's ball and reprimanded me so soundly. I had thought I could provide for them at a distance, but you reminded me that no responsibility is without personal cost. The boys will always have me fully and without compromise. No one else will be in my life except them.'

She frowned, strangely appearing not to like his answer, even though she'd been the one urging him to think of his family. 'Well, I didn't mean you couldn't have your own life, or marry yourself one day. Just that you would be the only father figure for the boys. Charles always said his own family were cold.'

A derisive snort escaped his mouth unconsciously. 'Cold? They have disowned him and Cleo entirely. Apparently, they have paid enough money over the years to raise an army, let alone four boys, and they refuse to give any more.'

Maggie gasped, her eyes widening in the lamplight to two black pools surrounded by a ring of blue. 'But that's impossible... Cleo said they received nothing from them for years!'

He sighed, lowering his voice to confess what he could never tell Cleo. 'He was a gambler and a rake, Maggie... A liar.'

She swallowed before giving a nod of acceptance.

'So you see,' he added with what he hoped was a reassuring smile, even though it felt too tight on his jaw. 'I am *well aware* of the fact that it will be myself, Cleo and the boys for the long road ahead. We will manage, but I need no reminder of my responsibilities. I know you are hopeful for Cleo and William, but the more I think on it, the more I realise it is impossible.'

'I am sorry,' she said softly, her eyes not quite meeting his, and his stomach twisted when he thought of her pitying him. If things were different, he might have even courted her. Between the fall in the garden and the day in the park, they had somehow formed a connection. Perhaps it was because of the fun and laughter they'd shared with the children, or the mutual pain of Cleo's outburst, but he felt strangely attached to her in a way that he had never felt before.

Would Maggie have ever considered him as a potential suitor?

The thought made him dizzy, but then he dismissed it quickly... She would *never* consider him. Even after she discovered he wasn't half as bad as she had originally imagined. Surely, she wouldn't want a dull man such as himself, who was bound by duty to live a life of quiet existence. She was a social butterfly and a woman of wealth who enjoyed parties and ribbons…not nights of drinking whisky and reading by the fire.

The confusion must have been clear on his face because she clarified it by adding, 'For reprimanding you…and for reminding you once again of your responsibilities—you must be sick of my lecturing you unfairly every five minutes!'

'I could never be sick of you,' he answered truthfully, unable to help himself, and being rewarded by the blossom of pink on her cheeks. Then, wondering if he had been inappropriate, he added, 'Even if you are a little maddening at times.'

She became flustered then and glanced towards the window overlooking the garden. 'So you will sacrifice a family of your own to raise Charles's brood?'

'I will.'

She bit her bottom lip as if hesitating, but he was familiar with her habit and waited for whatever question would follow. Sure enough, it came out a moment later in one quick rush of words. 'Is that why you said you weren't interested in me at the ball?'

A tonne of bricks could have fallen on his head and he would have been less surprised.

Chapter Eight

'You heard that?' His stomach rolled with embarrassment. She must think him a pompous ass!

'It was hard not to!' she exclaimed, 'There was a lull in the music and I think the entirety of London heard your quick rejection of me.'

He swallowed, understanding her frostiness the following day. 'Then I apologise *profusely*. I meant no criticism of you personally—'

'It doesn't matter. You wouldn't be the first.' She shrugged lightly.

But he could tell by the pinch to her mouth that she wasn't as untroubled as she pretended to be, and he was offended on her behalf. 'Whoever treated you badly in the past was either blind or a fool.'

'He was neither of those.' She shook her head with embarrassment as she quickly replied, 'And, I should have known better. You see, I spent my debutante years in Edinburgh, but after three years without a single suitor, my mother grew more desperate and sent me here for the season instead. During my first year in London, a Mr Beaston thought it highly amusing to court me as a jest. He had a wager with his friends that he would be the first to kiss me. In a way, it's not so bad. After all, he made the bet before he'd even met me. I guess my unlucky reputation arrived before I did. Thankfully, William found out about it—Mr Beaston wasn't very discreet—and we quickly put a stop to it. Eventually, he realised we were no longer ignorant of his schemes.'

Hawk recalled Mr Beaston from his university days—Hawk never forgot a face—especially an unpleasant one. The man was more than a fool, he was a cruel fool. The kind that delighted in pulling the maid's hair or tripping up younger boys. But he could also be charming when he wished to be, and he could well imagine how Maggie might have been tricked by him.

However, the idea of him kissing Maggie—well, anyone kissing Maggie, but particularly *him*—made his blood boil, and that was even before he thought about the cruelty of the jest.

She deserved better.

'Did you…kiss him?' he asked quietly, already vowing that he would teach Mr Beaston a lesson the next time he saw him.

Summer-sky eyes widened as she stared up at him. 'No… I've never been kissed.' She leaned back, her carefully coiffured hair pressing into the leather-bound volumes behind her head. 'Probably never will be, either.' She sounded breathless, and her eyes dipped to his mouth in an unspoken question. His heart was racing, the rise and fall of his chest matching hers for every ragged beat.

'Never?' They were so close to each other now that he was almost tempted to prove her wrong. Maggie looked up at him with her full lips slightly parted. Was she begging him for a kiss? Or was that wishful thinking on his part?

She shook her head, the copper ringlets around her face brushing against her collarbone.

'Would you like to be?'

She gasped, her bosom heaving as she stared up at him. 'I...'

This was so wrong!

She had admitted to being a hopeless romantic, and here he was trying to seduce her, *immediately* after telling her he would never marry!

He waited for a denial but it never came. Instead, she whispered, 'Yes...just once. I know it wouldn't mean anything.'

Hawk wanted to tell her that it *always meant something*. But he feared that would only hurt her in the long term. Her eyes were a single ring of pansy blue in the dim light, her pupils wide as she whispered the final words that broke him, 'I trust you.'

If he was a gentleman, he would have told her never to trust any man…

But he'd be damned if he let anyone else kiss her first!

Cupping her cheek, he tilted her face up and then brushed his lips against her mouth. She inhaled a small gasp as their lips touched, and her neck flexed beneath his wrist as she swallowed a nervous gulp of air.

He pressed against her, her body softening against his as he leaned her against the bookcase. He was about to kiss her more deeply but instinctively knew it wouldn't be enough to satisfy him. It would never be enough.

William's loud laugh filtered in from the other room and Hawk took a step back, suddenly realising the inappropriateness of his behaviour. Maggie must have realised the same because she dove to the side, walking a few steps away from him towards the desk.

'Uh…thank you!' she said. 'That was most…enlightening.'

She winced straight after speaking, obviously regretting her words.

Hawk ran a hand through his hair, trying to regain his own composure. It had been the sweetest of kisses, the type given by a groom to his bride in church. Hardly scandalous, and yet it had shaken him to his core. 'I am sorry. I should not have done that. I don't know what I was thinking.'

Maggie gave a nervous laugh and shrugged. 'No, honestly, think nothing of it. It was a nice experience... especially as it is unlikely that I will ever marry. Anyway, let us focus on the task of finding those papers!'

She began rifling through the many papers abandoned there. He had to admit the word *nice* offended him a little. But when she glanced up at him expectantly, he caught the momentary flicker of vulnerability in her expression and he quickly joined her.

'A man would be lucky to have you, Maggie,' he said firmly, and when she looked up at him for a second time there was a sweet pleasure to her expression that made him glad to have confessed it. 'I am sure one day you will find the perfect match. Sadly, I will never marry due to *my* circumstances.' He tried to make light of the situation. 'Unless...some wealthy young miss decides she can't live without me—which I highly doubt.'

Not everyone was as lucky as his friend Adam, who had managed to win the hand of a wealthy heiress in less time than it took Hawk to empty his bachelor rooms and move back in with his sister. A depressing realisation, but sadly true.

Maggie smiled, a sparkle of mischief in her eyes that distracted him from his gloomy thoughts. 'Or... you decide you cannot live without her?'

'I doubt that will ever happen.'

'Why?' she asked, a slight pout on her face that made him chuckle.

'Because... I am not the romantic type,' he admitted. 'I am a cautious man by nature, with a head for business. Much like Archie was. Why do you think Cleo fell so hard for Charles? He offered her passion and excitement. She was bored out of her mind at home. She'd been forced to mother a grouchy child, while also playing nurse to her sickly twin. The Hawksmere men are as dull and as dry as stale bread. Pessimistic, too. There is no cloud we do not spot.'

Maggie seemed offended on his behalf. 'I am sure you would not describe your enlistment in the war as a dry and dull choice? *Gallant* would be a more appropriate word!'

He stiffened at the praise; it felt like a lash against his heart.

He and his friends had barely survived, and there were many more men that had not.

'I enlisted because my friends enlisted... That is hardly *gallant*.'

'You were swept up in the excitement of it all,' she said. 'Many were. But you persevered and made a name for yourself on the battlefield. Archie was so proud of your exploits. And I can prove it to you. Remember that scrapbook I mentioned? It is here somewhere...' She walked over to the bookshelf and after a moment of checking the shelves, she dragged out a clothbound scrapbook and placed it carefully on the centre of his desk. Hawk came to her side as she reverently opened it to the first page.

Carefully pasted in were scraps from all manner of newspapers and pamphlets regarding the war. Glancing at the articles he realised a common theme pervaded each piece...the Thirteenth Light Dragoons and their exploits, including the horrors of Albuera.

Six bloody years of hell were carefully and beautifully marked on page after page. Maggie moved them gently, pointing out the clippings and making little remarks as to why they had been deemed worthy for the scrapbook.

'Look, this is about Major Mayhew's commendation from the Regent. Saving thirty of his fellow cavalry soldiers. Archie was convinced you would have been involved.'

Hawk shrugged. 'Adam is as reckless as he is brave. On that occasion he was right to go against orders. He saved a lot of men.'

'Och, so you had nothing to do with it?' Her soft accent washed over him like a warm melody.

'Oh, that time was all Adam. But I was there,' he answered, not wanting to go into the details in case she called him gallant again, but finding his mouth running away from him regardless. 'The top brass repeatedly failed us on the battlefield. This was one of the times we rebelled against their ineptitude. There were plenty of other times when we did as we were told…and men died. They should have *listened* to us. Some of those commanders should never have been put in charge of men. They couldn't even dress themselves, let alone make military decisions!' Hawk's bitterness rolled off his tongue with a hiss, and when he glanced back at Maggie he only saw sympathy in her eyes. He sighed. 'There was so much senseless death that could have been avoided. None of us are proud of what we did. We only wish we could have done more.'

Maggie turned the page and said gently, 'I think Archie understood that. He wanted to include everything, the good and the bad. He was very put out about the covert stuff. He wanted details, but even his contact at the war office couldn't give him everything…he left gaps here for you to fill in when you came home.'

Hawk rolled his eyes. 'They can stay blank.'

Maggie chuckled. 'There is one thing I want to know about…'

Hawk frowned; he suspected he would tell her anything. 'What?'

'The incident with the donkey…that ended with you all spending a night in the brig?'

Hawk winced, twitching his nose unconsciously. 'That damn donkey! I had my nose broken because of that beast! Then Adam thought it a good idea to punch my nose back into place. As you can see it didn't work.'

Maggie laughed merrily, and he couldn't help but smile in response.

'But *why* did you steal it?'

Hawk shrugged. 'It was taken from a family who needed it. We stole it back for them. Except the beast was stupid and ended up kicking me in the face for my efforts.'

He sank down into his brother's leather chair and began to carefully turn the pages. His own honours and medals were listed, as well as his friends'.

There were also lists of the fallen, with flowers of remembrance dried and pressed into the pages beside them. As if Archie knew Hawk would be pained by their loss and wanted to honour them.

But most heartbreaking of all were the drawings done by Archie himself. He'd been a talented artist and had drawn with meticulous detail depictions of Hawk and his friends astride their cavalry horses or charging into battle across the page.

His throat tightened painfully at the sight; they were idealistic and beautiful...nothing like the true brutality of war. 'I did my duty and I looked after my friends... at least as much as I could. Some of them were determined to put themselves constantly in harm's way.'

Like Ezra and Adam! he thought bad-temperedly.

Her head tilted as if she was examining him, her

hips brushing against the side of his chair, the rustling of silk whispering in the silence. 'You enlisted to protect them?'

He laughed, but it tasted bitter. 'Foolish... I could barely protect myself, let alone three grown men. But I will do right by Cleo and the boys. In a way it will be a far simpler task to keep them safe from ruin.'

'Archie was right about you. You really are a hero, through and through.'

Hawk squirmed like a worm on a hook. 'Maggie...' he said softly, a plea and a warning for her to stop.

She shrugged with a cheerful smile that quickly turned to a frown as she pointed down at the corner of the scrapbook. 'What's that?'

Chapter Nine

Hawk turned the page and found a letter amongst the pages, wax sealed and untouched. Carefully written in his brother's hand were the words *For the attention of my brother, Hawk, and Miss Maggie Mackenzie*.

Maggie gasped, shocked that Archie's final words would be written for two people who had never even met each other when Archie was alive. 'Why would he address it to both of us?'

'Let us find out.'

Hawk turned over the paper and broke the seal. He read it aloud for Maggie's benefit.

'To my brother and my dearest friend Miss Maggie Mackenzie. I am sure you are startled to find this letter hidden away as it is. But I hope you understand my need for discretion. I can feel my days in the sun are beginning to wane and I suspect I will not survive this latest bout of illness. My soul has been in debt to the reaper for far too long, and it is finally time to repay him. I am content to leave this world, so please do not mourn me for too long or regret the time we have spent apart. I would not change it. You have lived your life, which is the only thing I have ever asked of you.'

Hawk paused, his hands beginning to tremble. Gently, Maggie took it from his numb fingers and began to read the rest.

'I only hope that you return home safe and well. If that be the case, then know that I am happy, wherever I may be. Your return is all that I have prayed for in the remaining days that I have left. Now, let me explain the reason for my subterfuge and hiding of this letter...

Maggie, my dear and trusted friend, I know that you will be keen to show Hawk my scrapbook, knowing as you do how much it means to me. I also know that if the very worst should happen, and Hawk does not return from war, you will come, as instructed, and take this scrapbook as a token of our friendship, as we have spent many hours together compiling it. One thing is for certain; I can guarantee that Charles will not care to open it, for he is the reason I must keep this letter private. I am afraid of what will happen if even Cleo learns of this letter, which is why I will not mention it to you, for fear of her overhearing.

If the worst has happened burn this letter, Maggie, I beg you, and do what you can for my sister Cleo and her boys. A hard road lies ahead of them, and it is Charles who is to blame. I beg you, do not trust him. He has deceived us all.'

Maggie paused, glancing up at the door, still slightly ajar. But Cleo's music continued to filter in from the drawing room, so with a hushed voice she continued.

'He has run up terrible debts, sold their house and escapes a debtors' prison only because of my generosity. But that is not all. Money keeps disappearing from my accounts.

I suspect Charles is to blame and has forged documents on my behalf, but sadly Cleo is either complicit or fooled by his crimes... Perhaps even both, as strange as it may sound. She has been dazzled by him for so long that she can no longer see or accept the truth. The man she married was never real, and she and the boys deserve so much better than this poor illusion she has built her life around.

I have followed some of his larger payments to a Mr Wilkins who lives not far from our country estate in Castleton—maybe he will shed some light on the matter, although I suspect he is just another debtor. Unfortunately, I have been too unwell to travel to discover more. But I hope you will succeed where I have failed. Find Mr Wilkins and put a stop to whatever hold he has over Charles…or, better yet, remove Charles from our family completely, in any way that you can…'

Maggie swallowed, shocked by the implication. 'Surely, he doesn't mean…?'

A muscle flexed in Hawk's jaw. 'It seems fate or God has already made that decision for me.'

A shiver ran down her spine at the deadly look in Hawk's eyes; all gentlemanly visage had disappeared in an instant and she knew he would do anything to protect his family.

She hurried onwards with the rest of the letter.

'I have tried to keep the deeds to the country house and something else which will be essential to your future away from Charles and Cleo for as long as I can. You will find them amongst your treasures—I hope you still remember where they are kept. Sadly, I doubt they will stay hidden for long after my death. Charles has already been pestering my steward for details. But hopefully, they can be kept from him, at least until Hawk's return.

I leave it in your hands, dearest brother. I only wish that I could stay alive to help you. Know that I am proud of you. Raising you was my greatest challenge and my only reward in this life. Tell Cleo and the boys that I love them dearly. Mag-

gie, please help Hawk as best as you can. Be his comfort and his guiding hand, as you have been to me and Cleo for so many years.
All my love, Archie.'

Maggie wiped the tears from her eyes before they could fall onto the paper and smudge the precious ink.

Hawk took the letter from her. He stared down at the writing for a moment, then walked over to the mantelpiece and removed the cover of a lit oil lamp, his expression grim.

'Don't!' she cried, running to him and grabbing his hand to stop him from setting the paper alight.

Pained yet resolved eyes met hers. 'Cleo cannot find this.'

She nodded, peeling the letter from his hands. 'I understand. But these are the last words of your brother. You will want to keep them. Let me take them. They will be safe with me, I promise. And one day, perhaps Cleo will be able to read them, too.'

'She cannot...it would destroy her. She must never read it.'

'It will be safe with me.' Maggie quickly folded the letter tightly until it was only a small square and then tucked it down the side of her ample bosom. Hawk quickly looked away from her, a splash of crimson on his cheeks. He must think her very improper, so she explained quickly, 'My reticule is in the drawing room. But rest assured, I will keep your letter safely hidden in my home until you should want it back.' Her hand gripped his arm tightly. 'We must go to Castleton, *soon*.'

She was so small and yet so fierce. Determined to follow him in this battle no matter what. He was about to argue it, when a voice at the door startled them both, forcing them to take several steps apart.

'What has kept you so long?' asked Cleo sternly, her countenance disapproving as she looked between them, obviously surprised by their closeness.

'Oh, I was showing your brother Archie's scrapbook,' Maggie said lightly, guiltily glancing back at the book on the desk several feet away.

'Perhaps you will show us all?' said Cleo with a questioning look.

'Of course!' cried Maggie, rushing towards the desk to gather it up.

'No, it is in the past…where it belongs,' snapped Hawk, and everyone paused, shocked by the vehemence in his tone. He strode past Maggie to the desk and closed it with a thud.

Then, with slightly more care, he slid it back onto a high shelf, his fingers lingering on the binding before dropping to his side.

'Miss Mackenzie,' he said politely, offering her his arm, and she took it, allowing him to lead her past his confused sister with as much of a blank expression as she could muster.

She had never felt like this before…guilty, as if she were doing something wrong by being alone with a gentleman. But then again…she had never been alone with a gentleman before. Certainly, she had never been kissed…not until tonight, and she was still reeling from that revelation, as well as Archie's.

For all his bluster and pessimistic countenance, Hawk had kissed her sweetly, and if anything, she had been the one desperate for more, ready to throw everything away on five more minutes of blissful sensation. She had always dreamed of romance and love, but she had never imagined that something so sweet could also be filled with so much longing. Her body ached for him, and as her fingers touched the warmth of his sleeve, she realised how easily and far she could fall.

She had to remind herself that it was meaningless… at least to Hawk. He had plainly told her that he would never consider her. At least it wasn't because of anything that she had done. But it still hurt, because her soft heart hoped for more, and it had always wanted a man who would love her so fiercely that he would cross battlefields or oceans for her.

Hawk would never do such a thing, because he would never want her *enough*. His family duty came first and always would; he did not *want* her. Which was no surprise to Maggie; nobody had wanted her in the past, and as time marched onwards she grew more certain that no one ever would.

Such knowledge had always been a bitter disappointment to her, but it had never hurt as much as it did now—the pleasant smile on her face felt as brittle and as sharp as broken glass. Even the embarrassment with Mr Beaston had not hurt quite like this—for all his snakelike charm, he had never made her heart race like Hawk.

In fact, she had never met anyone like Hawk before, and perhaps that was why she was still unmarried. Were her standards too high? Strange to think that she might be the architect of her own unhappiness. But when Hawk kissed her, she had realised what she'd been waiting for all these years. A spark, a flutter of butterflies in the pit of her stomach, the quickening of her heart and the dizzying of her mind… *Passion*.

But it was all for nought, because he did not feel the same way and could never offer her anything more than kindness.

When the three of them returned to the drawing room, her uncle William spoke cheerfully about Cleo's playing and asked what had taken them so long. She explained about them becoming distracted by the scrapbook, and the conversation was quickly turned by Cleo on to other matters—probably realising that Hawk did not wish to speak of it. Maggie deliberately avoided looking at Hawk for the rest of the evening, in case it made them suspicious.

Hawk remained quiet, except when he said casually, 'After Ezra's benefit ball... I plan to visit Castleton.'

Maggie gripped her skirts, wondering if he would invite them. She was afraid he wouldn't despite it being obvious from Archie's letter that he intended for them to work together on this. He'd become cold and distant, as if shaken by all that had happened between them...as if he regretted it. Which not only stung her pride, but also dimmed the pleasure of their kiss with a veil of shame.

Cleo was her surprising saviour. 'Oh, the boys would love that! A short trip away before we find a tutor.' She looked pointedly at William and then Maggie. 'I know you have lots of plans, but...would you care to join us? Castleton is beautiful at this time of year, and I do not believe you have ever visited before, have you?'

Uncle William grinned. 'We have not!' He then glanced her way, his voice gentle as he asked, 'What say you, Maggie? Is there an engagement that we can't possibly wriggle out of?'

'None at all,' Maggie said, hoping she didn't look too eager. 'We would love to join you!'

A short time later, Maggie and her uncle walked back into their townhouse, weaving a little from the wine and brandy they'd drunk that night. William handed his hat and coat to the footman before turning to Maggie. 'Will you join me for a moment?'

Maggie nodded, a little confused but not overly worried. 'Of course,' she said, smiling as she handed her own coat to one of the servants. When his back was turned, she slipped Archie's letter from her gown and into her reticule before following him in their drawing room.

A small fire was burning and a footman rushed to light the lamps as William poured them each a glass of water from the carafe. They always kept some by the decanter of her whisky to mix it with, although William often enjoyed it neat.

Tonight the decanter remained firmly closed, as William handed her a glass and they settled themselves opposite one another in front of the fire. If it had just been to talk over the evening before bed, or to keep him company for a little longer, the decanter would have been opened.

It was the first indication that her uncle had something serious to discuss.

She waited, the ticking of the clock the only sound between them. Her uncle looked troubled; he shifted in his chair as if trying to make himself more comfortable and failing.

'Maggie, I want to…discuss something with you,'

he said eventually—when she had all but given up on waiting for him to speak.

'What is it? You seem...worried.'

William sighed and leaned forward in his chair. 'I am...worried.'

She held her breath. Was he concerned about her? About the time she had spent alone with Hawk? 'What about?' she asked lightly, clasping her hands together tightly to give herself something to focus on other than her uncle's piercing gaze.

'Are you really fine with us going to Castleton with them? If you need an excuse or time apart, I can easily say I forgot about some prior engagement.'

She frowned. 'I want to go. Why would you think otherwise?'

William leaned back in his chair and scratched his rusty head with a sigh. After a pause, he asked, 'Is Lord Hawksmere courting you?'

A hot blush flew up her face and she vehemently shook her head. 'No! How preposterous! He said so himself at Lady Bulphan's ball—he would never consider me in that way! We are friends.'

'Things change...' William said thoughtfully. 'And it is my duty—in your parents' absence—to protect you and your honour. You were alone for a very long time this evening. Cleo had to go find you. You must see how...improper that is.'

She laughed, but it was met by an uncharacteristic stony expression that caused her pretence to die in her throat. She decided to try another path, one of incredulity, 'Oh, come, William! We were only looking at the scrapbook Archie had made. You never had a problem with me spending time alone with Archie.'

'You were friends, and Archie was too weak to chase down a mouse let alone a woman,' replied her uncle tartly.

'There has been no *chasing* of any kind. I am not some silly debutante who needs to fear her reputation!'

'You are still unmarried, Maggie.' William's voice was low, but it was still a clear reprimand.

'I am aware of that fact, William!' she snapped, getting more irritated by the moment. Partly because a small part of her wished there *was* some scandal to speak of, but a polite brush of the lips did not warrant this! So she continued waspishly. 'For many years I have been unmarried. You cannot expect me to live my life still guarding against scandal at every moment! You were only a room away from us, and the doors were open. No one is going to question my honour. They will know that a man such as Lord Hawksmere would never wish to dishonour me.'

'True…' muttered her uncle, rubbing his jaw thoughtfully.

She flinched. 'Well, I didn't expect you to agree quite so wholeheartedly! But I suppose I should be grateful we are in agreement at least.'

'Och, lass,' sighed William, 'I meant no offence. But a man with a title...he has no need for a miss—not unless she comes with a heavy purse. However, that doesn't stop a man from taking other liberties.'

'For heaven's sake, Lord Hawksmere is a gentleman, and I am close friends with his sister. There is absolutely no fear of impropriety!' she hissed, and then with a forced smile she added, 'I am tired. I think I shall retire for the night. Perhaps in daylight you will realise the foolishness of such fears.'

'Perhaps I shall,' said William, leaning back in his chair and reaching for the whisky. As she left the room she heard him mutter, 'But why did he stare at you all night? That's what I want to know.'

Maggie didn't know the answer to that, and so she pretended she hadn't heard him.

Chapter Ten

'I imagine it's not far now,' said William cheerfully as they passed some cottages on the viscount's estate.

Hawk nodded with a polite smile. 'Thank you again for allowing me to join you.' He really wished William hadn't been quite so gracious or insistent that they travel with one another. It had been over a week since their dinner together, and so much had happened since. He'd attended Adam's wedding and had tried to untangle the web of debts left by Charles, while also being constantly distracted by the chaos…and fun living with his nephews gave him.

But when he tried to focus on his finances it always ended badly; his mind was constantly filled with thoughts of Maggie and her soft lips, until he'd struggled to concentrate on the numbers swimming on the ledgers in front of him.

'Oh, I insist!' declared William. 'Why bother with two carriages when we're going to the same place?

Besides, what if Cleo needs your carriage in our absence? Better to take only one.'

'I would have happily ridden. I feel as if we have taken advantage of you far too much already,' said Hawk, immediately regretting his words as his eyes instinctively sought out Maggie's, because he'd definitely taken advantage of her the last time they'd met.

She sat beside William, wearing a silk teal ball gown embroidered with gold thread around the bust and capped sleeves, with a few tartan Mackenzie bows added to her gown and piled up amber curls. Maggie's favourite colours seemed to be varying shades of blue and green. He absently wondered if it was because it suited her colouring or if it was due to family pride. Either way, she was particularly beautiful tonight with sapphires dangling from her ears. The constant jostling of the carriage caused the jewels to swing, softly brushing against her neck in a way that reminded him of how his own fingers had felt against her skin.

'Nonsense!' declared William, and reluctantly Hawk pulled his attention away from Maggie to her uncle, who was proudly wearing his traditional Scottish kilt, smartly paired with a military-style short jacket and waistcoat in matching Mackenzie tartan. Even his silver buttons were shaped into thistles.

'I expect you will be glad to see your friends tonight?' said Maggie, who up until now had said very little on their short journey out of London to Artington Hall.

He nodded. 'It will be good to see them—although, we do meet up once a week at White's.'

'They must mean a great deal to you.'

Again, he nodded, feeling more than a little awkward to be talking about such things in front of her uncle. He glanced out the window and was relieved to see the imposing viscount's home come into view. 'We're here!'

William and Maggie craned their necks to see and both gasped. 'By Jove!' declared William, and by Maggie's wide eyes he could tell she thought much the same.

Hawk was less impressed, not because the building wasn't outstanding in its grandeur and elegance. But because he knew how much the viscount who owned it had tormented his friend Ezra over the years. The man was difficult and cold, and manipulated Ezra with constant conditions—like finding a suitable bride at tonight's ball. It was distasteful and cruel, and Hawk pitied his friend because he deserved better than what that miserable old man could offer.

Lots of other guests had also arrived, and it took a moment for them to leave the carriage and make their way through the bustling crowd to the entrance, where they waited in line to be greeted by their hosts.

Miss Seraphine Mounier was a truly beautiful and

elegant hostess with kind eyes and beautiful golden hair with streaks of strawberry blonde hidden amongst the elaborate chignon. Maggie made a point of complimenting her on the flowers, and Hawk couldn't help but smile at the way her easy praise caused Seraphine to beam with pride. Maggie always seemed to bring joy to everyone she met.

Next, Hawk took them to greet his friend Ezra, who clapped him on the shoulder in a welcoming embrace. Hawk moved away a step, strangely nervous for the first time as he said, 'Ezra, I would like to introduce you to Miss Maggie Mackenzie and her uncle, Mr William Mackenzie.'

Ezra gave them both a warm welcome before asking him, 'Seraphine's done wonders with the place, don't you think?'

Hawk glanced around at the opulent splendour and glistening chandeliers. 'She's certainly brightened it up.'

Ezra grinned in agreement, but his face turned serious when the sound of trumpets announced the arrival of a very important guest—the Prince Regent, and Ezra had to step forward to greet him.

After the excitement of the Prince Regent's arrival, Hawk guided William and Maggie to the side of the ballroom to get some drinks, while the first dance began. Hawk wasn't much of a dancer; he was always too big and clumsy during the intricate steps. But he began to feel guilty for not asking Maggie when he noticed her staring wistfully at the dancers. She looked around the room, catching the eye of many acquaintances and giving them a cheerful wave, but then he noticed her quietly slip her empty dance card into her reticule.

'Will you do me the honour of the next dance?' he blurted out, a little shocked by the force of his tone. It sounded more like he'd demanded a duel rather than a dance.

Maggie blinked back her surprise and then gave a little nod of agreement. 'That would be lovely, thank you.'

'Put me down for the one after that,' said her uncle, and she gave them both a pleased smile.

Lord and Lady Wrexham joined them and asked after Cleo and the children. Hawk was quick to mention that Cleo was considering attending their ball later in the season, and Lady Wrexham seemed so delighted by the prospect, she said she would call on Cleo soon, saying that she was relieved to hear she would be returning to society.

William began to speak with Lord Wrexham about other matters of business, while Lady Wrexham chatted with Maggie.

Hawk, however, didn't join in on either conversation. He found himself staring at Maggie's profile instead. Occasionally, he nodded and laughed under the pretence of listening to what Lady Wrexham and Maggie were saying, but the truth was he only had eyes for Maggie.

It was almost a relief when the band began to prepare for the next set, and he was able to offer Maggie his hand. 'Our dance?' he reminded her gently, and her gloved hand slipped into his so that he could lead her to the dance floor.

He absently noticed Ezra and Seraphine had also taken to the floor a few feet away from them. Of course, Ezra would choose a waltz to dance with his beautiful lady, but for once Hawk was grateful for his scandalous friend's antics, because it meant he could pull Maggie into his arms and hold her tightly.

Maggie was floating.

Hawk was twirling her around the dance floor in a way that made her head spin and her heart race. He was so tall that she was certain he'd picked her up off the floor a couple of times, navigating them through the other dancers with confidence.

For once, Maggie didn't feel self-conscious. Her entire focus—in fact, her *entire* body—seemed to be captured within the embrace of Hawk's strong arms, and she couldn't have been happier.

At one point, his hand on her waist tightened and he fully picked her up in the air to twist away from their hosts, who for some reason had stopped dead in the middle of the dance floor.

Maggie gasped, gripping tightly onto his thick biceps. 'Sorry about that,' he said as he smoothly set her back onto her feet and continued as if nothing had happened.

'No, that's…fine,' she said, her heart still pounding. 'You're a very good dancer.'

Hawk's eyes widened in surprise, and a splash of colour stained his cheeks as he said with a shrug, 'I'm not really. I just pick you up if I miss a step.'

Maggie laughed at his confession. 'And there I was thinking I'd gained a few inches in height!'

He smiled, but as he opened his mouth to say something else, a loud shattering of glass came from behind them and Hawk pulled her close, turning her away from the bang and curving his big body around her like a shield.

A brick skidded past them followed by shards of glass that sprayed across the dance floor like glistening diamonds. People screamed in fright, and Hawk raised his head to glance over his shoulder.

'What happened?' she gasped, trying to look around him, but failing because of the sheer bulk of him pressed tightly against her. More people were running, scrabbling through the broken shards with whimpers and horrified faces. There were shouts to protect the prince, and she thought she heard Hawk's name being called to help.

With a grim expression, Hawk took one look at the glittering floor and swept her up into his arms, carrying her like a bride as he hurriedly crunched across the floor. She found there was one clear advantage of being so high up, as she was finally able to see what had happened more clearly.

A huge window had been smashed, presumably by the group of men that were running across the lawn towards them with weapons in hand, some with scarves wrapped around their faces, others openly displaying the hatred in their expressions.

She glanced back to where Hawk was carrying her, and spotted her uncle rushing towards them, forcing his way through the crowd like a salmon swimming upstream. The Prince Regent and many of the guests were being ushered by several men including the royal guards into the library. Already the doors were being firmly closed; people pushed away who hadn't made it in time.

Hawk swept the floor with one brush of his boot before he deposited her back on her silk slippers and into her uncle's now waiting arms. 'Look after her,' was all Hawk said before he was ripping off his jacket and running back into the fray.

He grabbed a sword from the wall and followed his friend Ezra into battle. Maggie took a step forward, horrified that he would put himself at risk. But William pulled her arm to tug her back behind him. 'Come away, Maggie!'

'I can't!' she said helplessly.

William hissed a curse and grabbed a cake knife from the pastry table as a makeshift weapon. 'I'll protect ye as best as I can, lass. But I'm no soldier.'

'I don't think you'll be needing that anyway,' she replied, more than a little awestruck by the heroism she was witnessing from Hawk and his friends, who were already engaged in battling the intruders.

Maggie rushed to the side of the ballroom to stare out the window, and her uncle joined her. 'Bloody hell!' he muttered with admiration, and Maggie couldn't agree more.

Hawk and his friends were not only fighting off their enemy, but also defeating them soundly. Disarming them with a few expert sweeps of their blades, and then wrestling them to the ground, or in Hawk's case knocking them out with a single brutal punch.

'Is that… Mr Beaston?' asked her uncle, and sure enough one of the intruders' scarves had slipped enough to reveal his identity. Mr Beaston scrambled back onto his feet after being disarmed by Hawk.

Hawk threw down his weapon after recognising him in an oddly deliberate movement, before bursting forward like an angry bear, grabbing hold of the man's jacket to pull him back before slamming a fist into his face. Mr Beaston slumped to the ground as if his knees had given in. But he was still being held up by his collar, which was twisted in Hawk's fist.

'He deserved that!' said her uncle sagely.

But it seemed Hawk wasn't done because after muttering something, he hit the man for a second time square in the face, and this time the man was knocked out cold. Hawk let him drop to the ground with a disgusted expression as if he'd just swatted a fly.

William chuckled beside her, seemingly less worried about their safety now that he could see Hawk and his friends in action. 'Well, that couldn't have happened to a nicer fellow.'

Quickly, their attackers were tied up, and their guests—including the Prince Regent—were allowed back into the ballroom as the royal guards forced the prisoners into a waiting carriage ready to take them back to London.

Hawk was still prowling around them, ensuring the bindings to their wrists were tight. She couldn't help but smile. *Such a warrior*, she thought with amusement and a heavy dose of pride. She doubted she had ever seen a man look more powerful and attractive than Hawk did at this very moment.

Her breath tightened in her chest when his eyes swept back to the house and saw her looking at him through the glass. He strode towards them and, blushing, she stumbled away from the window as William also turned away to greet him as he reentered the ballroom.

'Let me get you to your carriage,' Hawk said firmly, guiding Maggie by the elbow out of the ballroom, William hurrying to catch up with them—as he belatedly realised he was still armed with a cake knife, and had to toss it away.

'You should go before the rest of the crowd clog up the road,' Hawk said, ushering them straight to their carriage in such long strides that Maggie had to almost run to keep up with him.

'What about you?' she gasped as he helped her into the carriage and then stepped aside to allow William to enter.

'I will travel back with one of my friends. Do not worry.'

William leaned out of the window. 'Thank you, Hawk! Remind me never to annoy you in the future.' He laughed, and with a grim nod, Hawk called out to the carriage driver for them to go.

Maggie gripped the side of the window and leaned out as they left, staring back at the handsome figure of Hawk as they moved away. There was so much she wanted to say, but she couldn't find the wit or the words she needed.

She hadn't even had a chance to make another guess at his name.

Helplessly, she raised a hand in farewell, and Hawk

returned it. His figure grew more distant with each roll of the carriage, until they were out of sight of him and she sank back into the upholstered seat breathless.

'Well, that was certainly eventful,' said her uncle with a heavy sigh, and then, shaking his head, he added, 'Thank goodness Cleo wasn't with us. That sort of violence would have given her nightmares. Not to mention the fact she would never have come out of her house *ever* again!'

Maggie could only nod in agreement.

His eyes seemed to focus on her for the first time, and he took her hand gently in his. 'Are you all right, lass?'

Maggie nodded quickly with a bright smile. 'Yes, of course!'

Reassured, her uncle sat back in his seat with a relieved sigh and closed his eyes. 'I need a nap after all that excitement.'

Maggie chuckled in agreement, but she couldn't help shifting restlessly in her seat.

She took out her empty dance card and fanned herself.

She definitely wasn't anticipating any nightmares after tonight! In fact, she imagined she would be having many lustful and romantic dreams about her hero all night long.

And, really...what harm was there in indulging in some innocent fantasies?

Chapter Eleven

The day before they were due to leave for Castleton, Maggie met Hawk again in the most unlikely of places. They'd not seen each other since the Artington benefit ball, although she'd called on Cleo regularly. Hawk had always been busy in his study or out on business. She was almost glad of it, as her silly romantic heart had been reliving the drama of that night obsessively.

However, if she'd had hindsight, she would have picked a far better place for their next meeting.

She was at the basement entrance of White's, the gentleman's club that stocked her illicit barrels of whisky, and she was talking with the manager, a Mr Roberts, about her latest delivery.

The roll and murmur of passing carriages and gentlemen above meant that she kept her cloak firmly gathered around her head and shoulders. The constant drizzle helped to conceal her, too, as not many were looking at the faces of people that passed them, let alone paying attention to women dressed in servants' clothing as she was.

'What do you think of my first "aged" batch, Mr Roberts?'

'It's surprisingly good, miss. Not my usual taste—I'm a brandy man. But several of the gentlemen like it. One even asked for a barrel to be delivered to his home.'

Maggie had to stop herself from squealing with joy. 'Marvelous! Is it worthy of a second order, then, for next season?' She'd been hoping for this; she'd already sold to William's club in Edinburgh. If she could also sell a few barrels in London it would mean she had her foot well and truly wedged in the door when it came to legally distributing it later on. She might even need a bigger distillery if things went well.

Start small, dream big. That had always been her father's motto.

Mr Roberts smiled. 'It is indeed!' He paused, moving a little closer, his voice hushed. 'If you're willing, I can distribute it more widely for you as well...at a discount of course.'

'Of course!' Maggie grinned, and they negotiated for a few minutes more before shaking hands on an agreement that suited them both.

After saying goodbye, she lifted her skirts to walk up the steep basement steps to reach ground level. Carriages raced by and the rain began to pour more thickly. It was midafternoon, but it may as well have been dusk—the sky was so grey and miserable with dark clouds hanging low and heavy.

So much for a lovely summer down south! I might as well have stayed in Scotland! she thought bitterly as she hurried along the pavement, knowing by the force of the rain that she would be thoroughly soaked by the time she returned home.

She supposed she could try to flag down a hackney carriage. She turned to examine the road, but couldn't spot any of the yellow-painted coaches amongst the many private carriages—although it was difficult to see in the gloom.

One coach had to swerve to avoid a man on horseback, and its wheel dipped into a murky puddle at the side of the road. Instinctively, she turned her back towards it, the heavy splash of icy water hitting the back of her cloak and soaking her through the cloth. She was so distracted by the spray that she didn't realise she was about to walk directly into a gentleman who was leaving White's himself—although, of course, through the main entrance and not coming up from the bottom steps as she had.

Unfortunately, she barrelled into him, straight into his chest, covered in a silk waistcoat of peacock blue. He also wore an extravagant buff-coloured greatcoat with a three-tiered cape draped elegantly around his broad shoulders. Big and imposing, he wasn't one of the elegantly slim men who usually frequented White's, and he felt oddly familiar. Startled, she glanced up with a spluttered, 'Forgive me!'

To her surprise the dark brown eyes that stared down at her were ones she most definitely recognised…had, in fact, dreamed of only last night.

'Maggie? What are you doing here?' Hawk asked, his arms gathering around her as if to steady her, and it sent her heart down a merry path of excitement.

Another gentleman walked past them, glancing at them curiously. She dipped her head, not wanting to be recognised—it was bad enough that she'd walked straight into her handsome neighbour; she didn't need half the ton to realise she walked around in servants' clothing and visited gentlemen's clubs' cellar doors!

Hawk must have realised her discomfort because he led her by the elbow to the edge of the pavement. 'I sent a boy for my carriage. It won't be a moment—there it is!' A carriage rolled up in front of them, and he bundled her inside before anyone else saw them.

Bellowing, 'Home, please!' to the driver, Hawk took his seat opposite Maggie. The carriage jerked forward, throwing her into the back of the upholstery.

'I…uh…thank you,' she eventually said, wondering how she had managed to find herself in this predicament with Hawk of all people. Especially after their last dramatic encounter.

He stared back at her, his own chest rising and falling rapidly as if he was as perplexed by the situation as she was. 'Are you going home? I can stop somewhere else if you prefer?' he said, running a hand through his hair and then flicking the water on his hand away from him to the other side of the small space.

'No, I was walking home anyway. Thank you for the ride. The weather has really been abysmal this year, hasn't it?' She glanced out the window at the rain that was now pouring from the sky in sheets that bounced off the pavements and caused everyone to run for cover. The carriage began to slow as it struggled to move through the growing tide of carriages swarming in and out of St James's Street.

'What are you doing here?' he asked again, and the firm look he gave her meant there was no possible argument other than the truth.

'I have business at White's.'

'Business?' He frowned, obviously not believing her.

'Yes, my family's brewery stocks them… You must have seen our beer there.'

He nodded. 'Yes, but why on earth would you need to speak with them directly? Surely, your uncle and father deal with that side of the business.'

'Remember the special brew Cleo mentioned the other night? I was talking to them about trialling it there…but they refused.' She looked away, as if to end the conversation.

Hawk leaned casually back in his seat. 'I don't believe that for one moment. Maggie, are you distilling whisky, and smuggling it in through White's? Do not be worried if you are. I will not say anything. I am actually quite fond of your latest batch. I bought a barrel of it to keep at home.'

'That was you!' she gasped, and then blushed as she realised how badly she'd kept her illicit trade a secret.

Blurting it out after one simple question! She'd be in the dock by the end of the season if she carried on like this!

But Hawk didn't seem to mind; a slow smile spread across his face. 'Is that why you are dressed as a servant and wrapped up in that cloak? To avoid the scandal of being a whisky smuggler?'

She flinched at his amused tone. 'It is a very serious business, *my lord*. If I am ever caught, it would be disastrous for my whole family and for our *legal* business, too. Not to mention the fact that we could be sent away to the colonies for it.'

'That is true,' he said sombrely, although the twinkle in his eyes suggested otherwise. 'Then why do it? Surely, a few barrels here and there doesn't earn you much.'

It was a fair point. 'It is a passion of mine.' She hated having to justify herself. 'What are your passions, my lord?'

That caused Hawk to blink. 'Passions?'

'Hobbies and interests. Surely, you have some?'

She immediately felt sorry for him, because he seemed to struggle to answer her, mumbling something about riding, cards and meeting with friends. It was clear he had no passions, other than providing for his family.

She forged on with an explanation. 'When I was young, I was terrible at drawing and music, all the accomplishments of a young lady, actually. But it didn't really matter, because I was mainly looking after the children most days anyway... And isn't that the true role of a woman?' She asked the question bitterly, already knowing the answer and trying to brush aside the sympathetic look in his eyes.

'Duty to family is something I know all too well. But I only felt that responsibility recently.' He frowned, and she wondered if he was thinking about her, or his brother and sister, who had also been thrust into guardianship at a young age.

With a cheerful smile and shrug of her shoulders, she said, 'I have a lot of siblings. It would be churlish not to help, and besides, I like children. Anyway, my grandparents used to live in a little crofter's cottage at the very edge of our estate. My father and uncle had quite humble beginnings, you see, with only a small plot of land. My father worked hard to set up a brewery, and when my uncle was still only a lad, he went to help him. Now their brewery is a huge business, supporting most of our local community. My grandparents were very proud of their achievements. However, they still insisted on living in their cottage rather than moving into the big house my father had built for us.' Maggie paused and then chuckled. 'A wise idea in the long run. They were quiet, gentle people, happy with their lot and their cottage.' She closed her eyes as she imagined the pretty crofter's cottage she adored. 'It's simple…but has everything you need to survive. Overlooked by the mountains in a sweet little glen. In summer the glen is covered in heather and flowers… Well, it's idyllic, really…' She opened her eyes with a sigh. 'A lot of hard work, too, though—to manage alone. Which is why William suggested I go and stay with them occasionally, to help them in their old age. But honestly, they helped me.'

'How so?' Hawk asked gently.

Blushing, Maggie shrugged. 'Sorry, I'm rambling… You must be bored of my chatter. I only meant to say that my grandfather used to distil whisky with me, as a hobby. I found the process fascinating. But I also loved spending time with him. Papa was always so busy with work, Mama with the children… It was nice to have my grandparents all to myself… He was exactly like my father—I wonder if that's why my father wanted to start a brewery in the first place. From watching my grandfather make all his whisky, beers and fruit wines… Oh, I'm doing it again. You don't want to hear all this.'

'I do!' Hawk declared abruptly, and she smiled with relief at how genuine he sounded. 'I want to hear all about them, every detail. I barely remember my own parents, let alone my grandparents… I think they were long gone before I was even born.'

Her heart broke for him, having had so little family of his own; no wonder he felt compelled to protect Cleo and the boys.

'Well, my grandmother was a wonderful cook. She taught me how to make shortbread.'

'Did you make the shortbread you gave Cleo? I had some the other day, it was delicious.'

Maggie nodded with a blush. 'I enjoy baking.'

'I suppose it's a similar art to whisky and beer making,' said Hawk thoughtfully, and she nodded enthusiastically in agreement.

'Yes, exactly! It's all about the process and the right timing of things. They encouraged me to try new things, to find my passion. They showed me I didn't have to be a perfect *miss*. I could do whatever I liked, as long as I enjoyed it. I am forever grateful to them for that.'

'I take it they are no longer with us?' asked Hawk gently, and she could tell he didn't mean it unkindly, only to understand her situation better.

'They died not long after each other. I'd just had my

coming out season, and even on their sick beds they insisted I not mourn them for too long. That I lived my life and kept doing the things that I loved...like the whisky making. When I make the perfect batch, I'm going to call it Crofter's Glen, in honour of them and the home they loved so much. Anyway, that's enough of me. Now that you know one of my secrets, it is only fair that I know one of yours... I want to know your name, and I am quickly running out of suggestions.'

The amusement quickly fell from his face, but then an idea seemed to strike him, and he said, 'If you *swear* never to call me it in public... I will tell you.'

Excitement leapt into her throat and she leaned forward with a deep swallow and a hand on her heart. 'I *swear* it.'

With a deep sigh, Hawk relented and mumbled quietly, 'Well, if you must know...it is... Hercules.'

'Hercules!' shrieked Maggie, exultant with surprised delight. 'Your name is *Hercules*!'

'Bloody hell,' he groaned. 'Please don't shout it! It's bad enough as it is.'

'Why? It's a hero's name.'

'I hate it.' A dark shadow eclipsed the gold flecks of his eyes. 'I am not a hero. Archie picked it. Heaven knows why our parents let him choose it. He was only ten!'

A sudden realisation made her heart ache. 'Because

he wanted you to be strong and invincible just like Hercules.'

Unlike Archie himself.

Hawk shrugged. 'Archie took pity on me as I grew up, and when I asked to be called Hawk, he agreed. Now, are you happy?'

'Delighted!' She grinned, flopping back into her seat with satisfaction.

Hawk continued to smile at her in that lazy way of his. 'Back to the whisky... Why do you do it? Personally, I think you and your family like the danger. Your uncle seems complicit in your crimes.'

'It was his idea,' she grumbled, and he laughed.

'Are you not shocked?' she asked, more curious than offended. She had been dazzled by his own heroics for days and could barely sleep without remembering in great detail the way he had carried her across the dance floor to safety.

Hawk shrugged. 'Even reverends make moonshine in their bath at night. I suppose it is the price of grain, as well as other things...'

Maggie nodded. 'It is all so badly taxed! And I am only experimenting with my batches—I enjoy the... science, if that makes sense. It certainly isn't to put food on the table. Although, I know many who do rely on it for that. Half of Scotland makes it. William is hoping to get parliament to change its taxation and licencing rules so that we can produce my whisky without fear of reprisal. If you like this one, then perhaps you can add your voice to the call for change? A baron would hold far more sway in court and parliament than my uncle—although, he does his best.'

'I suppose that is why you are feeding it into places like White's? In the hope of influencing those in power?'

'Perhaps...' she agreed, looking at him curiously and wondering if he would view her schemes as clever or corrupt.

'Then I shall add my voice to your fight. I look forward to drinking a *legal* bottle of Crofter's Glen one day.'

Maggie relaxed into her seat with a pleased smile. 'Thank you. I hope so, too! You can have the first bottle.'

'I'd appreciate that,' he replied, inclining his head with a grateful nod. 'Are you still happy to join us at Castleton tomorrow?'

'Yes, thank you for inviting us. And, of course for your help at the ball... You were very *gallant*.' She said the last with a blush, and Hawk looked equally uncomfortable.

'They were just troublemakers. We dealt with them quickly because they were no better than fools. The law will deal with them now.'

'And how is Major Mayhew and his new wife? They

caused a lot of excitement at the Renshaw ball recently.'

'They are well,' he said. 'On the whole I think it went well.' There had been some unkind articles mentioning her previous scandal but the vast majority were more excited about the *Madly in Love Major*.

'I'm glad,' said Maggie cheerfully. 'They seem so wonderfully happy together.'

Hawk grunted an acknowledgement. 'I suppose so.'

After a moment of silence, he asked, 'Perhaps your scheme to match Cleo and William will come to fruition on this trip?' He then gave an awkward chuckle and she laughed in agreement.

A few more moments passed, and then Maggie took a deep breath before speaking. 'I meant to ask… Do you know what your brother meant by *your treasures*? He said that's where we will find the papers you need.'

Hawk nodded. 'I know where he means. But…there is no need to involve yourself. This is my trouble, not yours.'

She frowned, leaning forward to look at him better. 'He asked me to help you. I will not ignore the last wishes of a dear friend, no matter what you say.'

He blinked, his dark eyes pulling her into their depths until she was unaware of anything else in the carriage. *'Dear friend…'* he repeated darkly. 'Was there something between you and Archie? Something more than friendship?'

* * *

Hawk wasn't sure why he had asked the question, but he felt compelled to know the answer.

She stiffened, as if offended by the question. 'Of course not!'

'Because he was ill?' he asked softly, knowing it was the main reason Archie had never sought a wife.

Her pretty face contorted into a disapproving scowl. 'Do you think me so shallow?'

Hawk thought for a moment and shook his head. 'I do not think you shallow. But I can imagine Archie keeping you at arm's length because of it. He was never going to marry—he thought it unfair on a bride.'

'Because he would one day make her a widow...' Maggie answered, a sad look in her normally bright eyes.

'Yes.'

There was a moment of silence, and then Maggie shocked him by saying, 'There was a time when I *would* have married him if he'd asked me.'

'You cared for him?' he barked, surprised that such an idea angered him. His brother wasn't a bad man. Why would he begrudge his brother some happiness before death? Or was it the woman in question who concerned him? He had been thinking a little too much of his red-headed neighbour of late. It was one of the reasons why he avoided her, never leaving his study when she called on Cleo.

'He was a dear *friend*!' Her denial sent a wave of unexpected relief through him.

'But you wanted more?' he asked, unable to resist poking the hornet's nest.

In a sharp tone she replied defensively, 'So what if I did? It was after I realised the intentions of Mr Beaston, and well, I despaired...a little...for a short time...and Archie was so kind. Besides, if I had married Archie, it would have been an advantageous match for *both* of us!' She looked out the window, not meeting his eye. 'My debutante years are firmly behind me. And I have been so long on the shelf now that I am collecting dust.'

'You are believing the nonsense of men like Mr Beaston. That snivelling wretch does not speak for every man!' He snorted dismissively. Maggie wasn't *on the shelf*, she was lush and vibrant, and any man would be lucky to have her. But Maggie seemed to take offence to his reaction, because she turned on him with narrowed sapphires.

'It is not a laughing matter! At least not to me...' she grumbled, her eyes returning to the window, and he realised she couldn't look at him because she was ashamed. 'I am eight-and-twenty, without much of a dowry and no title. If that were not enough, I have four younger sisters and two brothers all of whom are already wed. If Archie had asked me to marry him, I should have immediately accepted and been grateful for the offer! But he never did. I take some comfort in the fact that it might have been to save me from a greater pain later on.'

'I am sure it was.' Hawk couldn't let her go on believing the worst of herself, but would it be just as cruel to give her false hope? He'd seen the admiration in her eyes when she'd looked at him after the attack, and she'd only moments before called him gallant for the second or third time. All of which was nonsense, but stupidly, he didn't want her to think badly of him by correcting her, and he definitely couldn't tolerate her thinking so poorly of herself. 'You are being too harsh on yourself. If you did want to marry, I am sure some man would be very glad to offer you a home.'

She frowned at him. 'You make me sound like a stray cat.'

He squirmed in his seat as he was forced to acknowledge that it *did* sound like that. 'Forgive me. I only imagined that a home and security were what every young lady desired.'

And he couldn't offer her any of it!

He could barely keep a roof over his own and Cleo's heads. He had four nephews, all of whom would need expensive education and guidance into careers and adulthood. She wasn't a wealthy heiress, and frankly he couldn't afford to marry, especially if it led to more mouths to feed…as it would with Maggie…because if he *were* to marry her…

God help him...he would never be able to keep his hands off her!

It was her turn to snort. 'At one time, yes,' she responded, and to his delight, mischief and joy once again returned to sparkle in her eyes. 'But not anymore... That's not what I want.'

His lungs filled with hot anticipation wondering what she would surprise him with next. 'What do you desire now?'

She grinned wickedly. 'I am relying on my *secret* business,' she declared. 'To ensure that I will be both independent and secure, without the burden of marriage. One day, with William's help, I am certain the rules surrounding whisky production will ease, and I will be ready with a refined and superior product. Mark my words. My whisky will be a triumph!'

Lightning split the sky, illuminating the carriage in white light before flickering out. Maggie had never looked more beautiful. Dressed in servants' clothing, a damp cloak around her shoulders, her face flushed with excitement and hope, and her red hair tumbling around her in messy waves. He had never wanted to kiss a woman more, and not with a chaste brush of the lips like last time, but with a far more passionate embrace.

Thunder rumbled overhead.

'I suppose a husband would only get in the way of that dream.'

She shrugged, untroubled. 'Probably... *Perhaps* I should consider myself fortunate, then—to be so plain?'

'You are far from plain. You are...bottled sunshine,' he replied, feeling as if the confession had been ripped from his throat.

A blush crept up her cheeks and she looked down at her hands in the sweetest of shy gestures. 'Well... thank you...that is kind of you to say so.'

They were both left embarrassed by his confession.

He opened his mouth, about to explain that he was not kind, but wicked. The kind of man who fantasised about kissing her, despite knowing that he would never marry her. A man who could never offer her what she deserved... But if he could, he would marry her in a heartbeat.

But before he could make a fool of himself, the carriage came to a standstill and he realised that they were home.

Chapter Twelve

Castleton was situated in the heart of the Cotswolds with its rolling hills, sheep farms and cloth mills. The area was beautiful—genteel England at its best, with wealthy spa towns, medieval churches and charming villages interspersed by soft meadows and woodland. Nothing like the dramatic landscapes of her Scottish home, and yet still just as mesmerising.

It took them one and a half days to travel to Castleton Manor at a brisk pace in two carriages, with plenty of stops for the children. It was a tight squeeze with their luggage and Maggie's maid and Daisy, as well—although, they took it in turns to ride with the coachman. They stopped often to stretch their legs at inns and friendly villages along the way. The area was prosperous and lively, but lacked the chaos and dirt of London, making it a most pleasant escape—even if the weather was dreary despite it now being June.

Hawk rode his horse alongside the carriages. 'To allow them more room,' or so he said. But Maggie suspected it was to give him more space and time away from them, although he always played games with the boys whenever they asked him—despite him having ridden for hours.

She supposed his years in the cavalry meant that he didn't mind or even notice spending all day in the saddle—he certainly seemed untroubled by it.

His long greatcoat and black top hat kept the rain off, and his gleaming black Hessian boots gave him a military flair that made Maggie daydream about how dashing he would have looked in uniform.

At mealtimes he was quiet and pensive—she suspected he worried over the missing deeds and papers his brother had mentioned in his letter.

He seemed happier alone with his thoughts than joining them in lively conversation. Which only made Maggie all the more determined to include him... much to his chagrin.

The journey passed reasonably smoothly with card games and books, the adults taking it in turns to sit with the children and entertain them.

As the distance from London grew, it was clear that Cleo's temperament also improved with every milestone they passed. She began to reminisce about her time growing up in Castleton, of the people and old friends that lived there, and Maggie began to look forward to meeting them—if only to help her friend reconnect with happier times. It was refreshing to see Cleo finally excited about something.

On the second day, as they approached the house, Cleo said with a wistful sigh, 'I miss the trees and the gardens...' She craned her neck up at the gnarled oaks that lined the manor's path, the dappled light flickering shadows across her face as she closed her eyes, seeming to happily embrace the light and dark. Maggie hoped it was proof that Cleo was moving on with her life.

'They are lovely,' agreed Maggie, although in truth she'd been staring at Hawk once again. She really needed to make an effort to stop admiring him. It was getting embarrassing and more than a little obvious—by the occasional frown her uncle sent her way.

As they drove through the iron gates of Castleton Manor, Hawk slowed his horse to let them pass. His eyes caught hers briefly, but he looked away quickly, his jaw tightening as he stared at his childhood home.

'Isn't it beautiful?' cried Cleo, leaning in close and moving the curtain aside to see better.

Maggie smiled in response. 'Yes, it is delightful.'

Castleton Manor was made from thick red brick and was framed by tall trees either side. The building was wide, with two clear protruding wings, and two rows of tall, narrow windows reflecting the last golden rays of the day. In the peaked roofs, you could see the smaller squat windows of the servants' quarters, and several large chimneys rose up into the sky like the medieval turrets of an enchanted castle.

Climbing white roses arched over the large oak doors of the entrance, and the surrounding gardens and stables looked tidy and well established as their carriages rolled into the driveway.

'The manor has been in our family since 1476. Although, of course, the current house was built much later,' Cleo reassured her quickly. 'Lots of light, plumbing and beautiful gardens, with a lake, orangery and even a small pinery! I wonder if we'll have any pineapples this year... Probably not. I imagine it's been pretty much left to go wild in our absence.'

Her expression saddened a little and Maggie opened her mouth to change the subject when Hawk—who had now ridden through the gates and was dismounting from his horse by the entrance—interrupted them. 'According to Archie's solicitor it has been well managed. So you needn't worry about that. I wrote to the steward and sent word to expect us as soon as we decided on our visit. So the staff won't be shocked by our arrival, either.'

'You're just like Archie, always thinking ahead!' Cleo beamed with approval, and was quick to open the carriage door as soon as the wheels crunched to a halt on the immaculate drive.

'Although, I doubt we'll have as many staff as our

guests are used to,' he said, inclining his head towards Maggie as he offered her his arm.

Taking it, she stepped down from the carriage with a cheerful shrug, placing her gloved hand on his thick arm and trying her best to look untroubled. 'I'm sure we'll be perfectly happy regardless.' She turned and took baby Matthew from Daisy as she was also helped down by Hawk.

He's a gentleman, with no interest in courting you! Stop reading into every look and action as if it means anything at all!

Maggie had been shaken by their talk in the carriage the previous day. *Bottled sunshine...* That was what he'd called her, but you could say that about a cheerful child or friend...*couldn't you?*

In the intimacy of that small space—all alone—she had felt as if each word and look held some greater meaning or weight that she couldn't quite comprehend. But of course, that was nonsense as Hawk had said plainly—and loudly on one occasion—that he had no plans to marry, especially someone like Maggie, who, although was not poor by any means, was not a *wealthy young miss*, either.

It was a passing fancy of hers—nothing more. The benefit ball had sent her romantic head into a spin, and frankly, she'd become infatuated with Hawk. It was a sweet crush, an idolisation that would soon wither under scrutiny or fade with time. There was no harm in her feelings as long as she did not embarrass herself with them.

She just had to keep them a secret.

'Well, now! Isn't this a grand country idyll!' declared William cheerfully as he unfolded his large frame from out of the second carriage and tried to hide his wince unsuccessfully.

'Let me show you around!' Cleo's face beamed with happiness as she gestured towards the house.

The children were fast on William's heels as they squabbled their way out of the carriage. 'Boys! You're going to love it here!' The answering grins on her sons' faces said it all.

Curious, Maggie asked, 'Why didn't you spend your summers here? You obviously adore the place.'

A shadow crept across Cleo's face and Maggie cursed herself for asking the question. But it was gone in an instant when she replied cheerfully, 'Charles liked to stay close to London, no matter the time of year, and Archie… Well, he preferred London, too.'

Maggie knew that wasn't entirely true. Archie stayed in London to be close to his sister and doctor. He'd also spoken fondly of their family home, so she imagined it was Cleo's absence that kept him away. Hawk, on the other hand, did not seem as pleased by their arrival as his sister; he looked at the house with a severe expression as if he blamed it for some ill will against him.

When the steward and other staff came out to greet them, Hawk began to speak with them, and Cleo hurried everyone else into the house, keen to begin their tour.

She showed them the many rooms downstairs, including a small ballroom perfect for country dances, and a library that was well stocked. Then she showed Maggie upstairs to her own chamber, pointing out all the many features including the fact that her own room was next door to hers—it had once been Archie's.

There was something peculiarly childish about it, as if Cleo were once again a young girl with ribbons in her hair showing off a cherished toy. Still, it was the happiest Maggie had seen her in a long time and so she was pleased to see it.

In Maggie's room, there was a large four-post bed with red brocade curtains hanging from the old oak frame. A dressing table by the window, and a washbasin stand, as well as a wardrobe with plenty of space for her trunk. She made her way over to the window to take in the views of the gardens and lake but was surprised to see the tall figure of Hawk striding across the lawn towards an elegant orangery that was situated a little away from the house.

The boys burst into the room, excitedly talking about the toys in the nursery, before running out again, dragging a laughing Cleo down the hall with them.

Maggie didn't follow.

Chapter Thirteen

Hawk stepped into the warm heat of the orangery, the smell of flowers and citrus heavy in the air. It reminded him immediately of Maggie and the warm, sweet scent she always wore, and he breathed it in deeply, savouring the pleasant smell.

The orangery was heated not only by the glass enclosure, but also by pipes that circulated hot air from furnaces through the back walls. As the weather had been poor this year the steward had seen fit to keep the fires burning once a week. Resulting in the hothouse living up to its name, and he felt as if he were stepping back onto Spanish or French soil despite the weak spring light.

He removed his coat and jacket, hanging them on a nearby peg by the door, then glanced into the smaller room to the side of the entrance. The pinery was so warm that condensation was running down the glass that sectioned it off from the rest of the hothouse. Inside, on a rectangular bed, were two small spikey bushes surrounded by shards of bark, each one topped with the beginnings of a very small and currently green pineapple. He chuckled to himself as he passed them—Cleo would be pleased—although whether any of them made it to a silver-plated centrepiece was anyone's guess.

He turned and made his way through the lush forest of plants and trees towards the centre of the building. There was more here than he remembered—he would need to thank the steward and gardener for their diligence in maintaining it. Potted trees of oranges, lemons and peaches as well as many flowering plants like camellias, hibiscus and even a couple of exotic lilies and orchids hid amongst the greenery.

White Greek statues and stone alcoves along the back wall decorated the orangery, making it reminiscent of an ancient palace and giving it an elegant serenity. The sound of the central water fountain trickling nearby forced him to focus on his task. He wasn't here to admire the building or pick fruit; he had something far more important in mind.

He walked towards the central fountain with its Aphrodite emerging from a clam, and dragged out the old wood-and-leather chest that was kept at the back wall. The lock was still intact, and he reached into the alcove above to retrieve the key hidden inside the stone urn. He hadn't been a particularly imaginative child, and had always kept it close.

Archie had known about its hiding place, and must have informed the steward of it, too, when he sent its contents for safekeeping. The steward had been warned to only reveal its location if Hawk's death in battle were ever confirmed. The extent to which Archie had gone to keep this secret was alarming and spoke more about his distrust of Charles than anything else.

Hawk knelt beside the chest, fiddling with the old lock for a couple of minutes until it eventually clicked open.

A rustle of movement from behind made him jump, and he turned to see a gasping Maggie skid to a halt a few feet behind him.

'Is this it? Is this where you kept your treasures?' She rushed forward, oblivious to the scowl he'd allowed to purposefully darken his face.

He didn't want her here for this—she was already far too involved as it was. Over the past few days, he'd begun to realise that he was developing feelings for Maggie, and it would be better for everyone if he distanced himself from her.

However, another part of him was relieved not to do it alone, and was deeply humbled that she would race to his aide. Even if it was simply out of curiosity and friendly kindness, it was nice to have someone with him…a silent witness to his grief as he obeyed his brother's final wishes.

Except of course Maggie was never silent; it was not in her nature. She stared at him, gasping for air, the sound of her panting filling the heated air between them. Cheeks flushed, a hand clasped to her heaving chest, coppery curls bobbing like ribbons of flame around her neck. It gave him uncomfortably erotic thoughts of how she might look and sound during lovemaking.

'Did you run here?' he snapped, not sure why he sounded so disapproving.

'I saw you from my window.' She swallowed deeply as if struggling to look composed, and then with a bad-tempered huff, she gave up and hurried forward to kneel beside him. 'You cannot deny me this. I must know what he left you!'

She was so close now that he could smell the sweet nectar of her scent. He found himself distracted by the gleam of her skin, the colours reminding him of strawberries and cream.

Why did she always remind him of fruit?

Was it because he dreamt of feasting on her, licking and consuming her like a ravenous beast?

Damn it! Control yourself, man!

'You're sweating,' he said, still transfixed by the sight of her and somehow unable to speak any sense.

'Ladies do not sweat!' she hissed before adding with a grumble, 'We glow...'

He couldn't help but smile at her defensive protest,

and he turned away to focus once again on the chest in front of them. Gently, he prised open the old leather lid and swung it back onto its rusty hinges.

Carefully wrapped in waxed linen was a package sealed with his brother's mark, and he lifted it out carefully, almost afraid that the world's ills would fly out of it like Pandora's box.

Maggie leaned closer to look, her breathing more even now, but her scent still as intoxicating as opium. To his surprise, she reached inside the chest and petted some of his childhood treasures abandoned there. A slingshot, a few marbles and a tin soldier. He spent so many days from sunrise to sunset, playing in here while his brother sat in his chair and acted as general. No other children to play with, just him and an adult brother who was too weak to do little more than watch.

She smiled at the toys but said nothing, and then twisted a little to watch him unwrap the parcel in his lap.

Easing his hand between the folds of the linen to break the seal, he took a deep breath before unwrapping it.

Inside were more folded documents and a little note written in an unfamiliar hand—presumably the steward's. It simply said, *For the attention of Lord Archibald Hawksmere's heir.*

He shouldn't have expected anything more; his brother would have sent the documents to the steward without mentioning its contents. But Hawk had a sinking feeling of disappointment when he realised there would be no other personal words from his brother.

A small hand gently patted his shoulder with commiseration, and without looking at her, he briskly began to look through the documents. There were the deeds to the house and its surrounding lands and farms, as well as details of a bank account he was unfamiliar with.

'The Bank of Scotland? Why would he have an account there?'

'Perhaps he wanted to keep it separate from his other ledgers?' said Maggie thoughtfully.

'And…away from Charles's eyes, too, I imagine. Although the Bank of Scotland is a little far…even for privacy's sake!' he said with a sigh.

The fact his brother was having to go to such lengths to protect his family, all while being so unwell himself, caused guilt to gnaw at Hawk's insides.

I should have been here.

But he hadn't been; he had to accept it. Now it was his duty to unravel the mess left behind and make all right again. He knew from the ledgers back in London that they were no longer affluent; were, in fact, on the edge of ruin. But…

He began to flick through the documents. An account had been opened with a sizeable sum deposited that seemed enough to keep them away from devastation.

'Is that property in Brighton?' asked Maggie, followed quickly by, 'And...look!' She pointed to a little scrawled note that he'd not noticed until now. It was the very last words of his brother...and they were actually rather dull, which was amusing in itself. She read it out loud. '"For wise investments on the exchange always follow the lead of Lord Mortram." How curious! I think Lord Mortram is dead...but I'm not certain. I don't know the family well. Oh, is that a list of possible investments...pottery, shipping—?'

'Canals and docks... Is there anything my brother *didn't* want to invest in?' he asked, more to himself than anyone else.

'Goodness gracious!' declared Maggie, grabbing his arm as if to steady them both, and he was glad of it, for he was more than a little lightheaded himself.

'Do you think...you're actually *rich*?' she asked, a little breathless and this time not because of her run to join him.

'Impossible,' he said, shaking his head vehemently. 'We can't be... Surely, he would have told the solicitor at least... And not telling Cleo after all her worrying, that would be...cruel. Perhaps this is just his advice, what I should do with whatever he managed to put aside for us. But at least there *is* something put aside for us.'

'True. I always knew Archie wouldn't let you down,' she agreed cheerfully, and for a moment they both languished in the happy lap of relief. There was still the issue with Mr Wilkins to uncover, but he would tackle that another day. At least he could go to bed in the peaceful knowledge that things were not as terrible as they first appeared.

'We won't have to sell Castleton,' he said, closing his eyes briefly as he accepted the happy truth; to no longer be constantly drained by the sheer weight of his burden.

She patted his arm, a sweet, consoling gesture that made his heart swell in his chest, but left him bereft when her hand moved away from his shirtsleeve.

Merrily, she went on to say, 'At least there is enough to keep the wolf from the door. That must have been Archie's intention. Some small investments, held in safekeeping until you needed them. After all, you can always trust us Scots to look after your pennies!' she joked.

He nodded with a chuckle, followed quickly by another sigh of relief. 'Indeed, I am sure that is the case. I mean, look at this Brighton development!' His relief turned into an incredulous laugh. 'It cannot be for the whole street! It's probably just a share in one of the buildings, and a small share at that! I shall write to the bank to find out more. But honestly, it is a relief to know that I don't have to sell Castleton. Cleo would have been heartbroken.'

Maggie nodded, looking around the lush orangery with admiration. 'It certainly is beautiful... But wouldn't *you* miss it, too?'

He paused before answering, unsure of what to say. Closing the treasure chest of his childhood and placing the parcel of papers on top of the lid, he eventually answered, 'I was...lonely here,' he admitted. 'Cleo and Archie were fully grown when our parents died. I do not have the same memories of this house as my sister does.' His family was reserved and shy; he'd been painfully aware of his lack of friends.

Even now, he struggled in large groups, preferring to spend time with a small group of friends, like his weekly trip to White's with Adam, Ash and Ezra. He couldn't imagine a bustling large family like Maggie had experienced growing up. No wonder she was such easy-going company.

Maggie's face crumpled with sympathy and he was quick to reassure her, placing a hand on her arm. 'Do not misunderstand me. I wasn't unhappy. I didn't even realise I was lonely until I made my own friends. I just...don't value it as much as she does. Cleo grew up here as a child with Archie—they had their own friends and they were always together. I came along so much later and didn't fit in with their social circle—because of the age gap between us. I've always been somewhat of a third wheel. But I was *never* badly treated by either of them. They loved me and did their best.'

'I'm glad.' She smiled, comforted by his words, and shuffled a little closer still on her knees. He thought the action strange, and his heart quickened, wondering if she wanted more from him...another kiss, perhaps?

But he was sure it was only his own desires leading his imagination; he was truly being driven mad with each day that passed in her company. He'd been grateful to have ridden his horse here, but even that hadn't stopped him from hearing her voice and everyone's laughter in the carriages... She truly did bring sunshine wherever she went.

'I have to admit...' she said softly, her voice hushed as if confessing something wicked. 'Growing up in Scotland... I sometimes *wished* to be alone. I used to daydream about it, of not having to share everything with my sisters, of not having to deal with their arguments and petty squabbles. Sometimes I even wished I were an *only* child... You must think me terrible for wishing such a thing.' She laughed nervously, glancing away with embarrassment.

'Not at all,' he said, distracted by the dusting of freckles across her nose. 'We always want what we can't have.'

Her blue eyes rounded as her gaze flickered back up to his face. 'Yes...that's true,' she whispered, her eyes dropping to his mouth, and his whole body stiffened with expectation.

'What do you daydream of now?' he asked softly, unsure why he would dare ask such a thing but unable to help himself. 'If you could have anything...'

Maggie swallowed deeply, her eyes flicking back up to his, and he wondered if she wanted the same thing that had plagued him daily since meeting her.

'I... I...' she stuttered, her face flushing.

Before his courage failed him, he asked, 'Would you like to know what I want...right at this moment?'

'What?' She wet her lips and it sent a shiver of heat down his spine.

'I...' His courage almost buckled as he leaned towards her, closing the distance between them and hoping she would not run away. It was wrong of him to do this, to take advantage of their situation, of her innocence. But he couldn't seem to help himself. The elation of his discovery combined with the allure of her scent was too tempting a prospect. 'I want to kiss you, Maggie...*thoroughly.*'

She inhaled a shallow little gasp that seemed to grab him by the throat, and then, ever so slowly she closed her eyes, tilting her face up in an open gesture of surrender. 'Then kiss me,' she replied softly, waiting expectantly for him to make good on his word.

He gave in to temptation, cupping her cheek in his palm and pressing his mouth against her voluptuous lips in a chaste kiss, conscious that he could not overwhelm her with his raw desire after their sweet first kiss.

But the scent of jasmine and peaches filled his head, and he gave in to a more primal thirst. His arm slipped around her waist and pulled her up to meet him. Not caring that they were both kneeling on a stone floor, or that she was now firmly pressed against his body in a lustful embrace that went far beyond a sweet kiss.

Her lips opened a little with surprise as she felt his hard body crush against hers; it was all the encouragement he needed. Deepening the kiss, he could taste the wet heat of her mouth and the velvety softness of her tongue against his.

She tasted of forbidden fruit and heavenly sweetness; he was consumed by her, unable to do anything more than worship her.

Chapter Fourteen

Maggie was in heaven...and yet, she felt everything so she couldn't really be dead.

It was divine, everything she had hoped for and more than she could have ever imagined, because of him. Instinctively, she knew that it would not be the same with any other.

The seductive stroke of Hawk's mouth and tongue were gentle. But the squeeze of his fingers against her waist hinted at a stronger and deeper emotion hidden just beneath the surface. The cold stone beneath her knees, the heat of their combined breath, even the smell of the exotic fruit and flowers blooming in the orangery, seemed to overwhelm her.

So blinded by sensation, she could barely think about the repercussions of her decision, let alone the reasons for his. All she knew was that this was the most thrilling moment of her life and she wanted to savour every second of it. Surrendering to his touch as if she were letting the tide take her out to sea.

His hand drifted up from her waist to cup her breast in a possessive touch, and she pressed and arched into the caress, gasping at the aching pleasure beneath his palm. He had such big hands, but they still failed to cup her fully. But it was more than enough to please her and him, for that matter, because the sound of her moan only seemed to enflame Hawk further. His kiss roughened, becoming more desperate and passionate as he pulled her closer, the mask of a gentleman finally dropping.

She wrapped her arms around his neck, encouraging him silently to do anything he wanted with her, and she was certain that she *would* have allowed anything. She did not care about ruin or scandal or even her future at that moment. Only that he *wanted* to kiss her and she desperately returned that wish.

Shouts and a flurry of shadowy movement along the windows startled them. Hawk dropped her so fast she had to slam her hands down behind her to steady herself.

It took her a second to realise what had disturbed them. It was the boys running past the orangery—no doubt playing some game or excited by the sight of the sprawling gardens and lake. She doubted the boys had even seen them through the thick foliage and misty windows, but her heart still raced with panic and other less terrifying emotions.

Nobody burst in through the doors, and after a moment the sound of the boys' voices became distant, and they were left alone in an awkward silence.

Hawk stood, raking a hand through his dark hair and looking out the windows with a panicked expression. He must have leapt to his feet as soon as he'd heard them, and even now he was staring into the fading light as if he was trying to figure out what had happened.

Hawk's reaction hurt her pride far more than she liked to admit. He did not want to be caught with her...which she could understand. Such a scandalous moment would result in some very awkward conversations with her uncle. But he didn't have to be quite so...

Horrified!

She rose to her feet, waving away Hawk's offer of help as he belatedly realised she was still on the stone floor. She refused to look him in the eye and instead took a moment to brush the dirt off her travelling dress, trying her best to rebuild a wall of composed dignity at his obvious embarrassment.

'Well, at least I know now what it is like to be *thoroughly* kissed,' she said cheerfully, hoping she sounded unbothered. When she dared to look up at him, he still looked mortified, and her skin crawled with humiliation, although she forced herself to appear untroubled.

She had felt this way once before, when she'd first

learned of Mr Beaston's jest, and she half expected to see him jump out from behind the foliage with a *Bravo!* At least this time she wasn't in a ballroom surrounded by knowing eyes and having to laugh it off.

'Maggie, I am so sorry. That should never have happened.' He looked so uncomfortable that she suddenly felt a strange sort of pity for him. Kissing her must have been an unexpected impulse. Probably brought about from the intense relief of finding out his family's circumstances were not as grave as he'd first imagined.

She shrugged with a carefully upholstered smile. 'Thank you. It was kind of you to…ease my curiosity.'

'Your *curiosity*?'

She hadn't imagined he could look any more shocked than he had a moment before, but it turned out she was mistaken, because he looked appalled now.

What did he want her to say?

That she'd been obsessively hoping that he would kiss her again, and that it had been the best moment of her life? Except, of course, when he'd pushed her away like a dirty handkerchief.

'I have compromised you,' he said gravely, his eyes once again drawn to the blurry dusk just beyond the window. As if he couldn't quite face her or the terrible future he now seemed to see for himself.

'Hawk!' she snapped loudly, pulling back his attention. 'Stop acting like you're about to be martyred! I have *not* been compromised. No one is here! No one saw anything! Let us pretend as if nothing happened.'

'Maggie.' He breathed her name as if it were a reproach. But she refused to be humiliated a moment longer.

'Please forget it. I already have. Now, back to more important matters. Have you learned of the whereabouts of that Mr Wilkins?'

He blinked as if startled by the question. 'The steward informed me that he is a farmer about half a day's ride from here. I thought I would visit him on Monday.'

'Perfect!' Maggie declared, striding past him to make her way back to the entrance.

There was only so much embarrassment she could take.

As she walked out into the fading light of the day, she saw the boys scampering around, throwing sticks for a young dog to fetch. Cleo was walking down the hill, William beside her. They were talking closely and then Cleo laughed at something William said and swatted his arm playfully.

Maggie smiled at the interaction, pleased to see her friend happy and carefree. Something she had not seen for many months.

Cleo then looked over to her and gave a little wave, but her eyes strayed to something over Maggie's shoulder and she realised it must have been Hawk leaving the orangery after her. Maggie hurried forward, aware that Cleo's smile had dropped and that she was now looking at them both with a heavy dose of suspicion. William didn't seem pleased, either, and he frowned at her as she stomped up the lawn towards them.

Maggie thought the best way to avoid any confrontation was to do as she had suggested to Hawk and pretend that nothing had happened. 'Lord Hawksmere was just showing me the orangery! It's beautiful!'

Cleo raised a single dark eyebrow, but followed her lead. 'Indeed, it is. Do we have any pineapples this year?'

Maggie hesitated, scouring her brain to remember anything other than Hawk's kiss. 'Ahh… Well… The pineapples…'

'The pinery is right by the door. You must have seen them.'

'Two,' Hawk said, his long legs catching up with her easily, and thankfully saving her from an awkward confession that she hadn't a clue if there'd been one or a hundred blasted pineapples. 'There's two growing, although neither of them are particularly big or ripe enough yet.'

'Two!' cried Cleo with a squeal of excitement. 'Oh, I must see them! Archie said they all failed last year. Something about the fertiliser not being quite right.' She tugged on William's arm. 'Mr Mackenzie, have you ever seen a pineapple plant before?'

William laughed. 'I have not!'

Hawk did not seem inclined to revisit the orangery, and she noticed he had put on his coat and jacket. She was sure she saw the bundle of papers peeking out from beneath his greatcoat. 'I have some matters to attend to with the steward. I will see you all at supper.' With a polite nod he strode up towards the house, the long coat whipping out behind him in the wind.

Unsure of what to do, Maggie decided to follow them back towards the orangery. A second viewing of the building seemed wise, in case she was asked any more pertinent questions later on...because, if she was honest with herself, she barely remembered what the orangery looked like.

They went to church as expected the following day, as it was a Sunday. The vicar gave a long and sprawling sermon on the importance of caring for the needy. Which was promptly followed by a hat being passed around for donations. Apparently, the old medieval church was in desperate need of a new set of benches. No one missed the disapproving glare the vicar had given the local carpenter when he mentioned the *surprising cost*, and wisely, the tradesman avoided his gaze.

As they were in the Hawksmeres' family box, they were the first to receive the hat. Hawk gave a generous note much to the vicar's sombre approval, and

William followed with a similar yet politely smaller donation. Maggie tried to hide her smile as she put in some coins of her own. They'd been warned by the steward that the vicar would probably expect some kind of donation after their years of absence, and this was obviously the beginning of their making amends.

Cleo swallowed nervously when she saw the notes go in, and Maggie tried to give her a reassuring smile as she patted her knee subtly out of sight.

Soon, everything would be resolved and her friend would no longer have to worry about any of it.

After the service they talked politely with the vicar for a moment before leaving. The boys were surprisingly well behaved, although Cleo had promised them a play with the steward's dog later if they kept out of mischief. The long walk to the village had also helped, the exercise and fresh air burning away some of their natural exuberance.

There had been a brief respite in the bad weather and now the sun shone brightly.

A group of women stood at the church gate and watched them with shy smiles as they left the church. Cleo grabbed Maggie's arm, pulling her forward. 'Come and meet some of my old friends, Maggie.'

She was introduced to a gaggle of sweet and friendly local ladies who were eager to meet her and reacquaint themselves with Cleo. A few even glanced admiringly at William and Hawk. Her uncle noticed and became even more charming and affable than normal, while Hawk seemed not to notice at all—appearing distracted and pensive once again. She imagined he still felt guilty about kissing her, and she was becoming more and more irritated by him.

'Oh, you must come to luncheon tomorrow!' said Cleo happily to the group of ladies.

Maggie stiffened. Tomorrow was the day Hawk would be going to visit Mr Wilkins.

But it appeared she wasn't the only one uncertain. Many of the women cast hesitant glances amongst themselves before one brave soul stepped forward. 'That is very kind of you, m'lady. But perhaps you would like to go to Tetbury's fair tomorrow instead? Some of us were planning on going—there's even going to be a balloon launch!'

Hawk chose that moment to join the conversation. 'Ahh, yes, I was going to suggest that for tomorrow. I think the boys would love to see it!'

The children all gave enthusiastic nods of agreement, and William was the first to agree. 'Sounds exciting!'

'Although...' Hawk added thoughtfully. 'Perhaps you should stay overnight at an inn there, rather than coming back the same day? The roads can be a little treacherous in the dark, and I hear the assembly rooms there are most entertaining.'

One of the women—a Mrs White, nodded enthusiastically. 'Indeed, my husband and I only have a horse and cart. So we have arranged to stay with some acquaintances.'

Cleo smiled warmly. 'I am sure we could squeeze you into one of our carriages—the boys don't take up much room. I look forward to seeing you ladies there. We shall have to do luncheon at Castleton Manor another day.' The ladies all beamed in agreement, and they began to make plans.

However, Hawk was quick to shake his head when Cleo mentioned taking both carriages as well as his horse. 'I am afraid I will not be joining you. I have business to attend to with the steward. But I wish you all a merry day.'

As they made their way back home, Maggie wondered how she was ever going to get out of the Tetbury trip.

'Tetbury is such a lively town, and those ladies are all so agreeable,' Cleo declared excitedly. 'Oh, Maggie, we are going to have such fun!'

'Sounds wonderful!' Maggie agreed with a polite smile, and she could have sworn she saw Hawk hide a smirk as he helped them around a puddle. Perhaps he thought her joining him to see Mr Wilkins tomorrow was impossible now? She gave him a curt glare before hopping over the muddy water.

She *would* wiggle out of this trip somehow.

Later at the evening meal she ate sparingly and

complained of a headache. Hawk shot her disapproving looks, but thankfully said nothing. She supposed him doing so would only incriminate himself as well.

Chapter Fifteen

'Oh, if only I didn't feel so terribly ill!' Maggie groaned, touching her head with a wince for good measure. 'I wish I could come with you, *truly* I do!'

They all stood in the manor's sweeping hallway, everyone ready to leave in their outdoor coats and jackets, except for Hawk, who was dressed in his usual dark blue attire and Maggie, who had thrown on a simple morning dress and then wrapped one of her family tartans around her shoulders like a bulky shawl. She'd even rubbed some rouge around her eyes and powdered her face to a deathly pallor.

All to aide her subterfuge and it had worked!

A little too well, unfortunately.

As Cleo asked for the third time, 'Are you *sure* you don't want me to stay home with you, or at least call a doctor?' Pointedly ignoring Francis, who was tugging on her skirts, eager to get going.

'Perhaps we *should* call a doctor…' said William, examining her with a concerned expression.

'Yes, perhaps we should,' agreed Hawk with a sour twist of his lips, and she resisted the urge to kick him in the shin.

'Nonsense! No need for a doctor. It's just a little headache, nothing serious. But I was tossing and turning all night. A long, restful sleep, and I will be as bright as a daisy by tomorrow. And please don't stay on my account—your friends will be waiting for you. And didn't you say you would be collecting Mr and Mrs White along the way? You can't disappoint them, and the boys will be terribly disappointed to miss the balloon launch.'

Francis looked horrified at the prospect. 'No! I want to see the balloon, Mama! Please, Mama, I want to see it!'

The other boys, who'd been kicking gravel in the open doorway to pass the time, rushed back into the manor to add their own tugging and pleas to that of Francis's. Cleo was helplessly dragged out to the carriages by her children, muttering apologies and well wishes to Maggie as she left. Daisy followed closely behind with baby Matthew.

William was the last to leave, taking a moment to ask her quietly, 'Are you sure you don't want me to stay behind, lass?'

'No! What a miserable day that would be for you! All I am going to do is sleep!' Maggie gave a weak laugh before pushing him towards the door. 'Away with you. I want to hear all about it tomorrow when you return.'

After a moment of hesitation, he said, 'Well, I suppose you have your maid to keep you company if you wish it.' Then he gave a weighted glance at Hawk. 'And you will call for a doctor if she grows any worse?'

A twinge of guilt made her squirm a little, but thankfully, Hawk was quick to reassure him, 'Of course. She is safe with me.'

Before the carriages had left the driveway, Hawk muttered bad-temperedly, 'You have missed your calling for the stage, Miss Mackenzie. But I'm afraid it will all be in vain—you will *not* be joining me today.'

She did not miss the formality of his address, or the frostiness of his tone, and so she turned towards him with an equal helping of scorn. 'I *will* be joining you. It was Archie's last wish that I be involved, and nothing you say or do can stop me from doing as he wished. Besides—' she smiled, slowly and deliberately, his eyes dropping to her mouth and the muscles in his jaw clenching, as if he knew her final blow was coming '—you do not want me to tell Cleo that you went out today. Do you?'

He looked away. 'Fine!' he snapped. 'But as both the carriages are gone, we will need to take the old phaeton. I must warn you it has seen better days, and there is no hood. You might have wished you stayed indoors.'

Maggie shrugged lightly as she walked away. 'It doesn't look as if it's going to rain. I am sure we will do just fine! Let me change into something a little warmer.'

Hawk called out to her as she began to mount the stairs. 'You might want to wash your face, too. The sight of you might make Mr Wilkins think the angel of death has come for him.' His jibe was followed swiftly by a grumbled, 'Considering the amount of money sent his way, he might be wishing the reaper *was* with me.'

Maggie didn't respond, but she took some time to scrub her face clean.

'Are you sure about this, miss?' asked her worried maid as she helped her change into a more appropriate walking gown and green pelisse.

'Of course! Lord Hawksmere and I are going on a secret errand that will benefit my friend and Cleo's family in the long run. But it is essential my uncle does not hear of it until later—he always spoils surprises.' Maggie liked to think this wasn't a complete lie. Betsy was trustworthy, and had been with her since her debutante years. But the details regarding Mr Wilkins was not her secret to tell, and so she had been vague about the reasons for her deceit.

'Well, if you're sure...' said Betsy with a troubled

expression, and Maggie took her bonnet from her with a smile.

'I am certain of it! Besides, we'll be back before nightfall!'

A couple of hours later she was feeling a little less optimistic. The phaeton was perilously high and rickety; it squeaked and bounced with every bump and dip in the road. She'd been thrown into Hawk's shoulder so many times she was sure they would have matching bruises.

Eventually, after several winding country lanes, they rode through a village that was little more than a church and an inn, with a large crowd gathered outside the church.

'Oh, look, a wedding!' Maggie gasped, craning her neck to try to see the bride.

'Hold on to your bonnet!' snapped Hawk, and then he cracked the reins.

'What—' Before Maggie could ask the question they were jerked forward, and Maggie did have to grab hold of her bonnet for fear of it flying off her head.

Hawk steadied their pace just as they were passing the inn, and from behind there was a loud cheer as a newly wed couple came running out of the church to be showered with well wishers. Hawk sat back as if pleased. 'We might have been stuck behind the crowd if I'd not hurried us forward.'

'Why would that have been an issue? It would have only delayed us a moment—and it's not as if it's Rotten Row down here, is it? I haven't seen another soul for miles,' she grumbled, glancing back towards the church and disappointed when she saw nothing but people flooding the village thoroughfare. 'And I wanted to see the bride...'

Hawk huffed bad-temperedly but didn't apologise; instead, he reprimanded her with a cold, 'We are not here for leisure, Maggie!'

'I do realise that! I am not stupid!' And then she turned in her seat to glare at him more fully. 'Why are you so angry with me?'

'I am not angry with you.'

'Really? Because you barely said more than two words to me at dinner last night, and today you've been nothing but *beastly* all morning! Is it because of what happened in the orangery?'

'No!' he yelled.

Maggie blinked at the harsh tone. 'Well, I am glad to have clarified that, then!' She shifted in her seat, drawing her tartan closer around her shoulders. It was freezing in the wind with no hood to shelter them and she was glad she'd brought it with her.

Hawk slowed the horses down and turned to look at her. 'You should have trusted me to do this alone.'

'I do trust you! But you shouldn't have to do it alone. That was *why* Archie wanted me involved.'

'It might not be safe.' He pursed his lips and stared straight ahead at the muddy road. 'I was worried... about bringing you.' After a moment, his tone softened. 'I suppose it *is* because of what happened.'

She stiffened. She had been dreading this conversation. He would want to explain that she meant nothing to him, that he'd had a *moment of weakness* and was embarrassed by his behaviour. But she didn't want to hear any of it because it spoiled the sweet fantasy in her mind. She wanted to continue on in blissful ignorance and treasure their moments alone, as if they meant the same to him as they did to her.

'I do not expect anything from you,' she said, hoping it would be enough to end it.

He nodded. 'I know that. But... *I* should have behaved better. I put you in harm's way, and I fear I am doing it again.'

Maggie leaned close so that she could catch his eye. When she did, she said firmly, 'I make my own choices. Every single one of them. Good or bad. Understood?'

He nodded, although he still looked terribly guilty, and his eyes once again strayed to the road. 'We should be there soon. The steward said it was the first farm after the village. Let's find out the truth and get out of here quickly.'

They travelled in silence until the bumpy road turned to the east, a wooden signpost proclaiming

Wilkins Farm reassured them they were going in the right direction—if nothing else.

As they approached the house and cluster of barns, they saw that it was well kept, if small. Geese squawked in the yard, and a young man was pulling water from a well. He looked up and moved his long brown hair away from his eyes to squint up at them. 'Are you lost?' he asked in a thick country accent. 'The village is further down the lane,' he added, pointing back to where they'd come from. But something about his sharp eyes made Maggie wonder if he already suspected why they were here. He was eyeing Hawk with thinly veiled disdain; that was very unusual for someone of his standing or someone so young.

'Mr Wilkins? My name is Lord Hawksmere,' Hawk said curtly.

The lad straightened his spine and squared his shoulders, looking at him firmly and without a scrap of humility. 'You'll be wanting my father. You better come inside.' He then turned towards the nearby barn and bellowed, 'Charlotte!'

A little girl, no older than six or seven, came running out of the barn. She had a cloud of messy blond curls and a sweet face that seemed eager to please. 'Yes, Rob!'

The lad who answered to Rob nodded towards the

phaeton. 'Look after their horses while they speak with Pa.'

She nodded, taking the bucket of water he offered her and then quickly walking over to them.

'Will she be all right with them?' Hawk asked, a little concerned that such a young child would be given the task of looking after the horses.

'Your carriage will be perfectly fine,' snapped Rob, misunderstanding him.

Hawk stood up and jumped down from the carriage, in a display of strength that Maggie was sure was meant to intimidate. 'She's only a child.'

'I can drive the plough by myself,' said the little girl proudly as she heaved the bucket of water to the horses. 'Do not worry, mister. I'm real good with animals!'

Rob made a strange sniffing sound—a mix of scorn and approval. 'I will be back out to help her in a moment. She won't be on her own for long.'

Hawk didn't seem impressed by the reassurance, but he turned and offered Maggie his hand so she could dismount. It was awkward to climb down after sitting for so long, and she wobbled a little as she moved closer towards the edge of the carriage.

Firm, large hands gripped her waist, and then to her horror Hawk plucked her from the carriage and placed her down on the cobbled yard in one swift motion. She was gripping his arms so tightly it took a moment to unsnarl them from his coat.

Had he really just picked her up like a doll? Why was he making a habit of picking her up all the time? It was most disarming!

She busied herself with readjusting her bonnet to avoid him seeing her blush, and then followed him and Rob towards the farmhouse.

The lad opened the kitchen door and called inside, 'Ma, Pa, we have a visitor.'

He held open the door for them, and they stepped inside the hot kitchen with its large fireplace and flagstone floor. The furniture inside was strong and solid. It looked old, but as if it had been well loved and cared for over the years. Pots and homely touches lined the shelves and dressers.

A middle-aged woman with salt-and-pepper curls straightened up from the kettle she'd been placing over the fire to turn and look at them. A bald man with a weathered face stood up from his seat, his body not quite fully straightening as if his spine and legs were slightly bowed from hard labour.

They both looked startled to see them and glanced nervously at each other for a moment.

Hawk quickly introduced them with a curt bow that the couple struggled to return. 'I am Baron Hawksmere of Castleton, and this is… Miss Mackenzie.'

He seemed to struggle a little at her introduction, and Maggie quickly added, 'I am a friend of the family.'

Mrs Wilkins gasped and steadied herself with a hand on the mantelpiece while her husband's eyes merely narrowed. 'Take a seat, although... I am sure it is not what you are used to. It is all we can offer you, my lord.'

Maggie couldn't understand the hostility, but she took a seat at the kitchen table, as did Hawk, and turned her body to face them.

'Can I offer you some refreshments? Tea, perhaps?' asked Mrs Wilkins, seeming to realise that politeness might be the best course of action despite her husband's bad temper.

'That would be lovely,' Maggie said cheerfully.

Mrs Wilkins went about making tea, carefully taking her best china from the top shelf of her dresser, as well as a small precious tea caddy. She placed them all on the table, and everyone watched in uncomfortable silence as she busied herself with setting out the cups and saucers.

She began to pour the milk into the teacups and then hesitated, an embarrassed blush blooming on her cheeks when she realised she had poured the milk first. The upper classes never poured their milk first, only the lower classes did—for fear that the hot water would crack their precious china.

'I adore milky tea,' Maggie said, hoping to ease the

woman's dismay, and Mrs Wilkins gave a weak smile and continued to pour out the milk before going to get the kettle from the fire.

'Sugar?'

When they shook their heads, Mrs Wilkins's shoulders relaxed a little with relief.

Mr Wilkins had joined them at the kitchen table, although he didn't touch his cup and stared at Hawk with hostility. If anyone needed a dose of sugar it was Mr Wilkins, but Maggie decided to reserve judgement until she knew more.

'Mr Wilkins, are you aware that my brother died last spring, and that my brother-in-law Charles died not long after in the early summer?'

Mrs Wilkins gasped and set down her teacup. It rattled in her saucer before settling into place.

'I knew of your brother... It's local knowledge, as your family owns most of this area,' said Mr Wilkins coldly. 'But I did not know of your brother-in-law.'

There was no offer of condolences from either of them.

'Mr Wilkins, may I be frank?' asked Hawk.

Mr Wilkins's lips pursed, but he gave a quick nod of his head.

'Why did my brother-in-law send you two large sums of money, followed by several smaller payments?'

Mr Wilkins chewed on the inside of his mouth for a

moment, his granite stare never faltering from Hawk's face. Mrs Wilkins began to twist the cloth of her skirts with her fingers.

'May I also be *frank*, my lord?' asked Mr Wilkins.

'Of course.'

'The first sum was to pay off several debts in the area that your *brother-in-law* had accumulated.' It was as if Mr Wilkins could not even bring himself to say Charles's name. 'I had many tradesmen and other more *unsavoury* men demanding payment from my family. It took some time, but I managed to get payment from *him* eventually.'

Maggie couldn't help herself. 'Why? Surely, you could go to the Castleton steward or write to Charles directly?'

Mr Wilkins's scowl deepened. 'We didn't know his true name at that point.'

Mrs Wilkins interjected quietly. 'We thought him a friend of your family, that he occasionally did business for your family—he said he was unmarried and owned a gentleman's club in London.'

'He stayed at Castleton alone?' asked Hawk, confused.

They both shook their heads, and then Mr Wilkins said, 'No, Tetbury, and sometimes at the village inn… when he called on Jane.'

Maggie's heart sank, and Hawk seemed to suspect the same thing as he asked, 'Tell me everything.'

Mrs Wilkins began to cry, and Maggie quickly offered her a handkerchief.

Mr Wilkins spoke plainly and without emotion, his heart hardened to stone. 'Jane, our youngest, believed he was going to marry her. We all did. They courted and were engaged. Jane adored him, and we never had any reason to doubt his word. It was as if...he *believed* it himself... His business meant he had to travel and stay in London often, but he always came back and promised to take our Jane with him once they were wed. The banns were read...we didn't know until later that the man he claimed to be never existed.'

Maggie exchanged a horrified look with Hawk.

But Mr Wilkins was not done. 'When he disappeared for good we thought all was lost. I managed to find a friend of his in Tetbury, a man he'd confessed his true identity to. I wrote to him, demanding answers, and received a purse of coin instead. We thought that was the end of it, but it was just the beginning...'

'Charlotte...?' asked Hawk, pausing tactfully.

Mr Wilkins's face pinched with distaste. 'Yes, that's his whelp.'

Maggie stiffened at the unkindness of his tone, and Mrs Wilkins sobbed a little louder.

Mr Wilkins bristled in his seat. 'The second sum paid for Jane's funeral and our silence. She died delivering Charlotte. The smaller payments are for her daughter's care... But we'd look after her regardless, if that's why you've come, my lord. We will care for her even if the payments stop.'

Hawk, who had not drunk from his cup, took one polite sip before setting it down in its saucer. 'Thank you for the tea, Mrs Wilkins. Please be assured that I will now be taking over the payments to your family. Please write to me directly via the steward at Castleton if you require anything more for her. My sister Cleo is unaware of any of this, and it would greatly trouble her to learn of it... I hope I can count on your discretion?'

Mr Wilkins nodded, his expression softening a little. 'We meant no harm to your sister, my lord—we never knew who he was until it was too late. And we would never go out of our way to embarrass a lady. However, you should know there are no secrets in this part of the country... Although we may not speak openly of such things, it is well-known about Charlotte, *and* who fathered her.'

Hawk gave a grim nod as he rose from his seat. 'Thank you for your time, Mr and Mrs Wilkins.'

Maggie stood as well and brushed away Mrs Wilkins desperate attempt to tell her that she would return the handkerchief freshly laundered. 'No need. I have far too many as it is. Keep it, as a thank-you for the lovely tea.'

They left the house and walked across the yard back

to the phaeton, where Maggie braced herself for another few hours of uncomfortable bouncing. Not to mention the pain of realising she and her friend had been so utterly deceived by the black-hearted Charles.

If Cleo learned of this, it would break her heart.

But... Wouldn't it be better to know the truth?

Charlotte was stroking the velvety nose of one of their horses as she fed it a bucket of vegetable peelings, and she beamed up at them as they approached. 'What's their names?'

Hawk paused and then crouched down to speak with her. 'I don't know... What would you name them?'

The girl grinned, her front teeth missing, causing her to lisp a little as she declared, 'Midnight...and Twilight.'

'Then that shall be their names from now on. Thank you for naming them, Charlotte.'

'Come along, Charlotte. Go check if the hens have laid any eggs,' barked Rob, and with a sweet smile the child gave a wobbly curtsy and ran off back to the barns.

Hawk turned to Rob with a scowl. 'Treat her well, or there will be hell to pay.'

Rob gave a light snort before replying, 'This is a farm, my lord. Everyone works, even the children. Both Jane and I worked as children, too. She is treated well, and will never want for owt. But it would be better all round if you just let sleeping dogs lie. My parents have been through *enough*.' The lad then turned away from them, and neither of them had the heart to reproach him for it, not after the pain Charles had caused.

Maggie and Hawk clambered up into the phaeton one at a time, Hawk helping her with a gentle hold of her waist that had her blushing all over again.

As they rode out of the yard, Maggie said quietly, 'Charlotte... She looks just like him... Charles.'

Hawk nodded grimly. 'She does.'

Chapter Sixteen

'What are we going to tell Cleo?' asked Maggie quietly when they returned to the main track, leaving the Wilkins farm behind them.

Hawk's expression was stony. '*We* are going to tell her nothing.'

Maggie stiffened in her seat and tilted her head and body to see him better. 'Nothing? Surely, you don't mean that. There's a child involved. This wasn't some mere dalliance... He was about to commit bigamy!'

He cracked the reins, hoping the horses would go faster so that he wouldn't be trapped any longer with Maggie. She spoke too plainly, knew too much, and this stain on his family's honour would cause irreparable damage for years to come. Even if he *did* manage to keep it a secret from Cleo, the shame would follow them like a shadow.

It would be better if Maggie was left out of it entirely.

He'd already compromised her repeatedly, couldn't

seem to keep his hands off her—if the kiss in the orangery was anything to go by. This was yet more proof that he needed to distance himself from her. He couldn't allow Maggie's reputation to be tarnished by his, or Charles's behaviour. If society found out about this, his sister would be shunned or at the very least openly mocked, as would anyone else associated with her...including Maggie.

'What do you want me to do, Maggie? Inform Cleo that her *beloved* Charles fell in love with another woman while he was courting her? So much so that he planned to marry her under a false identity? That her eldest son is almost the same age as his illegitimate daughter? That her husband was an adulterer, liar and a gambler who sold their house from under them to repay his debts and silence his crimes? How can I tell her all this when she still grieves for him? How can I add yet more pain and torment to her misery?'

Maggie nodded, clasping his arm as if to comfort him, and he shrugged it off. But she persevered anyway. 'The man she loved never existed... I am beginning to wonder if she would be happier knowing the truth. At least then he would not be such a...hero in her mind. She might even be able to move on... remarry even—'

'You are thinking of your uncle,' he snarled, and she flinched at his tone.

'I think...he loves her.'

'I will not hurt my sister to pave an easier road for your uncle!'

'I did not ask you to!' she snapped back, the colour high in her cheeks. 'But surely, it is better to be honest. Cleo cannot continue to mourn and idolise a man who cared nothing for her!'

'Who is to say he did not care? You know nothing of men. Perhaps he loved them both?'

She sank back in her seat, horrified. 'Are men truly so fickle? Could *you* behave so cruelly, profess undying love to more than one woman?'

He stiffened, but replied honestly, even though he could not meet her eyes and instead stared ahead at the road. 'No... But my behaviour hasn't always been gentlemanly.'

To his surprise she gave an indignant huff. '*That* again! I think you should trust us women to make our own informed decisions.'

'Informed?' he asked with a raised brow. 'You know nothing of the real world. You have lived a sheltered life and know nothing of true hardship—' He would have said more, but the phaeton hit a dip in the road more heavily than he'd anticipated. It was followed by a loud crack and an alarming tilt to the entire carriage.

'Whoa!' he yelled, pulling on the reins to halt the horses while simultaneously throwing out an arm to hold Maggie in the carriage. She grabbed hold of the frame as she tipped precariously to the side.

'What was that!' she cried, pushing her bonnet backwards as it had fallen forward almost covering her eyes.

Hawk had thought this day couldn't get any worse, but he was obviously mistaken. He got down from the phaeton to check the wheel, and unsurprisingly it was badly damaged. 'Damn it!' he shouted at the sky.

Maggie peeked over the side. 'Do you think it will last until we get to the village? There's bound to be someone at the inn who can help us.'

He sucked in a deep breath. He'd not wanted to bring her in the first place, would have ridden here himself if he could have, and then he wouldn't have had to use this old rickety phaeton. As it was, the smaller wheel at the front had four spokes broken and was dangerously close to coming off altogether.

Muttering a curse, he said, 'It might be best if we both walk. I'm worried any weight will break the wheel at the back, too.'

Maggie nodded and hurried to clamber down, looking more than a little flustered. 'Of course, sorry!'

He immediately went to help her and she practically shrieked at him, 'There is *no* need!'

'What's wrong? I won't drop you.'

Her face was crimson as she stared down at him. 'I... I am a little heavy.'

Deliciously curved were the words he would have used to describe her.

'I have never had a problem carrying you,' he said as he continued to offer her both arms.

Hesitantly, she placed her hands on his shoulders and sucked in a deep breath as if preparing herself. Gripping her around the waist he plucked her off the phaeton and set her down as carefully as he could, mainly to reassure her that she was no burden. He'd moved artillery carts and canons; a pretty Scot was the least of his worries...at least, physically.

They walked to the head of the two horses and Hawk began to lead them carefully the rest of the way down the lane.

Rain began to fall, gentle at first, but it was enough for Maggie to drape her tartan over her bonnet and shoulders. However, soon it began to fall with more ferocity, soaking them both down to the bone.

'The village is just over the next hill,' said Hawk, the rain pouring off his hat in a steady stream.

Maggie nodded beneath her blanket. 'It could be worse...' she said, her voice trembling with cold. 'We could be miles away from anywhere.'

'True,' he grunted, but he couldn't bring himself to be grateful.

A short time later they arrived at the inn, and already they could hear the sounds of jubilant celebrations within.

'The wedding,' he grumbled. 'Go in and warm

yourself by the fire. I will speak with the farrier. He might be able to help me fix the wheel.'

Maggie went off to do as he said, and Hawk spent the next hour sorting out the carriage wheel.

Maggie waited patiently inside and listened to the stream of rain pouring down the inn's little windowpanes. The large dining room was thick with people who were all revellers celebrating the wedding, and she smiled at the bride, who was blushing prettily in a corner with her groom.

She wore flowers in her hair, and a light pink silk gown that looked as if it had been originally designed in an older style and had been reworked, possibly a family heirloom passed down from bride to bride.

Maggie thought she looked beautiful.

She ordered them each a beer from the bar and waited to see if Hawk would return before ordering anything else. There was no way she could reach the fire; people were all gathered around it. She sat by the door instead, warming her hands by rubbing them briskly, and stared at the menu board with increasing hunger, allowing the chatter of the nearby celebrants to wash over her.

They hadn't eaten since breakfast, and she'd eaten sparingly to *prove* how ill she was. Hawk had partaken of a large breakfast, she recalled, and she wished she'd thought to pack some food for the journey.

They were about two hours away from Castleton, and that was being generous considering the roads were not particularly straight or well kept in this part of the countryside.

When the door eventually banged open an hour later, Hawk strode into the inn in a rush of cold air and rain. The inn quietened for a moment, a little shocked by his commanding entrance as he searched the crowd for her. The men and women stared back at him with wide eyes as he glared around at them in a bad temper.

'Hawk?' she called quietly, and he spun back towards her.

'There you are!'

'I bought you a beer,' she said weakly, pushing the tankard across the old oak table towards him and shuffling a little along the window bench to make room for him.

'You should be by the fire. You're soaking wet!' he grumbled, even though he looked far worse than she did. His top hat was so saturated with water that it poured off him in little streams.

'They're celebrating!' she whispered, not wanting to draw any more attention from the crowd. 'Now, sit down before you make a spectacle of yourself!'

Hawk glanced behind him and must have seen the curious looks of the locals because he quickly took his seat.

'How's the carriage?'

It was obviously the wrong thing to ask because he scowled at the question and drank heavily of his beer. 'It can be fixed.'

'Great!' She paused at his dark frown. 'Why isn't that great?'

He shook his head. 'Apparently, it's such an old carriage, he has to pretty much make a new wheel from scratch.'

'Oh… How long will that take?'

'A couple of hours…perhaps longer.'

Maggie winced. 'That would mean travelling back in the dark.' She then brightened, glancing back to the menu board hungrily. 'At least it will give us time to eat first. I'm famished!' She waved at the serving woman to get her attention.

'We can't travel on these roads in the dark and in this rain! We'll end up overturning in a ditch somewhere.'

'Oh, that won't do,' Maggie said, although she was trying to decide between the chicken or beef pie, and didn't really care to hear any more bad news until she'd eaten.

The serving woman came to join them. 'Can I help you, madam?'

'Please, can we order one beef and one chicken pie for myself and Lord Hawksmere?'

'Of course. Anything else, m'lady?'

Hawk sighed. 'Can we trouble you for two rooms for the night?' There was a loud cheer from the wedding party, and a fiddler began to play. 'And perhaps we could take our meals in them?'

The woman smiled. 'You're in luck, m'lord. We still have one room left tonight so it's no trouble—we've been ever so busy, what with the Spencers' wedding. But our best room is still available. It's plenty big enough for two, if that's your worry?'

'I would like *two* rooms.' Hawk's expression remained firm.

The serving woman squirmed uncomfortably before glancing back at the wedding party, 'I suppose I could—'

'Darling!' Maggie implored sweetly, placing a gloved hand on his arm. 'We will be fine with one room—after all, it is only for one night. Let's not put these people to any more trouble...not during their celebrations.' She then turned to the serving woman. 'Please, could we have some hot water sent up, too?'

The woman nodded with obvious relief and bobbed a curtsy before leaving. 'That's very kind of you. I will put your order through to the kitchen and fetch the key for you.'

After she'd left, Hawk turned on her and hissed, 'What have you done? They think we are ma—'

She interrupted him quickly. *'For goodness' sake!* These people have come from far and wide to celebrate Miss Harris's wedding to Mr Spencer. I will not be the one to throw her aging grandmother or her blind uncle out of their bed!'

'How do you know so much about these people?'

She huffed with a shrug. 'I listened! I had very little to do while I waited for you. I am cold, wet and hungry. I just want dinner and a bed for the night. We will be perfectly fine with this pretence—it is only for one night. A few hours, really—as we'll have to leave by dawn to make it back before the others return.'

'Maggie!' he warned, 'it is improper. We are not—'

'Hush!' she snapped, and she proudly crossed her gloved hands primly on the table. 'No one will know, and there's no way I'm remaining in cold, wet clothes, or throwing a member of the wedding party out of their bed tonight. We will *manage*!'

The serving woman came back to them and Maggie was relieved when Hawk stood up without argument and followed her to the stairs.

They were shown into a large and cheerfully decorated room, and the woman quickly lit the fire and left. There was a large bed, a table with two chairs and a screened-off area for the garderobe. There were dried flower arrangements dotted around, and she walked around lighting the candles to brighten up the room. It was dark because it only had one small window, and also because of the miserable weather outside.

Hawk took off his greatcoat and hat. The coat he

shook out and hung on a peg, the hat he had to vigorously shake and then reshape with light punches of his fist. She tried to hide her smile at his bad humour. He really was the most foul-tempered fellow at times.

He moved both chairs from the table and positioned them beside the fire before he sat down on one and took off his tall Hessian boots, which were no longer gleaming and looked caked in mud and hay from the farrier's stable. He poured out the rain from inside them, peeled off his stockings and then stuck them by the fire to dry.

Maggie sat on the chair opposite him and shivered with pleasure as the heat began to slowly seep through the wet cloth. Even moving seemed to hurt, her bones frozen right down to the marrow. 'It's meant to be June,' she said with a sigh, knowing that weather was always a safe topic when she was nervous, and she took a moment to busy herself with reshaping her own bonnet—which looked a lost cause.

Had she really insisted on this? For the two of them to spend the night together...alone?

'You should take off your wet outer clothes. They will only make you feel colder,' said Hawk, not meeting her eyes.

Maggie nodded, but bit her lip. She was thoroughly soaked, more so than even Hawk, who was taking off his tailcoat, waistcoat and cravat so that he sat in his shirt and buckskin breeches. But they seemed reasonably dry, while she was sure even her lungs were wet through. The greatcoat he'd worn was obviously very practical in poor weather.

Tentatively, she placed her tartan blanket on a peg, as well as her long pelisse—which was not one of her winter ones and therefore was about as warm as any promenade coat. She looked down at her walking dress beneath, and sure enough, it was soaked through. She peeled it a little away from her chest, and then, deliberately avoiding his gaze, she returned to the chair to unlace and remove her boots.

'I must look a fright!' she said, self-consciously tapping her curls and knowing by the touch of them that they were a ruined mess.

Hawk was staring at her, his large body draped in the chair opposite, his half-naked legs spread out but turned slightly away from the fire, so that she felt the benefit of the heat first. Oddly, that action warmed her far more than the burning logs. It suggested that he was thinking of her comfort almost unconsciously, and she doubted anyone else would have done the same. Perhaps with the exception of her uncle.

However, his expression made a lump form in her throat. His gaze seemed to burn through her, his eyes lingering over everything from her wet gown to her tight throat, to her flushed face, and, of course, the cloud of wet hair.

A knock at the door startled her, and she called out quickly, her voice sounding slightly strangled. 'Come in!'

The serving woman entered with two steaming pies, and she placed them on the table as a young lad followed with two buckets of hot water that he put behind the screen.

'Oh, that's wonderful, thank you,' said Maggie, rising from her seat to look at the food with anticipation. Her stomach was in knots, she was so hungry.

'Would you like anything to drink, m'lady?' the woman asked, and Maggie jumped a little when Hawk suddenly rose from his seat, grabbed a blanket from the bed and made quick work of draping it around her shoulders. It was a very large blanket and swamped her.

'Two bottles of your finest claret, please,' said Hawk, turning away from her as quickly as he'd arrived.

After the serving woman and lad had left with a few coins from Hawk, Maggie asked, 'Would you mind if I used the water while it's still hot? I feel terribly cold still, and I honestly don't care what pie I have. You pick whichever one you prefer.'

'Go ahead,' he replied, carrying the chairs back over to the table, and she wondered if she'd imagined his heated gaze.

Biting her lip, she said, 'Do you think...if I just wrapped myself in this blanket that I could give my clothes to the laundress to be cleaned before tomorrow?'

He stared at her, and she had the distinct impression

she'd gone too far. 'It's just...after traipsing through the mud and rain, I don't see how these will dry in time solely in front of that small fire.'

He looked away from her and sat down at the table to eat. 'Do as you wish.'

Maggie took that as agreement and busied herself behind the screen peeling off her wet dress and using the cloth and soap provided to clean off the worst of the mud and sweat. After warming her body with the hot water, she finished by tipping the dirty water out the window and pinning the blanket around her like a badly fitted toga with one of her brooches, so that one shoulder was bare while the other was pinned. She then grabbed one of the bed ropes to tie it around her waist to keep it closed and reasonably decent.

It was enough to make her feel human again, but she took a moment to unpin her messy hair and run her fingers through it to ease some of the knots.

She had made quick work of her washing, because she was eager to get back to the table to eat her meal.

The claret arrived, and Hawk instructed the serving woman to take their wet clothes and clean them for the morning, although his breeches and shirt remained on.

Was she being scandalous?

She had to admit she was, but the heated gaze he'd given her earlier made her no longer care anymore. She wondered about poor Jane, and the love she must have felt for Charles to place herself under such terrible circumstances.

For years, she had been warned about men's terrible *lustful urges*. But now she was beginning to wonder if women had such feelings, too. She certainly felt a strange obsessive longing for Hawk. Had presumed it was one-sided until that kiss in the orangery.

Part of her, a wickedly wanton part of her, enjoyed his heated gaze, revelled in how he seemed to enjoy the sight of her. It was baffling—as no one else had found her desirable in the past.

Kind and sweet, charming and entertaining to be around, yes. But desirable? Definitely not.

The fact that Hawk might actually return her feelings… It was too wonderful a prospect to imagine, and she found herself pulling at the loose threads of his composure deliberately, almost to reassure herself that she was not imagining it.

She couldn't seem to help herself around him, and frankly, she *did* want to wear freshly laundered clothes tomorrow.

'You must think me very spoiled,' she said quietly as she tucked into the delicious pie and roasted vegetables.

Hawk had almost finished his meal and sipped on a glass of the claret while picking at the remains of his food. 'No, I do not.' He smiled and gestured with a tip of his glass towards her *clothing*. 'I have to say I am impressed by your ingenuity.'

'Thank you,' she laughed. 'I should have made you one, too. That way you could have had the rest of your things laundered.'

He shook his head. 'What a sight we would make, two Romans in the centre of the Cotswolds.'

She grinned, raising her own glass of claret in a toast. 'At least we have wine!'

'Indeed!' He clinked his glass with hers, and they sat back to enjoy a sip, their eyes locked in an intimate embrace that left her heart beating wildly in her chest.

Hawk sighed and looked away from her towards the fire. 'This is a grim business… Charles, I mean.'

She blushed, realising she probably shouldn't be enjoying this as much as she was. 'It is. For him to lie like that, and we cannot blame Jane. Even if they did lie with one another… She must have thought him honourable, and that…he *was* going to marry her. And poor little Charlotte. It's not her fault what he did.'

'I do not blame Jane or Charlotte.'

Maggie sighed with relief. 'Many would. Even Jane's own family seemed to condemn her for it. But she wasn't the only one misled… They believed him, too. And it is obvious that she loved him. Unfortunately, it is inevitable that a child will always follow from such…lapses in judgement.'

Hawk shook his head. 'Not necessarily.'

She imagined he'd spoken without thinking because when she asked, 'How?' he suddenly looked very uncomfortable.

Chapter Seventeen

'*How?*' Hawk swallowed nervously as he repeated her question.

'Yes, how?' She took a deep breath. 'I *know* how children are made. My mother was not shy about the details, she wanted my sisters and I to be informed of the...*mechanics*.' She coughed, but rallied on regardless, even though he really wished she wouldn't. 'Thankfully, I am not like those poor young ladies who go into the marriage mart completely unaware of what will happen to them on their wedding night. But my mother did insist that lying with a man almost always resulted in a bairn—especially if both man and woman were young and healthy. And she should know. She's had seven children!'

'I do not think we should be talking about this,' Hawk said sombrely before throwing half a glass of claret down his throat.

'But if there is a way to...*satisfy* lust...then surely

that should be spoken of more widely? To ensure young women such as Jane do not face the same fate.'

Hawk closed his eyes and sighed deeply. 'It is… *complicated*…to explain.'

'Then…show me,' she eventually said and then sucked in a shocked breath of her own, no doubt wondering why she'd dared to utter such a scandalous thing.

His eyes shot open, and he stared back at her for a long moment, waiting for her wits to return and with it a quick denial of her request. But it never came. If anything, her chin rose up a little in defiance. 'You do not realise what you are asking,' he said.

Maggie released her breath slowly, the sound a trembling whisper on her tongue. But there was still hope. He had not laughed or become disgusted by her suggestion. If anything, he seemed tightly wound with anticipation, his chest beginning to rise and fall with deep breaths.

'Maggie…' he warned, although it sounded more like a plea.

'I am curious.' She shrugged, pretending indifference, when she was as fizzy as an unopened bottle of champagne.

Unfortunately, it was the wrong thing to say.

'Then you can remain curious!' he snapped, thudding his glass down so hard the scarlet liquid sloshed over the rim. 'Would you have me behave no better than Charles?'

'Oh! I'm sorry, are you already married?' she asked with mock-seriousness.

'No,' he acknowledged, but his eyes still shone brightly with emotion. 'However, it would still ruin you all the same.'

'This—' she gestured to the room around them '—if it were to ever get out, would also ruin me.'

A growl escaped his throat and he leaned forward to glare at her. *'It will not get out!* Not unless *you* say something, as I surely won't!'

Her jaw tightened at the implied insult. 'So you think I am trying to entrap you?'

'No! But…you were the one who insisted on coming with me today. You were the one who asked to be kissed, and you are the one sitting in front of me wearing nothing more than a blanket! You deliberately tempt and toy with me every single day!'

Embarrassment clawed at her throat and she stood up in such a rush that the chair rocked back, dangerously close to falling over completely.

Had she been trying to tempt him?

Possibly, she admitted to herself. Shame and anger at her own foolish behaviour burned her pride so hotly that she could only see red fury in that moment.

'You think very highly of yourself! You may have a title, but you have nothing else to tempt me! I have the privilege of being protected by my family. I have no desire to entrap you in marriage. I just...*liked* you! An emotion that is currently fading with the miserable light of this day. It is strange how men are allowed to freely indulge themselves in pleasures of all kinds. But when a woman tries to do so, she is considered a villain! Well, let me take all temptation out of your sight—by retiring for the night! I am sure the chair will serve you well!'

She flounced away from the table with as much dignity as she could manage in a robe made out of a blanket and a bed rope. But as she passed him, Hawk's arm shot out, barring her path.

She stared down at his arm in surprise and then looked to Hawk, whose face still stared straight ahead, his expression dark and solemn, as if he was making a heavy choice. Then, when she was about to step out of the way of his arm, it moved. Hooking around her hip and pulling her quickly and decisively into his lap.

She let out a shocked gasp as she flopped into his arms.

'You *like* me?' he asked, turning her a little in his lap to see her better.

Still flushed and shocked by his behaviour, she looked away, embarrassed. 'Yes... But... I expect nothing—'

Her words were cut off by the unexpected brush of his knuckles across her cheek, drawing her attention back towards him. Dark pools of chestnut brown stared back at her, reflecting some of the glow of the nearby fire. His arm tightened around her waist, pulling her closer, and she braced a hand against his shoulder, unsure of what to say or do, but praying he would at least kiss her.

It seemed the heavens were kind, because his knuckles stroked up her face, and then he cupped the back of her head, pulling her down to meet his lips. The kiss was soft and gentle, with light exploring brushes. Then he pulled away slightly, hesitating as he said, 'Are you sure you want me to show you? Because…honestly…you are right—I have nothing to offer you. It is not I who should be worried about entrapment…but you. We are on the edge of financial and social ruin. You are courting disaster even by associating with my family. If it all comes out into the open, we will be shunned and ridiculed by the entire ton. It really would be better for you and your uncle if you distanced yourself from us.'

She smiled at his words, which clearly contradicted the way he was holding her.

Allowing her palm to smooth up from his shoulder to the back of his neck, she leaned forward, repeating breathlessly as she did so, 'I do like you, Hawk, very much, more than anyone.' She wanted nothing more than to be in his arms. To feel his kiss once more, and ease the longing she had suffered with since first meeting him at Lady Bulphan's ball.

He covered her mouth with his, the kiss deeper and more passionate, and she mimicked his actions, desperate to please him the same way he was pleasing her. His hand dropped from her head, no longer needing to guide their kiss.

Wrapping both hands around his neck, she pulled him close, burying her fingers through the silk of his dark hair and drowning in the taste of him. Rich fruit wine, combined with the salty musk of rain and man. The arm around her waist dropped back to her hip and squeezed her lightly as his other hand stroked slowly up from her knee beneath the cloth of the blanket.

His hips shifted beneath her, and the hard bulge of his groin rubbed against her thigh as his fingers slipped beneath her slightly open legs. She shifted her legs a little wider, breaking the kiss, a little worried she might topple off his lap, and gripped the back of his neck tighter for purchase.

'I have you, my darling,' he reassured her with a smug smile, and she realised she needn't have worried. In Hawk's embrace she was always safe. He held her firmly in place with one arm while the other explored her intimately, sliding down between her thighs, his index finger gliding over her silken flesh until it touched an intimate spot that made her gasp and tighten her hold on the back of his neck.

'Do you like me touching you there?' he whispered and she moaned as he stroked again, more firmly this time, and she arched up, desperate to allow him complete access to her body.

'Undo the brooch,' he commanded, and she quickly fumbled with the latch, dropping it on the table, and then allowing the blanket to puddle round her waist. She tried her best not to look embarrassed or flustered, but she had never been naked in front of another before, let alone a man.

But then his hand stroked between her legs and she groaned and arched again, his head dipping to kiss her breast. Sensation shivered down her spine, and her nipples tingled as the rough stubble of his chin rubbed against her skin. He pushed her back a little so she lay against his other arm and held her up, and then he licked and kissed her breasts until her nipples hardened and she was whimpering at the rush of sensations.

Despite his focus on her breasts, his other hand didn't stop its gliding motion back and forth between her thighs, and she began to rock against his fingers as tension and anticipation began to build within her.

His head lifted and he began to watch her, his breathing heavy and his eyes piercingly sensual and black as midnight. She clutched at his neck, wanting to kiss him, but being unable to think or speak her request as tension steadily built within her as if she were a rope twisted and tightened to the point of breaking.

Sudden delirious and overwhelming pleasure rushed through her as the spiralling tension suddenly broke like a crashing wave and she cried out, dragging him close, unable to take any more, but unwilling to let go. Their eyes met through the fog of pleasure, and she clutched at him, desperately wanting to hold him and never let go.

He gathered her close and held her for a long time, until she finally caught her breath and he murmured in her ear, 'Go to bed, Maggie. I've shown you all that I can.'

She pulled a little away to see him better and then hopped off his lap, gathering the blanket back around her. Suddenly uncertain, she asked, 'Can't you come with me?'

He sighed. 'I cannot. This is as far as we can go.'

'But...' She paused, looking down at him, not sure how to explain herself. 'You don't seem as pleased...'

He laughed, but it sounded hollow. However, when he looked up at her his eyes burned with desire. 'This is as far as *I* can go. Anything more...there would be no going back.'

She nodded, understanding his discomfort, if nothing else. If he said there was nothing more, he could do to find his own pleasure, then she would have to trust him at his word. 'It seems...terribly one-sided.'

His eyes reminded her of her favourite drink, black coffee, sweetened with plenty of sugar, his voice equally deep and rich as he replied, 'Tonight I have had more than I could have ever hoped for.'

Still uncertain, she gave a little nod and went to the large bed to sleep alone. She lay awake for most of the night, wondering about what he'd said before kissing her.

Did he really consider himself a poor offering?

She could not imagine it. Not only was he an English baron, he was also a war hero, a protective and kind family man, who also happened to be devilishly attractive and a fine figure of a man. He could melt her heart with a single look and steal her thoughts with a kiss. He was everything she wanted and more.

But could she bring herself to admit it? To fight for it, when the potential humiliation of his rejection would break her? And she knew it would, her heart beat only for him, and if she ruined things between them, she knew she would not even remain as his friend. There would be no going back…as he had so eloquently said.

He said he could go no further, that anything more would bind them together, and it seemed she was the only one who did not mind such a fate.

Had she been wrong, then? To think that there could be more between them? She was so confused.

Were lust and love two separate desires?

They were not for her. But they had been for Charles, or perhaps he had never truly loved either of his brides?

But what of Hawk? Did he feel lust or love?

His kisses and worry for her reputation made her think he might be falling in love with her. But...he had not once offered her anything more than pleasure. No courtship, no promises, not even a glimmer of hope for a future together, once all the mess of his finances and Charles were put to rest.

In fact, he had said more than once that he never planned to marry or have a family of his own. Should she ignore his words just because they no longer suited her?

Maggie could not face another humiliation like Mr Beaston, who had seen her as nothing more than an amusement. Hawk was not cruel like him, but she was beginning to fear that Hawk and Mr Beaston had one thing in common.

Neither of them had ever wanted, or *would* ever want, to marry her.

But unlike Mr Beaston, Maggie could not lose Hawk as a friend; she was determined to put aside her adoration and enjoy whatever remained between them... Perhaps one day he would change his mind?

There was no harm in hoping.

Chapter Eighteen

They arrived back at Castleton well before the return of her uncle and his sister. Hawk had made certain of it. He'd not bothered to sleep—he wouldn't have been able to manage it anyway. But at least that meant he was ready to go by first light.

Thankfully, the laundress had been true to her word, and their clothes were ready for them as soon as he rang the bell.

They were gone with a basket of bread rolls and a pot of honey well before any of the other patrons rose from their slumber. He couldn't even blame the lack of sleep on the revellers or the hardness of his chair. He would have slept badly regardless, knowing that the object of his frustration was only a few feet away, wearing nothing more than a blanket.

The ride home was reasonably smooth despite the bad weather previously. Maggie chatted cheerfully about her home in Scotland, and offered him bites of the bread and honey as he drove. It was pleasant, and he was glad she had decided to make conversation; it avoided any awkwardness between them and reminded him that they were, first and foremost, friends.

She seemed accepting of his rejection—could he even call it a rejection? He had said he could not go any further, and he could not. The temptation and risk of ruining her was too great. But *damn it*! He *wished* he could have joined her in that large bed. Thoroughly taken her without regard to propriety or good sense.

Thankfully, he'd had enough wits left to stop when he had. He dreaded to think of what would have happened otherwise.

You would have had to marry her.

The thought hit him square in the chest, not because it horrified him—although it should—but that he was a little disappointed he *wouldn't* have to.

You have no business taking on a wife! he admonished himself sharply. *You can barely afford your nephews and sister! Not to mention if the scandal of their poor finances and Charles's secret child ever got out, it would ruin Maggie and her family by mere association.*

Even with the property to sell in Brighton and the strange shares mentioned, it might not be enough to see them right. It would keep the *wolf from the door*, as Maggie had put it, but the wolf was not gone; it still lingered like a shadow, ready to claw them at any moment.

Indulging himself by pleasuring Maggie had been a terrible mistake, but it was done, and perhaps after this visit to Castleton they would both be done with each other... Or at least she would be done with him, her curiosity satiated.

As they rolled up the Castleton driveway he said, 'Can your maid be trusted to keep your absence from your uncle?'

Maggie nodded with a dismissive shrug. 'Of course, but I will give her some coin to sweeten the deal.'

'Good.'

'Are you still set on not telling Cleo the truth?'

He stiffened defensively. 'I am.'

Maggie sighed. 'Well, I do not agree with it. But I suppose she is your sister.'

The knots in his neck and shoulders loosened a little and he begrudgingly said, 'Thank you.'

'But if you do decide to tell her, please let me know first...so that I may help her through it?'

'That is fair. But I doubt I will change my mind.'

He stopped the phaeton at the entrance, and one of the footmen came to take the reins. He jumped down and made his way over to the other side to help Maggie down. With a cheerful and confident smile, she braced her palms on his shoulders and leapt into his arms.

The sheer brilliance of her smile dazzled him and he wondered how he would ever recover from this terrible mistake. He caught the eye of the footman, who was watching them with a knowing smile. But as soon as the servant realised his mistake, he straightened his face and looked away. Hawk dropped his arms from her waist as if she were a hot coal.

He had to put a stop to this madness!

'You should go in. Have a bath drawn for yourself and rest. You will need to look fully recovered by the time they return. I want no further delays to our return to London. I must be back by Wednesday afternoon at the latest.'

He had whist to play with his friends...not to mention catching up with their whirlwind love lives.

Maggie's face was now painted with a blush and he wondered if she was also embarrassed by the footman's gaze or by his own curt manner. 'That won't be a problem.'

'Good,' he replied, hating how cold he sounded but unsure of how to behave otherwise. He did not want the servants gossiping...although, it was already far too late for that...

Still, best not to add fuel to the fire.

When Cleo, William and the boys returned later that morning, Cleo was full of good cheer as she entered the drawing room where he'd been sleeping in an armchair, a token book in his lap for when they returned.

'We had such a wonderful time! Maggie will be so

sad she missed it!' She then paused, taking a moment to inspect him closely. 'You do not look well, brother. Perhaps you have the same illness as poor Maggie?'

Bloody hell! Did he look that bad?

Maggie had painted her face with ash and coal; he'd done nothing more than sleep in a chair! 'I am tired. Perhaps I will go for a nap.'

Concerned, Cleo nodded emphatically and pushed him towards the stairs. 'Yes, go, I have invited the Whites and Carpenters for dinner. I want you well enough to receive them!'

He allowed her to push him away, a little relieved that he could have some time alone before facing society again.

The evening was as he had expected…painful. Their guests were jovial, but he felt like a stranger at the dinner table. Worse than a stranger, as even William and Maggie seemed to find conversing with them easy enough, while he brooded over his past mistakes.

William knew them from the trip to Tetbury, and Maggie was always agreeable in any company, he'd come to realise. He, however, struggled to do little more than pretend to listen. At least Cleo was enjoying herself.

'Oh, I did love going to Tetbury,' declared Cleo with a smile that made him glad they'd come to Castleton for more reasons than discovering the papers or finding out the dark truth about Charles. She really did seem happier here. 'Although, I am surprised that tavern we stopped at for lunch wasn't more welcoming.'

Mrs White exchanged a look with Mrs Carpenter before answering, 'It was a little odd... But it isn't the best place to eat. I wouldn't recommend going there again.'

William looked uncomfortable for a moment, and Hawk wondered if the tavern was one of Charles's debtors. He suspected as much. He remembered seeing many names of taverns and inns, as well as gentlemen's clubs, in the long list of payments his brother had made. Now that he knew Charles had used Tetbury as his base to visit Jane Wilkins, he wouldn't have been surprised if people knew more about the Hawksmere connection with Charles than Cleo did. There was some comfort in the fact that, as Mr Wilkins had said, people would never openly speak of it. So Cleo could remain blissfully unaware of her husband's crimes.

Cleo seemed unconcerned, though, which was a blessing. 'True, I much preferred the Kings Head, a much more friendly establishment. It is a pity Miss Brown couldn't join us, though. I do love her company.'

Miss Carpenter, who was barely older than eighteen, nodded enthusiastically in agreement. 'Miss Brown is such fun! But she had a wedding to attend—

not far from here. She's returning tomorrow, so perhaps we should go on a picnic together? If the weather doesn't turn again?'

Hawk flinched at the mention of a wedding, and his eyes darted to Maggie, who sipped her wine and deliberately avoided his gaze. Quickly, he interrupted before any plans could be made. 'We should begin our return to London tomorrow.'

'Oh! But couldn't we stay a little longer?' pleaded Cleo.

'No, I must be back before sunset on Wednesday. We will need to leave very early tomorrow.'

She tutted at that. 'Only because you always go to White's on a Wednesday evening! Surely, you can miss *one* week!'

'I cannot,' he said firmly, and when Cleo looked put out by his comment, he added, 'But you can return here after the season ends. Spend the rest of the year here if you wish.' Silently adding to himself, *But I will not!* If Miss Brown had seen him and Maggie at the inn together it could cause a scandal that would embarrass Cleo terribly, in the very home she obviously adored, and put his own reputation in the mud... *where it belonged!*

Miss Carpenter's face flushed with excitement. 'How wonderful! Perhaps we could even have a ball?'

Mrs Carpenter stared at her daughter in horror. 'Rebecca, you cannot ask that!' she admonished her with a hiss.

But Cleo was quick to smile and ease her worries. 'Perhaps when I am fully out of mourning, I shall host a ball here. But until then, the best I can offer is a luncheon or dinner.'

The fact that Cleo was even willing to consider a time when she was no longer in mourning seemed a miracle in itself, and Hawk had to admit, even with the potential scandal looming, it was enough to know that his sister was considering a future without the ghost of Charles haunting her.

Later, while he and the other men were drinking port and playing billiards, William approached him. He looked strangely nervous, which did nothing to alleviate his own discomfort.

How could he face this man after his own behaviour?

'Lord Hawksmere,' he began formally, followed by a coughed, 'Um—may I speak with you privately a moment?'

'Of course!' he said with such uncharacteristic enthusiasm, it made William blink and swallow deeply, but Hawk couldn't seem to help himself—guilt was gnawing at his insides. He half hoped the man would demand satisfaction and put him out of his misery.

He may not have bedded William's niece, but he'd done everything else to ruin her. He could no longer claim he'd offered her a chaste first kiss as a friend. The kiss in the orangery alone had disproved that argument—who was he trying to fool? Nothing they had ever done together was *chaste*!

He showed William into the library and promptly poured them each a very large brandy. 'I suppose you would prefer whisky, but I'm afraid I left Maggie's latest batch at home.'

'You know about that?' asked William, wide-eyed, and Hawk realised his first mistake.

'I guessed as much…' He decided not to mention how he'd found out the truth in an unchaperoned carriage ride.

Bloody hell. When had he not been inappropriate with her?

William chuckled, a blush blooming over the top of his red beard, making him look even more ruddy. 'I am not a subtle man, which is why I wished to speak with you.'

'Really?' said Hawk, taking a very deep draught of his brandy and trying to brace himself for whatever demands William would make. He must suspect Hawk and Maggie's relationship had become inappropriate. Had Maggie's maid spoken to him? Was he about to demand he marry her? Or had he merely noticed Hawk staring at her constantly?

'Yes…' William paused as if he was struggling to find the words. 'It is…a delicate matter… I…'

Hawk waited...

And waited...

Hawk was sure duels were not as agonising as this. Would the man ever finish his sentence? It seemed unlikely.

'Go on,' Hawk eventually urged. Although, why he would encourage his own reprimand he wasn't sure.

Hawk usually prided himself on seeing problems well before they arose, but since meeting Maggie he seemed to constantly be caught off guard by the twists of life, as he was now, when William finally said in a rush, 'I want you to know that I respect and value your family and friendship. Maggie—'

'I also respect and value Maggie,' he said sharply—even though, frankly, he had no right to make such a claim, and William also seemed surprised because he hesitated before nodding in agreement.

'Yes, my lord...' William scratched his head, and Hawk had the horrible feeling they were on two very different paths in this conversation.

'Speak plainly, William,' he urged, and William nodded decisively.

'I care greatly for your sister,' the man blurted out, and then took a large gulp of his brandy.

'Cleo?'

William nodded, sucking in a sharp breath as the liquor hit the back of his throat and almost choking on it before regaining his composure. 'Yes, Cleo...

And, I *know* that she is still in mourning for Charles, and that I have no business courting her. But I have admired and loved her for many years... Even, God forgive me, when she was still married to that...*man*. But...even though I did not like him, I respected her love for him... And I am determined to be patient and considerate of her mourning, allow her the time to grow accustomed to me before I declare myself. But know that I will declare myself eventually—that I am not being insincere—only cautious in my courting of your sister. And frankly, I would feel a wretch if you did not know my intentions from the start or were not reassured that they were completely honourable. I mean to marry her—' he gave a wincing shrug '—eventually...if she will have me.'

'Yes...quite...' agreed Hawk, feeling like the worst of wretches—*this* was how a gentleman behaved. 'But... Cleo is a widow. You do not need *my* permission to court her.'

'I know,' said William with a dismissive shrug, his usual cheerfulness returning now that he had confessed his feelings. 'But...it felt only right that you should know. I do not plan on rushing her. If anything, I think my mentioning it to you now is rather presumptuous of me. I imagine it will be months, if not years, until Cleo would consider me as a suitor—if at all. I only wish to make you aware of it, because... well, Cleo seems keen to return to Castleton. Perhaps you will let me rent a house nearby for some months… so that I may call on her?' William looked a little nauseated and he quickly added, 'If Cleo is amenable to it, of course!'

'I cannot see why not. She adores you and Maggie.'

William smiled guiltily. 'I confess that is one of the reasons I have insisted Maggie join me each season. I would be lost without her.'

That made Hawk flinch a little, and he smiled weakly in response. Would Maggie no longer be his neighbour, then…if William decided to spend time in Castleton instead?

'Well, you have my permission to court or not court her for as long as Cleo does not mind. *If* that is any comfort to you,' Hawk said, not sure of the point of this strange request to *potentially* court his sister in either a few months, years or never. But he saw no reason to refuse him, as he genuinely did like William and thought they were well suited to one another—if Cleo would ever allow it—which he doubted.

William seemed pleased, however, and toasted his glass with a grin. 'Thank you. Your approval means a great deal to me!'

That night Hawk retired early, claiming to be tired from the mysterious bug that had claimed Maggie the day before. Maggie gave him a curious look, but said nothing. In fact, she'd said very little since Cleo's and William's return.

Perhaps that was for the best.

He had made a terrible mistake. One he deeply regretted, never more so than now. After speaking with William, he'd realised how a true gentleman should behave, and he was sorely lacking. Not only did he have very little to offer Maggie, he had also opened her up to a possible scandal that could ruin her chances of happiness forever.

The ton were not forgiving—unless you had both a title and wealth. Even then people were openly shunned for far less than what he had done to Maggie.

It would be best if he removed himself from her circle entirely. A plan he hoped to put into action as soon as he was back in London. Perhaps if she was no longer his neighbour it would help matters?

If Cleo moved to Castleton, he could sell the townhouse and take back his rooms in the Albany. Go back to the bachelor life.

For some reason, that idea only made him more gloomy. Despite the chaos his nephews brought, he enjoyed their company, and he had felt closer with Cleo in the recent weeks than he ever had before. And Maggie...

How could he live without her sunny disposition in his life?

The newspapers were claiming this had been the worst summer on record, that it would be known forever as *the year without summer*. But he did not feel that way. In his mind, the sun had always been present in Maggie's dazzling smile, and this was the only summer he would remember and cherish for the years to come.

Could he really go back to the bleakness of before? But what choice did he have? He could not harm or disappoint Maggie any further.

Perhaps he shouldn't rush things...he still had his financial situation to look into, and who knew what the next crisis would be?

Chapter Nineteen

William peeked out the carriage window and said, 'Not long now, Maggie. We just passed the Wrexhams' house.'

'Should I wake the boys?' asked Betsy quietly.

Maggie smiled weakly and glanced at the sleeping children before whispering, 'Let's not wake them yet. They'll only be bad-tempered.'

'True.' William nodded and went back to cheerfully staring out the window.

Maggie sighed, resting her head against the lush upholstery. The journey back had been a lot quicker than the journey to Castleton. Hawk had seemed determined to return to London at a breakneck pace, and that, combined with the rest of his behaviour, had made her uncomfortably aware that he deeply regretted that night at the inn.

Leaving her feeling about *as wanted as a trollop in church!* That was one of her grandfather's sayings, which had always made her giggle as a child and her mother purse her lips in disapproval. Even though, when she'd been young, she'd barely understood its meaning.

Now she understood why, and it no longer made her smile. It made her feel sick and ashamed of herself because of her own wanton behaviour. Hawk had barely spoken to her since, had ridden ahead of their carriage at all times. He deliberately sat far away from her at all mealtimes, as well as the few rest stops he allowed.

What made it even more humiliating was that no one seemed to notice his sudden coldness towards her. William was as cheerful and as chatty as ever, entertaining Cleo and the boys, barely noticing how withdrawn she'd become.

Cleo's disposition had brightened considerably and she was eager to talk about her old friends and organising another, much longer, trip to Castleton. Completely oblivious to how close her husband's actions had come to their almost losing it.

Nobody noticed Maggie's sadness, or perhaps she was just too good at hiding it. Putting on a sunny smile had always come so easily to her. If she pretended to be happy, she usually felt better in the long run. But her current smile felt particularly brittle today as they neared London, because Maggie knew her time with Hawk was over. It was clear he had no intention of continuing their close friendship or anything else for that matter, and it hurt...*considerably.*

Their townhouse came into view just before the sun began to set, and Maggie sighed with relief. Soon, she could go to her room, shut the door and take some time alone to accept Hawk's clear rejection of her.

This is as far as we can go.

Now she fully understood what he'd meant by that.

It was over...before it had even begun.

After all, she had been the one to tell him that it meant *nothing*. So it was really her own fault if she'd allowed her hopes to get out of hand. He did not want to ruin her...because he wanted nothing more. He did not care for her in the way that she might have hoped...wanted...yearned for.

The carriage stopped outside their houses, and after a few moments spent waking Francis and Thomas, they were stepping out onto the pavement, ready to say their farewells.

Hawk handed his reins to a footman and was now helping Cleo out of the carriage, while the boys' nurse, Daisy, stood carrying Matthew and holding Peter's hand.

'Thank you for such a lovely trip. I loved Castleton. You have such a beautiful ancestral home,' declared her uncle.

Cleo opened her mouth to thank him when a very loud shout rang out from the doorway of their townhouse. 'Maggie, William, where have you *been*?'

Everyone turned, including Maggie, although she

knew precisely whose shrill voice that belonged to, and her heart sank. 'Mary? What are you doing here?'

Her youngest sister came flying down the steps with her usual anxious excitement and lack of grace, hitching up her skirts and jumping the last couple of steps to join them on the pavement. Mary was a curious mix of a nervous disposition, an impulsive nature and a complete blindness to most manners. She seemed to merrily throw caution to the wind, only to lament her poor decisions for months after, as if someone else were to blame for them. The latest was Mary's elopement to an officer not long after her sixteenth birthday; apparently, being married wasn't as exciting as she'd hoped it would be.

But then...was Maggie any better? Throwing caution to the wind and letting her passions control her as she had?

Their mother was quick to follow, elegant as always and looking particularly beautiful in her dainty muslin gown, with a scarlet spencer jacket decorated in gold military tassels that matched the jaunty cap on her head. Her mother had the ideal figure and taste for fashion. 'We were just about to go out when we heard you had returned. Did you enjoy your trip?' she asked casually, although by the sharp examination she gave Hawk from top to bottom it was clear she thought him a potential suitor.

How wrong she was!

'Catherine, dearest!' cried William, giving her mother a fierce hug that Maggie knew her mother would not enjoy, but would bear gracefully purely out of politeness.

'It is a shame that we missed you! We must have arrived just after you left. More's the pity, we could have joined you!' said Mary with a thoughtful frown. Maggie was very grateful her sister *had* missed them. Mary then went on to grumble, 'Although, I might not have enjoyed yet another long trip after coming down from Scotland. Perhaps we could have planned something else instead?'

'Oh, Mary,' interrupted her mother with an embarrassed laugh at her youngest's thoughtless chatter. 'We weren't invited in the first place—nor would we be! Lord Hawksmere hasn't even met us until now.' Her mother readjusted her tassel with a slightly defeated sigh.

Her parents had always said Maggie was no trouble compared to her sisters. A ray of sunshine. But the truth was her parents—and herself to some extent—were so outnumbered by the rest of their brood, that their only option had been to surrender to the chaos, and try their best to limit the damage caused by their wayward children.

Of course, Maggie was trusted to do as she was told and behave well without complaint—she'd had no choice as the eldest to at least try to set an example. She had always succeeded in avoiding scandal—until recently. But it was galling that despite playing by the rules, she was the only one of her siblings to fail at finding a match.

Thankfully, William was quick to take charge of the situation. 'Well, let me rectify that immediately! Lord Hawksmere, please let me introduce you to my sister-in-law Mrs Catherine Mackenzie, and my niece Mrs Mary Bell. I am sure you remember them, Cleo, from their previous trips?'

'I do indeed!' Cleo said warmly, although she gave Maggie a commiserating glance.

'Perhaps you will join us for dinner sometime to reacquaint ourselves? It's been so long since I was last in London,' said her mother, and Mary was quick to nod in agreement.

'Indeed, it has been *ages* since I came to London.'

'You came two years ago,' grumbled Maggie—not that anyone was listening to her.

'We thought it would be nice to enjoy the last month of the London season all *together* before returning to Scotland,' said her mother with an indulgent smile that did not match the horror Maggie felt.

'Together? Who else has joined you?'

'All of us are here—except Anne. She has her husband's townhouse, of course. But the rest of the girls are here. Not all of their husbands have joined them, and your brothers have decided to rent a house in Mayfair for some unknown reason. Although, I did say William's house is always open to all of us.'

Uncle William gave a flinching nod of agreement. 'Indeed.'

'But...why?' asked Maggie incredulously.

'Oh, a couple of reasons...' said her mother breezily while winking at William, and Maggie had a terrible feeling William had told her something he shouldn't have in his latest letter to her mother.

'Besides,' declared Mary, drawing the conversation back to her favourite subject, '*I* am a *married* lady now—which will give me greater freedom when it comes to London's entertainments.' Mary's pride was quickly overshadowed by a multitude of worries. 'Oh! But... I clear forgot that I now have a different name! Oh, Maggie, you will have to train me like a dog so that I do not forget my new name and embarrass myself in front of the ton. Now that I am a married woman, I will have to be sure to represent my darling Gregory well! I wouldn't want to embarrass him or his regiment. And what if he has family in town? I didn't even ask—'

'I am sure it will be fine, Mary. There is no need to fret!' interrupted William quickly, and Maggie wished she could pat his arm in sympathy. William, much like Maggie, came to London to get away from the daily dramas and worries of their family. To have them all descend on them unexpectedly was a bitter blow.

It made an already miserable end to the season ten times worse! She was still licking her wounds after Hawk's abrupt change in manner towards her. To be hounded by her family's presence seemed an unnecessarily cruel fate. The idea of pretending all was well, when her hopes had been so thoroughly dashed, made her stomach churn with dread and nausea.

'I look forward to hearing all about your trip, Maggie. With such pleasant company—' her mother's eyes slid curiously to Hawk. '—I am sure you had a wonderful time.'

Maggie was saved from having to roll her eyes by the dramatic inhale of her sister. 'But we were just on our way to the theatre! Oh, Mama! Please tell me we will not have to cancel tonight, purely because Maggie and Uncle William are home? We see them all the time as it is.'

Her mother looked a little uncertain—not wanting to disappoint her youngest, but also being painfully aware of how badly Mary was behaving in front of an English lord.

'We insist you still go out!' Maggie cried, trying her best to look as cheerful and as unbothered as ever. 'We are so tired from our journey. We would not be good company for you anyway. Are the others out, too?' she asked hopefully.

'Yes, they were invited to dinner…but only if you're sure?' her mother asked hesitantly.

'Oh, Mama, she said it was fine! We can find out about their trip tomorrow—after we visit Madame Devy, of course. I am in desperate need of updating my wardrobe and she is the finest modiste in London, and Papa did promise I could get two new gowns.'

Maggie peeked a glance at Hawk, wondering what he thought of this spectacle. As suspected, he appeared disapproving and aloof.

He caught her eye and straightened up a little. 'Please excuse me. I have business to attend to. It was a pleasure to make your acquaintance, ladies.' He then turned to the tired children, who looked fed up and bored by the adults making small talk. 'Come along, boys. Let's get you inside.'

Cleo also made her goodbyes, clutching Maggie's hand tightly before she left—as if wishing her strength and fortitude. She might have even said something to that effect. But Maggie was distracted, watching Hawk stride up the steps to his house, the boys following after him like sleepy ducklings.

After her own wanton behaviour, and then meeting her indulgent mother and dramatic sister, he must think himself lucky to have escaped her.

Chapter Twenty

*B*loody hell, it had been one thing after another!

Hawk had gone to White's last night expecting to drown his sorrows about the events at Castleton, the uncovering of his unsavoury family secrets and his own poor behaviour with a woman far too good for him.

Except, he wasn't the only one to face a grim truth, and he'd had to hold his tongue and comfort Adam, who had had a terrible argument with his new wife. He'd not had the heart to tell his friend of his own woes. He would tell him later, when his own burdens weren't so great.

Adam had discovered the truth about his bride's true intentions in marrying him. Apparently, the *convenient marriage* was only that, and she had no intention of having a real marriage with him. She had hoped only for him to father a child with her and then promptly leave her so she could get on with her life and furniture business alone.

Adam, who rarely did as he was told at the best of times, was greatly put out by such a deceitful revelation—and, in fact, seemed strangely devastated by it. So much so that he had refused to go home and had spent the night at Hawk's house, drinking every bottle of alcohol he owned and grumbling over his poor luck in marrying such a *deceitful witch* for hours.

Hawk had listened with sympathy, but suspected that Adam simply needed to work through his emotions before he decided on a course of action. He had clearly grown to love his wife, and Hawk could understand his hurt at her deceit.

After all, Adam had even considered returning to the war office in a job he would most definitely hate, all so that he could repay his wife for the money she'd used to clear his brother's debts. It had meant giving up on his plans to go into law for the second time in his life, which was a bitter blow indeed.

It must have stung that a woman he'd given up his dreams for didn't actually want a future with him.

They'd slept off the booze for most of the day, until Hawk had said goodbye to a rumpled and miserable Adam, who went off to fulfil his duty as the *happy groom* at yet another social function.

Hawk winced and rolled his neck and shoulders to crack the stiffness in his joints; even after a bath and dressing properly for dinner he felt like an old rag. Perhaps it was the guilt that made him feel this way?

Had he behaved much better to Maggie?

Pushing her away, after he had been intimate with her?

Still, she had not seemed miserable afterwards and had appeared even cheerful on her return to London, except perhaps when her mother and sister were introduced to him. She'd seemed a little distant then…but that could be due to the tiredness from the journey.

As he walked into the dining room, he was surprised to see that Cleo had already started eating, piling up her plate with plenty of food, the boys doing much the same.

'Has Adam left? Mrs Wimple said he was here,' she asked lightly as she began cutting into her roast beef after passing Peter the salt.

'Yes,' he answered, taking the seat beside her. 'Sorry about that. He's had a tough time of it lately.'

'No problem at all. He's always welcome here,' she replied cheerfully.

Hawk frowned. Something about her appearance startled him, although he couldn't think what. Due to the fogginess of his whisky-soaked brain, it took him a moment to realise what it was.

Cleo was no longer in her customary black.

Today she wore a lavender-grey gown; it was still sombre and dull in colour, but it brightened her face considerably, giving it colour and life where once there had been only an empty shell before.

'You look—' he struggled to find the words to express his relief at her appearance '—lovely.'

Cleo smoothed down her skirt in a nervous gesture and glanced at the boys, who were too busy eating to pay attention to their conversation. 'It has been over a year… It would not be seen as improper to go into half mourning now, would it?'

'Of course not,' he reassured her, even adding an awkward smile in the hopes of easing her discomfort. The truth was she should already be out of half-mourning by now, but he didn't want to put further pressure on her.

Cleo sighed with relief. 'Good.' She sipped from her wine glass. 'I was thinking that I really should try and attend some social events—Maggie will need me. And I have lost touch with many of my acquaintances…' She paused, and he sensed she was becoming uncertain again.

'I agree,' he said decisively, remembering how Maggie had pointed out his own reclusiveness when they'd first met. 'In fact, I think we *both* should attend more social events—I have been absent from society for far too long. I was unsure at first of what would be expected of me now that I am the Baron Hawksmere, and I will *need* your guidance in that regard. I am actually relieved to hear you suggest it. I would be afraid to go out otherwise. You know how I struggle with such things.'

Cleo's expression warmed considerably with a genuine glow of good humour. 'You *struggle* to suffer fools or idle small talk. That does not make you *afraid* of social events. I doubt you have ever been scared of anything in your life! You went to war without even a backwards glance.'

Hawk had been about to take a bite of his meal when he slowly lowered his fork. 'I know, and I am sorry for that, for not thinking more of how it would affect you and Archie.'

Cleo's expression did not falter. 'I am *proud* of you for it. I have never been able to do anything so brave.'

He looked deliberately at her gown. 'You have been brave today... I am sorry, Cleo. For not helping you sooner. I kept my distance because I was a coward and didn't know how to help you through such a difficult time. I have never been very good at expressing myself.'

Cleo stared down at her plate, and he was afraid he had upset her, until she said quietly, 'Maggie is right. I shouldn't blame you for that. You were grieving, too.'

Hawk was surprised that Maggie had defended his actions to Cleo. 'I promise to always protect you and the boys. I swear it. You never have to worry about money or...anything else ever again.'

This was one promise he could make without fear of disappointing anyone. He wished he could make such a vow to Maggie, but there was still so much uncertainty about their future.

Cleo looked up at him, her eyes full of unshed tears. 'I have heard that before…and, although I believe you, I think… I should try to take responsibility for my own life and decisions. I have left my happiness in the hands of others for too long.'

He nodded, a little surprised by her answer. 'I understand. Just know that you are not alone.'

'Thank you.' Cleo went back to enjoying her meal, chatting to the boys about the games they'd played that afternoon.

He noticed the box of shortbread on the sideboard, which was probably going to be served with tea at the end of the meal.

How many boxes had she given them?

It seemed like an endless supply.

It made him wonder about Cleo's mention of Maggie earlier. 'May I ask you something? Why would Maggie need your help at social engagements?'

Cleo brightened, and it reminded him of how much she had once adored gossip and society. 'Her family are a *nightmare*!'

'William seems—' he started to say, but he was quickly interrupted.

'Oh, no! Not dear William! He's a sweetheart!' she said with a dismissive wave of her knife before reaching over for another helping of potatoes. Hawk filed away her comment about William as another white ball in the man's favour. He really didn't have a problem with William courting Cleo, but any mention of her disliking their neighbour in any way would instantly blackball him.

'Her mother and sister seemed a bit...' He struggled to find the words.

'Oh, they are a handful, that's for certain! Especially Mary!' declared Cleo with a chuckle. 'Poor Maggie, having them all descend on her without notice. I bet she thought she would enjoy a London season without them. They don't always come, you see, or if they do, it's only one or two of them. But the whole brood? She'll be tearing her hair out by the end of the month!'

'How so?'

'Well, as you know, Maggie is the eldest, and she's become a second mother to most of them, there are so many of them! Twins run in her family, too. Isn't that funny? Except, Mrs Mackenzie had a boy and a girl as twins, *twice!* Straight after each other, and I thought I had it bad.' At his wide-eyed look, she shrugged. 'I digress... So Maggie has had to care for many children over the years—even when she was only a young girl herself, and well, she *still* has to care for them in a way. Mary is the greatest mischief-maker, although, perhaps her marriage has tempered her spirit. That was apparently a big scandal—an elopement with a soldier. They are quite *something* as a group, well-meaning and good-natured, but Maggie can feel a little...overwhelmed by them sometimes, and she does tend to sink into the background when they are near.'

He remembered how quiet she had become in her mother and sister's presence. 'I wonder why? She is so confident normally.'

Cleo sighed and then looked at him firmly, as if she were explaining a simple fact to a dull-witted child. 'You will understand when you see her sisters. She can become...*overlooked* when they are around, and she never really has a chance to shine amongst them. Why do you think she never made a match in Scotland? It wasn't because she isn't pretty or pleasant to be around. But when it was her time to come out into society and shine, they delayed her coming out because her mother couldn't cope without her. Then foolishly sent three girls out into society within the same year! It was no wonder that poor Maggie missed her chance—she's such a romantic, and I imagine she was so focused on ensuring happiness for her sisters, she quite forgot about herself!'

Hawk frowned. He couldn't believe someone as vibrant as Maggie could fade into the background, but he had to concede she had seemed different around her mother and sibling so it must be true.

Cleo was still chattering to herself. 'At least Anne's presence will be some comfort to her.'

'Anne?'

Cleo nodded before launching into the family tree. 'She's the eldest sister after Maggie and has always been a good companion and friend to her. Then there's Eleanor and Robert—twins, James and Elizabeth—also twins—they all call Elizabeth Beth, and finally Mary.'

'The Mackenzies like royal names, then... I presume Maggie is for Margaret?'

'Yes,' chuckled Cleo, 'I believe it is a family tradition. Thankfully, they stopped producing children before they had to resort to the rest of Europe's monarchy.'

'I will have to carry a list around with me to remember them all.'

Cleo laughed and then her expression sobered into a frown. 'I was probably a little harsh on Maggie... for not being here for me when Charles died. Anne's baby wasn't well that year, as I recall, and perhaps I have relied on her too much—I suspect I am as guilty as her family in that regard.'

'You have me now,' he reminded her. 'You—'

But Cleo shook her head and interrupted him. 'I shouldn't have to rely on anyone. Now that I am finally able to look to the future, I have realised that I cannot allow things to slip as they did before. The boys are *my* responsibility, and even though I cannot support them financially without your assistance, I must do all else that I can to build a happy and bright future for them. Which starts with me reentering society and finally finding them a tutor.'

Some of the boys groaned and Cleo tried and failed to hide a smile of amusement.

'What about yourself?' he asked, again wondering at her sudden change in perspective, but also suspecting it only went so far.

'What about me?' she laughed. 'I am a widow and a mother of four boys. There is no time for *me*, nor should there be.'

Hawk nodded with understanding. It was what he had told himself daily in regard to Maggie. She was better off without him. She had enough family scandal and chaos to deal with without adding him to her problems.

Except…the thought left him feeling…hollow and miserable.

Chapter Twenty-One

It was a rare sunny day in a summer of constant chill and rain; unfortunately, it did not match Maggie's sour mood. With the weather brighter, Maggie had escaped into the garden to find some peace and quiet. She sat on her garden bench and closed her eyes.

Part of the reason she appreciated coming down to London was to enjoy the entertainments of the city *without* her family. But this year it seemed she couldn't escape them even for a couple of months.

It had been a whirl of activity since they'd returned from Castleton nearly two weeks ago. Balls, dinners, soirees, opera and theatre performances as well as *lots* of family dinners…too many, in Maggie's mind.

The excited sound of children playing next door caught her attention and made her smile. She craned her neck towards the wall, wondering if she might be able to hear who was with them. She breathed a sigh of relief when she heard only Cleo's voice. She got up to go and climb through the gap in the wall, safe in the knowledge that Hawk was not with them and would likely avoid her anyway.

Maggie had only seen glimpses of Hawk since their return. Usually, it was of him leaving through the front door and climbing into his awaiting carriage or mounting his horse.

She could see the street from her current room, having given her usual bedchamber to her mother because it was bigger and she preferred the garden view.

It was no hardship to her, as it had the advantage of allowing her to see the comings and goings of their neighbours. To her horror, she had become obsessed with Hawk—even more so than before.

In fact, she spent most of her days when she wasn't with her family, reading in her chaise by the window and wondering if she might see him…which was a foolish pastime as it was clear he wanted nothing more to do with her.

Occasionally, she saw him at society events, although Maggie was always so busy with her family that she rarely spoke to Cleo for anything more than a few minutes and rarely to Hawk at all. He was always occupied, talking with his friends whenever she joined Cleo.

Two of his friends were now happily married, and although their ladies were friendly, witty and beautiful, she always felt a bit lacking in their presence, mainly because Hawk seemed to deliberately avoid her when they were near. It was clear that what had happened between them in Castleton was a mistake he deeply regretted, and he wanted nothing more to do with her or her loud family.

Hawk never called on her.

Which had not surprised her, but had disappointed her mother greatly. Apparently, William had written informing her of their new friendship with Lord Hawksmere, and her mother had taken that pinch of knowledge and concocted a fanciful courtship between Maggie and Hawk in her mind.

Her mother had similar hopes for William and Cleo and made constant remarks about it. Remarks that she probably thought were encouraging and might give her uncle the push he needed to act, but in fact, only seemed to make him incredibly uncomfortable and nervous. He'd spent many hours at White's avoiding her.

Maggie had no such luck when it came to avoiding her mother. She was dragged to every social event and outing that her mother and sisters could think of. Her only respite was seeing her sister Anne—whom she adored, and who understood the strain of their family like no one else. But Anne had children of her own, so her husband had rented a townhouse in Mayfair for the month; close, but not close enough in Maggie's mind.

Today she had managed to escape yet another trip to the modiste by saying she had already spent her allowance on gowns upon her arrival. This wasn't entirely true, but she was sure her mother and sister would not notice her lack of new gowns anyway.

She climbed through the snug gap between the two walls and waved cheerfully at Cleo, who was on a blanket with Matthew. The boys appeared to be building a fort with some of the logs and branches that had been piled up after the new gardener had set the garden to rights.

'I hope you're going to put those back when you've finished with them,' Maggie said sternly as she passed them.

Peter gave a long-suffering sigh. 'Yes, Maggie! Mama has already told us!'

Maggie grinned and took a moment to admire their work. 'It's looking good, though!'

'Thank you, Maggie!' crowed Francis and Thomas in unison as they continued to build.

She made her way to Cleo and was glad to see that she no longer wore black and had continued to branch out into the lavenders and greys. Her current dress was the most colourful she'd seen her wear. 'You look nice.'

Cleo smiled nervously before brushing at her skirts. 'I think it's time… I can't wear black or grey forever.'

'I agree,' Maggie said, 'and black cloth is such a terrible pain to maintain. It fades so quickly in the wash and does nothing for the complexion!'

'True.' Cleo chuckled, ducking her head to shake a rattle at Matthew until he managed to grasp it.

Maggie was afraid she might be pushing her too soon, but she was desperate. 'Cleo, please tell me you're coming to the Wrexhams' ball. I don't think I can manage it on my own.'

Cleo gave her a sympathetic look. 'Are they driving you mad?'

'Just a little,' said Maggie with a pained look, and Cleo giggled before her face became serious again.

'It would be my first ball…since…well…years! Even before Charles died, I didn't attend many.'

'Oh, please!' Maggie begged. 'I would never normally ask it of you. But I am desperate!'

'Won't Anne be there?'

'No,' Maggie sighed, 'she doesn't like to leave her bairn. I can understand it. She gets nervous about leaving little Maggie—although I tell her she worries too much.'

Cleo's eyes widened. 'I never asked! Her baby was sick after Charles died, wasn't she? What did she have?'

'Scarlet fever…but she survived and has gone from strength to strength!' Maggie insisted, not wanting Cleo to worry. 'However, Anne is still a bit nervous to leave her at night. It's a miracle to get her out to the theatre as it is. Her husband and I have to practically drag her from the house!'

Cleo didn't laugh with her, and she was acutely aware of how similar it had been with Cleo. But then she surprised her by saying, 'After a shock like that, getting back to normality is a struggle...but it is for the best...in the long run.'

A look of kind understanding passed between them, and Maggie wrapped an arm around her thin shoulders, pleased to feel a little more flesh on her bones than before and gave her an affectionate squeeze. 'Is that a...*yes*? Please say it is,' she asked hopefully. 'Otherwise, I will send Mary round, and you can answer her questions about the *expectations* of a married woman.'

Cleo laughed. 'Goodness gracious! Yes, I promise I will come to the Wrexhams' ball. But save me from *that*, I beg of you!'

Maggie hugged her tightly and then stayed with them for a while enjoying the uncommonly pleasant weather.

Hawk stood in his study, looking out onto the garden where Cleo, Maggie and his nephews were enjoying the sunshine. He'd just returned from speaking with his new solicitor; he'd thought it prudent to change them. He did not like how his brother had not trusted their last one in the final weeks of his life.

He was rereading the letters from the Bank of Scotland and his new solicitor in his hands. He wasn't sure what to make of them. His brother's investments seemed to have been a success. So much so that the row of Brighton houses were, in fact, *his*. But they were still being built so there was nothing he could do with them now.

The large sum in the account had been used on the exchange by a trusted banker who had been instructed to follow all of Lord Mortram's investments, and it had proven very fruitful indeed over the past year. He was not overly familiar with a Lord Mortram, but if he did ever meet the man, he'd have to shake his hand!

All his problems and worries had been resolved by the foresight of his elder brother, who was still looking out for his family even after his death. It was humbling and Hawk only hoped he could be as impressive a Lord Hawksmere as Archie had been.

But their new-found wealth did change things.

He had been convinced that he would never marry because he could not provide for a family. But now that problem was solved… He *could* marry if he wished.

Except…would the woman he wanted…want him back? She never seemed troubled by his presence. Always smiled and appeared pleasantly friendly…if a little quieter than normal—but that could be due to her loud family, who were lively in both appearance and temperament, and seemed to command the entire room wherever they went.

Meanwhile, he had avoided Maggie since their return and even now continued to do so. He was worse than Cleo had been—avoiding his problems and hoping they would disappear.

Why?

He couldn't understand it; he wanted her and yet, he found himself paralysed by doubt and uncertainty. He prided himself on being able to look to the future and see all possible problems... But in this, he was blind.

Because the truth was he could not control or truly know how Maggie felt. Perhaps she did love him, or maybe he awakened only lust in her?

Did she pity him?

That thought made him feel like he'd swallowed a lead weight. He could not bear it. But what else would she feel towards him, after she'd witnessed the grief, sickness and shame of his family's secrets?

She had admitted to wanting to marry his brother at one point. Was he just a poor replacement for his much nobler, yet frail, brother?

And yet...she had clung to him and trusted him with her passion and her reputation. Only for him to immediately distance himself from her.

Had he ruined things between them?

Would she even consider him, after his behaviour? Not only that, but when would he ever be able to speak to her alone? He'd considered calling on her, but had thought better of it after meeting her family. He imagined it would be a gruelling affair for all of them if he did call on her, and it would put Maggie in an awkward position if she decided to refuse him. Which he had to concede was the most likely outcome. After all, she knew every dirty secret in his family, the debts, the adultery... Charlotte. She must realise that if it ever got out, there would be a terrible scandal, one that would shame her by association.

You are a coward! hissed a voice inside his head. *You're just scared she doesn't love you!*

Hawk threw the papers on his desk and took a moment to compose himself, gripping the leather and mahogany tightly as he took five deep breaths.

However, the pull of Maggie's presence was too much.

With his mind set, he strode forward, opening both doors of the patio with one swift movement to join his sister and Maggie in the garden. But Maggie was already gone, the swish of her skirts the last sight of her as she slipped away through the wall.

He closed his mouth, which had been half-open, about to announce his arrival, and swallowed the ball of nerves in his throat.

'Uncle Hawk, come see our fort!' shouted the boys, and he walked down the steps to join him.

Cleo glanced up at him with a smile before delaying him by reaching up to touch his sleeve. 'Would you mind if we attended the Wrexhams' ball this week? Only Maggie is desperate for some friendly company.'

'Of course!' he said, trying not to seem too eager and obviously failing by the raised brow from Cleo. He turned his attention deliberately to the boys and entertained them for a while before returning to sit beside his sister.

'Did you hear from the solicitor? Will we be keeping Castleton?' she asked softly, and he stared at her, shocked she had even realised it was in danger.

'Yes…but…how did you know?'

'I've always known… I was just too afraid to ask. That's another reason why…' She paused and took a deep breath. 'I tried to cut my own allowances. I hoped it would help…but I see now how silly I have been.'

He gave her a sympathetic smile. 'You weren't to know that scoundrel debt collector was taking from both of us.'

'But if I'd confessed…'

'You don't need to worry about any of it anymore. Archie made provisions. We don't need to sell Castleton or any of our land, for that matter. He has made investments that will very comfortably secure our future. I am sure he didn't tell you about them because he wasn't sure if his risk would work out. But they have. We do not have to worry about the future. All will be well.'

'Do you really mean that?' Cleo asked. 'I don't think I can bear any more…disappointment. Our family has never been very good at talking to each other. But I would rather know the truth of it.'

Hawk put his hand on his heart. 'I swear it. Our financial troubles are over.'

Cleo sighed. 'What a relief. Especially as... I would like to spend more time at Castleton. I had forgotten how much I missed the place and the people, and it would be nice for the boys to live in the countryside.'

He nodded. 'As you wish.'

'Would you join us...occasionally?'

He laughed. 'Of course. Where else would I be?'

A soft smile graced her lips as she looked away from him to the bottom of the garden. 'Perhaps you will have a family of your own one day.'

He stiffened. 'What if... I only wanted you and the boys to be my family? After all, no one knows what troubles we might have to face in the future...'

Cleo remained silent for a moment before answering. 'In a loving family...there is always room for more. Sometimes it is wise to take a risk. Archie proved that.'

Take a risk?

Hawk wasn't sure if he was brave enough.

Chapter Twenty-Two

The Wrexham Ball was always a highlight at the close of the London season. Lord and Lady Wrexham loved to entertain in their grand house just south of the river. The Wrexhams liked to theme their parties, and this year their inspiration was Mount Olympus with lavish decorations, flowing wine fountains and extravagant decorations. It always ended the season with a bang.

'Isn't it wonderful? It's like a palace from a fairy tale!' cried Mary in an embarrassingly shrill voice as they handed their cloaks to the waiting servants.

'Yes, very grand,' agreed her mother, staring up at the glistening chandeliers. Paper clouds hung from the ceiling with mirrored raindrops and gold thunderbolts cascading from them.

A servant offered them olive wreaths for their hair, including William, who took his with a broad smile. All the other guests had decided to wear them, or had already created their own impressive headpieces, which they displayed with pride as they glided around the gilt rooms.

Tonight's theme suited the style of the house, as there were plenty of marble and stone pillars to resemble an ancient Greek temple on display. She presumed that each room open to their guests was inspired by a god or goddess and decorated as such. As they passed the drawing room, Maggie noticed many people playing cards, and the room was heavily decorated with peacock feathers for the goddess Hera.

It was all very clever and beautiful. Normally, Maggie would have loved it.

But she wondered where Hercules was…her dark Hercules, not the golden demigod, but Hawk, the man who seemed about as real to her as those Greek myths did now.

Had she imagined it all?

Would she go back to Scotland soon as if nothing had happened? She suspected she would, and it felt like a thorn in her heart.

Maggie straightened her wreath, glancing in a nearby mirror as she passed it. William paused beside her, taking a sip from his whisky flask before tucking it away. He'd been pale and silent the entire journey here. At first, she'd thought it was because her mother and Mary were dominating the conversation as usual, but now he seemed almost…nervous.

'Are you well?' she asked quietly.

William gave a brisk nod before asking, 'Did Cleo really say she was going to come tonight?'

'Yes, and I am sure Lord Hawksmere will be joining her,' she replied, wondering if he was craving friendly company after spending so much time with her mother and sisters. The fact Hawk's presence would actually make Maggie uncomfortable she tried to hide with a breezy smile.

William only nodded gruffly and she noticed for the first time that his beard was neatly trimmed and glossy, as if he'd taken great care with it.

'Am I wrong to reassure you about Lord Hawksmere? Is it actually Cleo you are concerned about? This will be her first ball in a long time…but I will keep her company—do not worry.'

William nodded thoughtfully, but he did not seem reassured.

'Is there something else—'

She was cut off by Mary insisting, 'Oh, do move along, Maggie! I want to dance!'

Her mother and sister were determined to go straight to the ballroom to discover the rest of their family. It didn't take long to find them, and Maggie cringed at the sheer volume and space her family seemed to consume.

But she pasted on her best smile and welcomed each of them with her usual calm enthusiasm that seemed to put even the most highly strung amongst them at ease, because that was her job, even if she found it exhausting.

It wasn't long until she spotted Cleo and Hawk as they entered the ballroom a short time later.

Cleo wore a deep purple gown and shone in the candlelight like an exotic jewel. Maggie couldn't have been more delighted. 'You look beautiful, Cleo!'

'Thank you!' Cleo replied with genuine delight before glancing around the twirling dancers. 'I feel as if I have been away from society forever, but also... as if nothing has changed! Is that odd?'

'Not at all,' Maggie reassured.

'The music is lovely. Do you not agree, brother?'

Hawk nodded grimly as if he were agreeing to the execution of a convicted man. His eyes caught hers and she was shocked by the uncertainty within them.

'Perhaps...' interjected William with a spluttering cough, 'you would like to join me for the next dance, Cleo?'

Cleo looked uncertain for a moment, but then seemed to draw confidence from nowhere. 'If... Hawk and Maggie join us, I will?'

Maggie's stomach dropped about ten feet, and she could tell by the way Hawk stiffened that he was equally uncomfortable. William was looking at them with hopeful eyes, and Maggie waited with growing nerves to see what Hawk would say.

'I would be honoured… Will you join me for the next dance?'

She gave a little nod of agreement before wincing as Mary sidled into the conversation. 'What? You are all going to dance? Oh, please ask me, as well! Nobody knows me here, and not a single gentleman has introduced himself or asked me to dance.'

Maggie admonished her with a hard look. 'Mary, married women tend to dance with friends and acquaintances of their husbands only… Gentlemen do not pick an unknown woman out of the crowd!'

'Well, they should! There is nothing unseemly about it! I merely want to have fun! Lord Hawksmere, you are an acquaintance of mine—if not my husband's. If you were to ask me, I am certain others would follow.'

Hawk looked like a fish on a hook, but gave a polite nod. 'I would be honoured, Mrs…' There was a sudden rush of panic in his eyes when it was clear he couldn't remember Mary's married name. Followed quickly by another rush of relief as it appeared to arrive just in time, '*Bell*. The next quadrille will be yours.'

Mary looked delighted and not at all embarrassed by the fact she'd fairly pulled the offer out of him like a backstreet dentist. Maggie was horrified by the whole interaction, but tried her best to remain cheerful, in case people around them listened more carefully to their ridiculous conversation. The one good thing about being a member of such a large family was that the people gathered around them tended to be relatives anyway.

William wisely chose that moment to say, 'Let me introduce you to the rest of the family...'

The next half hour was filled with small talk, as each member of the Mackenzie brood was introduced to Cleo and Hawk.

The current dance came to an end, and there was a lull as dancers left the floor and people began to gather for the next.

Hawk offered her his hand and she took it, the warmth of his fingers beneath the white cotton of her gloves sending a familiar shiver of longing down her spine.

They walked onto the dance floor with several other couples including Cleo and William. A country dance started and they began the steps of the cotillion, each group dancing in a circle, exchanging partners with elegant turns and skips.

Maggie's eyes constantly searched for Hawk, regardless of whose hand she held or in whose arms she was turned. As the women came together to dance in a circle before switching partners again, she noticed that Cleo's face was bright with amusement.

'William almost forgot the turn!' she laughed, and when Maggie glanced over her shoulder at William, she smiled, understanding his nervousness a little better. He was staring at Cleo with a mixture of awe and desperate love.

They returned to their partners to turn and spin, and Hawk held her hand firmly, guiding her with ease. 'Do you think there is any hope for William?' Maggie whispered, nodding towards her uncle and Cleo, deciding it was the only safe topic of conversation she could think of.

Cleo let out a delighted laugh at something William had said. But when Maggie looked back up at Hawk, she realised he wasn't staring at them, but at her. His face was sombre as he said, 'To complete the dance correctly?'

'Do not be obtuse!' Maggie hissed. 'I meant for him and Cleo?'

They broke apart then, Maggie dancing through the circle of partners before joining the women once again in the centre.

Maggie asked Cleo with a teasing smile, 'Has my uncle improved?'

Cleo nodded eagerly. 'So far, so good!'

There were more turns and skipping between partners before Maggie returned to Hawk, who gripped her waist tightly with one hand as he held her other in a feather-light grip. 'It is too soon,' he warned in a hushed voice.

'Nonsense!' Maggie argued. She bit her lip, uncertain for a moment, before quickly deciding that she would not behave as he had done, or discourage her uncle. 'The problem with your family, my lord, is that you fear change.'

His eyes widened as he looked down at her. 'And what do you fear?'

Pain split her heart in two, but she answered honestly, 'Not being liked.'

The dance came to an end, and they respectfully bowed and curtsied to one another before clapping their thanks to the musicians and gracefully leaving the dance floor.

Cleo fanned herself and gasped, 'I must get some punch. I am not used to all this exercise!'

William offered her his arm. 'I may be rusty with the cotillion, but I can certainly help a lady to the drinks table.'

Cleo laughed and took his arm. Maggie looked awkwardly at her feet, wondering if Hawk would offer the same, but when he opened his mouth to speak, Mary was quick to interrupt. 'The next dance is mine, is it not, Lord Hawksmere?'

He nodded.

'Well, you must stay close by me so that we are ready when the next dance begins. Maggie, as you've had your dance, can you get me a drink if you're getting one for yourself?'

Maggie was glad of the excuse. 'Of course. Thank you for the dance, Lord Hawksmere,' she said, plastering as unbothered a smile as she could hope to give on her face.

She had no intention of returning anytime soon. Mary probably wouldn't even notice, and she doubted Hawk would care either way. His coldness towards her was obvious. Whatever he had felt for her in Castleton was over…if it had ever existed in the first place.

She was beginning to believe she had imagined it.

As she made her way through the busy crowd of guests, she stopped to speak with friends and acquaintances along the way, so it took her a long time to reach the punch bowl. When she did eventually reach it, she poured herself a glass, quickly drained it and then poured another, glancing around to check if anyone had seen her guzzle the first.

Hawk was leading Mary off the dance floor, so their dance had obviously finished in the time it took her to reach the refreshments table. Their eyes met through an unfortunate parting of the crowd, and she spluttered as she choked on her punch. It was far stronger than she'd realised, and seeing Hawk pointedly staring straight back at her had given her a fright.

The garden doors were open and braziers were lit along the patio. So she quickly slipped out, hoping that Hawk didn't think she'd spent the whole time watching him dance, because she *hadn't*! She'd been too busy speaking with friends!

Occasionally, she'd glanced his way, but only to check Mary wasn't making an utter fool of herself. Which, by her exuberant dancing, she had—Hawk had looked as if he were herding a cat.

This was turning into a nightmare of an evening!

A bit of fresh air would do her good, even if she was meant to be keeping Cleo company, or Cleo was meant to be keeping *her* company. Either way, she'd not seen her since the first dance.

Usually, she didn't mind flitting around like a butterfly from one group to another. William was usually with her, or some other companion, but tonight felt different somehow. As if she were no longer a merry butterfly, but an insect skewered with a pin for other people's amusement.

One lady had stopped her only to ask that she repeat an amusing story about her life in Scotland. Maggie would have gladly obliged normally, but with all those eyes staring expectantly back at her, and her sister gambolling around the dance floor, she'd suddenly felt less like an entertainer and more like a punchline. She'd told the joke with little enthusiasm and had left them looking decidedly unimpressed by her tale.

Frankly, she was tired of being other people's entertainment, of never being celebrated for anything other than how amusing or cheerful she could be.

She sucked in a deep breath of cool night air, grateful to finally be alone.

'Maggie,' said a husky voice, and she was startled to see Hawk standing behind her.

'My lord.' She gave a little curtsy before turning away with a muttered, 'Cleo isn't with me. She's probably still inside.'

'Maggie.' This time her name was a plea and she turned a little to face him. The brazier lit up his face with a flickering flame. He was so handsome in his gruff, sombre sort of way, and it hurt her heart to see him and know things were over between them.

Irritated, by her reckless emotions, she snapped, 'What is it? What do you want?'

'You are right to be angry with me… I know I have been…distant.' He seemed genuinely perplexed and confused by his own behaviour, which only irritated her further.

'You have barely seen me since our return from Castleton. I understand, and do not worry, I have taken the hint!'

'No, Maggie, that's not what I want—'

She interrupted him angrily. 'What do you want from me?'

'I want…to pretend that the last couple of weeks did not happen.'

'I thought that was exactly what we were doing? Pretending nothing had happened between us?'

'No, that's not what I meant… Pretend that I have

not behaved like a distant...dithering fool for the last two weeks... That's what I meant.'

'There is no future for us... *You* said that. We are friendly neighbours—nothing more.'

'You are not being very friendly now,' he grumbled, running a hand through his hair and causing some dark strands to tumble to the side.

How she wanted to brush them away!

To touch his face and kiss his lips, but she clutched her skirts to stop herself from reaching out.

'You cannot have your cake and eat it!' she snapped, turning sharply away so he would not see the pain in her eyes.

'Maggie.' Her name was soft on his lips. 'I never meant to hurt you. I want to tell you—'

'I was speaking of myself!' she snarled, wishing more than anything that he would leave her alone. 'I cannot be like a man. To take pleasure and feel no bond. I thought I could, that if I told myself it did not matter, then it wouldn't. But as always, I have failed in matters of the heart, so please leave me alone. I would dearly love to be your friend, Hawk, but I cannot. So I *beg you*—' Her words trembled a little as she lost control of her composure and had to brush a tear from her eye '—do not ask me to go back to how we were. I cannot...not yet. When the season ends, I will return to Scotland, and I am sure this obsession I have for you will dull with time.'

'Obsession?' He inhaled sharply as if shocked by the word. It only made her feel more pitiful.

'It will pass, like all things.'

He grabbed her arm and turned her towards him. 'What do you mean *obsession*? Maggie, I think... I would like to court—'

A sudden flurry of purple silk from the garden drew Hawk's attention away from her. Cleo came running out from behind an ornate hedgerow, her skirts fisted in her hands as she ran full pelt back towards the house.

'Cleo, wait!' cried a desperate voice from behind the hedge, followed not long after by a flustered William.

Cleo had made good progress, however, and was already halfway up the steps when she spotted their shocked faces. 'I want to go home, Hawk. *Now!*'

'What the devil happened?' asked a shocked Hawk, who was staring back towards William with growing confusion. 'Did he...*compromise* you?'

Cleo's face was scarlet and she glared at her brother as she screeched, 'Don't even speak such a thing! I want to leave *now*!' And with that she stormed past them both without a backwards glance.

'I...' Hawk looked truly horrified. 'I do not know whether to follow her...or beat William senseless.'

Maggie rolled her eyes. 'Follow her, you idiot! I will deal with William.'

With a nod, Hawk left and William arrived, walking up the steps as if he were going to the guillotine.

'Blast it, William. What did you do?' asked Maggie, not sure if she should slap him or hug him. She was inclined to hug him, he looked so miserable.

William sighed heavily. 'I have made a serious error in judgement. I doubt she will ever forgive me.'

She smacked his arm, trying desperately to make him focus. '*What* happened?'

'She wanted to see the fountain. It was romantic and perfect, and I just wanted her to know that I cared for her...that she was the only woman for me...that I would follow her to Castleton if she wished it.'

'Oh, you pudding-heided clod pate! Tell me you didn't kiss her!'

'No,' he said firmly, and then his face softened into an awe-filled expression. 'She...kissed *me*...'

'Oh...well, that changes things. But why did she run away?'

'I said... I wanted to marry her.'

'Oh... William!' she growled in frustration. 'It is too soon!' She was more than a little irritated when she remembered Hawk had said much the same thing earlier that night.

He gave a miserable grunt of agreement. 'You're probably right.'

Maggie wrapped her arm around his and said quietly, 'Shall we go home early?'

'What about your mother and Mary?'

'We'll send the carriage back for them. Believe me, they'll be here until dawn anyway.'

With a mournful nod, William allowed Maggie to lead him home.

Chapter Twenty-Three

Maggie decided it was best not to let things stew, and so she went through the garden wall to visit Cleo the next day just before luncheon. Unlike her own household, she presumed they would be up, as they had not been at the ball all night like her family.

As she entered the kitchen, she said her usual greetings to Mrs Wimple and was told that Cleo was in her parlour.

Mrs Wimple gave her a meaningful look as she busied herself with preparing the next meal. 'She's taken two steps back—that's all I'll say on the matter... Weeping in her room for hours, she was. And back to wearing black this morning—more's the pity! And m'lord? Well, he hasn't been much better. Bad-tempered and irritable. I'm surprised his study floor isn't worn straight through—he's been pacing back and forth so much!' She then finished her litany of information by asking, 'Would you like me to bring up some tea, miss?'

'It might be best to wait for the bell,' Maggie said. She wasn't sure how Cleo might receive her.

It wasn't long before she was tentatively knocking on her door and then peeking around its edge. 'May I come in?'

Cleo looked up from her embroidery and nodded, her eyes red from crying and her lips pinched and pale.

Maggie hesitantly walked in and took a seat in the armchair next to her. 'How are you?'

Cleo stabbed her needle through the cloth. 'Fine. I presume William told you what happened. Heaven forbid he *ever* keep a secret!'

Maggie decided to tread carefully. 'He wishes things had gone differently...and he cares for you, I know that much.'

'I do not *want* him to care for me!' snapped Cleo, and there was a desperate anguish and doubt that seemed to overshadow her for a moment before she briskly shook her head. 'It was a mistake! I'd had too much punch, and the night air... It went straight to my head.'

'I am sure William will understand.'

'I was lonely, that is all. It was a mistake. One I deeply regret.'

'I see.'

Cleo glared at her, throwing aside her embroidery. 'But you don't! I know that you would love for us to be together! That you think romance will make me happy again... But when it's gone, when it's taken from you...' She covered her face with her hands and began to weep.

Maggie didn't say anything. She moved closer and gathered her friend close.

Cleo began to hiccup through her tears. 'I *do* like William, but how can I ever betray Charles?'

Maggie stiffened. 'Is *that*...the only thing holding you back?'

'Of course! I would be betraying him to even consider another man!' She sniffed miserably, wiping at her face. 'Charles once said our hearts and souls were linked—that our love would never die! I cannot betray that kind of love!'

'I am sure...he did not mean...' Maggie struggled to find the words. This was far more difficult than she could have ever imagined. How could she reassure Cleo to move on, when the false words of her husband bound her in chains? 'If Charles truly loved you, he wouldn't wish for you to live the rest of your life alone.'

'Oh!' Cleo bristled, pulling away from her. 'You will never understand! Charles was a devoted husband and father. For all his mistakes he truly loved us. I cannot betray that love! Already, I am thoroughly ashamed of what I have done!'

Maggie frowned and then tugged on Cleo's arm to force her to face her and look her in the eye. 'If you do not care for William, that is one thing. And you do not need to worry about…indiscretion. My uncle may be the worst at keeping secrets, but when it comes to you, he would protect you with his life! So do not worry about that at all.' Cleo's eyes widened at her words, and so she continued firmly. '*But* if you have started to care for William as more than just a friend, then I beg you, do not waste time! Love is too rare and precious to be cast aside. Cleo, you are still young. You have your whole life ahead of you. Are you certain that you want to spend it alone?'

Cleo shook her head firmly, pins falling from her hair as she once more began to cry, clutching her hands as if Maggie were her port in the storm. 'But… Charles would hate me… I cannot…'

Maggie bit her lip and then decided she could no longer stand idly by and allow her friend to ruin her future. Not out of love for a man who betrayed her! 'Charles is *not* this paragon of virtue you believe him to be. You were a good wife to him. Loyal and caring, you gave him four beautiful boys. But that does not mean he owns your heart and soul! Charles was no angel!'

Cleo's mouth dropped open as she stared at her in horror. 'How can you say such wicked things?'

Maggie sighed. 'Surely, you have begun to see that already…with the sale of your house…the debts…'

'How dare you!' Cleo rose to her feet, dropping her hands like they held a hot coal. 'Get out!'

Maggie rose but knew she couldn't leave without revealing the truth. 'Charles was a gambler and a liar, Cleo. Ask Hawk to tell you about the money he has to give Mr Wilkins back in Castleton. You will quickly realise that Charles never deserved your love before, and he sure as hell doesn't deserve it now.'

Cleo screamed at her then, her eyes burning with anger. 'I said *get out*!'

As she left the room, Maggie heard the embroidery hoop bang against the door, and simultaneously Hawk came charging down the stairs.

He took one look at her face and the loud sobbing coming from Cleo's parlour and asked, 'What have you done?'

'I'm sorry…' Guilt gnawed at her insides, but she raised her chin. 'She needs to know the truth.'

He closed the distance between them, his eyes dark with anger. 'What *truth* did you tell her?'

'Only that Charles is not all he appears to be and that…' Her stomach twisted at the next confession. 'She should ask you about Mr Wilkins…'

His nostrils flared, but he only said with a frightening calmness, 'Go! And do not return unless you are *invited*!'

Maggie turned and fled, realising that she was the very worst of cowards.

* * *

That afternoon when she went out to sit on her garden bench to think about how she could possibly make amends, she heard loud hammering from beyond the wall. Following the sound of banging, she realised a trellis was now being put up to cover the gap in the fence.

Mr Wimple gave her a sympathetic look. 'Master's orders,' he mumbled by way of explanation, and Maggie felt as if she had been thrown out onto the street as the last nail was hammered into the wall.

At the ball, Hawk had said *I think... I would like to court—* before he'd been distracted by Cleo running from William. Perhaps he'd wanted to start courting her, or perhaps he was confessing about courting someone else? She had agonised over those words ever since, a pointless endeavour considering his feelings about her were now crystal clear.

Whatever feelings he'd had towards her were now as closed to her as her friendship was with Cleo.

She decided to wait.

Hoping by some miracle that Cleo would come round to call on her. But nothing happened, and she waited in all day and evening while her family went out.

At noon on the third day of waiting, there was movement from their neighbours. Maggie saw it from her bedroom window. The Hawksmere carriage rolled up outside, and then the family and maid stepped out the front door. Huge trunks were carried out and placed on the back and roof of the carriage, implying they would be leaving for some time.

Maggie ran down the stairs, shouting for William, but he was already at the bottom of the stairs wearing his coat and hat. He had a bright green pelisse and a flamingo-pink bonnet in his hands. They didn't match, and must have been one of the many discarded ones that Mary left around the house, as was her custom. 'Hurry!' he urged, pushing them towards her.

Without caring what she looked like, she threw on the clothing and breathlessly hurried outside holding William's arm. The pair of them already knew what the other wanted as they turned at the bottom of their steps and pretended to be surprised when they saw the Hawksmeres walking down to board their carriage.

'Good day!' William said with a cough as he tried to measure his breathing, his eyes drinking in the sight of Cleo as if he were a man dying of thirst.

In contrast, Hawk refused to even look at her, and Maggie was horribly aware of the difference between the look of love and the look of…hatred…indifference? She wasn't sure what it was, but when he only turned his attention to William, her heart broke.

They were truly strangers now.

'Good day,' Hawk said quietly, and Cleo said nothing, busying herself with the boys and muttering some apology about them being in a hurry.

'We are going to Castleton,' said Hawk.

'Oh?' replied William, and she squeezed his arm tightly. 'Another trip so soon?'

'Not a trip. Cleo has decided she wishes to live there...permanently.'

There was silence, as the statement slowly sank in for all of them.

Hawk was the first to recover. 'I will be in London occasionally, but only for business. I imagine I will sell this house and take rooms elsewhere.'

Pain knifed through Maggie and she fought to keep her composure.

William was staring at Cleo, trying to catch her eye. 'Well, I wish you all well. You will always have a friend in us.'

Cleo stiffened. She'd been busily straightening Francis's collar, when he whined, 'Can William and Maggie come to visit?'

'Perhaps...although, I am sure it is too far for them,' said Cleo, but the smile was false, and she ushered him into the carriage, turning to say a polite farewell before quickly ducking inside.

Hawk tapped the side of the carriage and it rolled forward, just as his horse was brought around the corner. 'Goodbye, Mr Mackenzie, Miss Mackenzie. I wish you both well.' He gave a polite bow to each of them and then mounted his horse in a confident swing of his body that would have made her swoon previously, but now only made her miserable because she knew it would be the last memory she would have of him.

Maggie and William continued to walk slowly down the road until his horse went out of sight, and then she couldn't hold it a moment longer and began to cry.

William stopped walking and gathered her into a hug. 'Perhaps we just need to give them time?' he said, but from the pain in his voice she could tell he didn't even believe it himself.

'Can we just go home?' she whispered through her sobs, praying that they wouldn't see anyone they knew, and that none of the ton were watching through their windows at the odd behaviour of people who had once been close friends.

'Of course.' William turned her back towards the house, and then in a lighter tone—that was an obvious attempt to make her smile—he said, 'I mean, what were you thinking? Pink and green should never be seen!'

She chuckled through her tears, dropping her head to his arm as she tried to brush them away. 'It's your fault.'

'I know,' said William in a miserable tone, and Maggie quickly looked up at him.

'I meant the ugly fashion choice, not everything

else. *I am* as much to blame for that as you. I pushed her too soon…when I shouldn't have.'

Maggie hadn't told William everything; it was not her secret to tell—if only she'd realised that sooner. But she was sure William suspected he wasn't the only one hurt by all of this, and she'd told him that she'd spoken some harsh truths to Cleo about Charles… He'd simply presumed it was about the debts.

'As did I,' said William with a heavy sigh as they made their way back up the steps to their house. 'And, worse… I have made things impossible for you and Lord Hawksmere, too.'

She stared up at him, shocked. 'I don't know what you mean…'

'Oh, come along, Maggie. I am not as blind or as stupid as you think I am. You cannot paint yourself in flour and rouge and think I would believe you were ill. I allowed it because I knew he was a gentleman…' His steps faltered a little. 'He *was* a gentleman? Wasn't he?'

She nodded numbly. 'He was… But he doesn't… feel the same.'

William opened the door for her. 'Then, I am sorry for him.'

Chapter Twenty-Four

Three days after leaving London, Hawk drove the now very much fixed phaeton to Mr Wilkins's farm. But this time he had his sister beside him.

Cleo was silent as she had been for days. Only speaking to talk with the children or about them. She had been like this since her falling out with Maggie and his reluctant confession.

She had asked him to tell her about Mr Wilkins, and he had done so, stating the facts and hoping that the quickness of his delivery would somehow lessen the blow.

It had not. She had wailed and cried, shouted denials and curses at him until she had finally fled to her room where she had stayed for two days.

Then, as coldly and as calmly as he had ever seen her, she had left her room, only to demand that she and the boys be moved to Castleton permanently. That she would arrange for a local tutor or school for the boys, as well as more help. But that she no longer wished to stay in London.

It was clear that she was cutting all ties with the Mackenzies, and he could see the wisdom of it. Even though his own heart twisted painfully at the thought, he knew it was for the best. They were better off alone, and all hopes of his making amends for his earlier behaviour and finally courting Maggie were gone with it.

How could he be with Maggie if his own sister could no longer be in the same room as William? Not to mention that Cleo had practically thrown Maggie out of her house.

It was all such a mess, and he knew that he was as much to blame for it as Maggie. He'd not communicated well with either his sister or Maggie about his feelings. He could already be courting Maggie if he'd just allowed himself to take a risk on happiness. And perhaps he could have softened the blow regarding Charles, too. Informed her more gently over time, or insist that William do nothing until his sister was in a better position to consider him.

There was so much he could have prevented simply by being more open. But all hope for that was now gone.

Not long after their arrival at Castleton a special delivery arrived direct from London. Inside, carefully wrapped in waxed tissue paper, was his brother's last letter to him. The one Maggie had taken that night, to stop him from burning it. The note attached simply said, *For your treasures.*

It seemed Maggie accepted the situation, and at least wished him well. She would be wise if she had nothing more to do with his mess of a family. What could he offer her except family scandals, a quiet life away from London and a pointless title?

After all, he envisaged a long and difficult road ahead for his family, in which Cleo would slowly have to accept the truth about her husband, and grieve all over again for his loss.

However, his sister had surprised him. Rather than taking time to settle into Castleton and meet with old friends, she had simply asked him to take her to see *the child.* Adding that she did not believe for one minute the lies spouted about her husband, but that she could not rest until she saw *them* for herself.

He had tried to dissuade her, but she had insisted, and so they travelled the country lanes in silence towards the Wilkins farm. Thankfully, the weather was largely dry, if not overly pleasant, and they made good speed on the roads, reaching the farm before midday.

Hawk stepped down from the phaeton and looked around the empty yard. 'They are probably eating their midday meal. Let me—'

'I wish to speak to them alone,' Cleo said firmly,

climbing from the phaeton so quickly he didn't have time to help her down.

'Let me tie up the horses.'

'No need!' she snapped and then turned on him with a glare. 'I am sure I will not be long, and frankly, I would rather you were not present. I want the truth, something you have failed to give me in the past!'

Hawk could only nod numbly in agreement.

He then waited for over an hour before the door finally cracked open again. Cleo's face was pale, her eyes bloodshot, as if she'd been crying heavily. But there was also determination there. To his surprise she was holding Charlotte's hand in hers.

Hawk hurried over to them.

'She is coming home with us,' said Cleo firmly.

Helplessly, Hawk looked towards the Wilkins family, but they seemed in agreement. Mrs Wilkins gave Charlotte a tearful goodbye before pressing a basket full of belongings into his hand. He noticed Maggie's handkerchief had been pinned to a dolly like a makeshift dress. His throat tightened painfully as memories of Maggie wrapped up in a blanket flooded his mind.

'We will come and visit her often,' Mrs Wilkins said with a tearful sniff before hugging Charlotte goodbye and saying thank you to Cleo.

Hawk stared at his sister, who simply said, 'I have decided to adopt her.'

Strangely, Charlotte did not seem as concerned

by the change in circumstance; she smiled up at him cheerfully. 'Can I bring my cat?'

A short time later they were trundling back down the road towards Castleton, Charlotte clutching her basket of possessions with a kitten also tucked inside. The little girl had fallen asleep against Cleo's side, who had an arm around her protectively.

Hawk had to ask, 'What are you thinking, bringing her home with us? She's—'

Cleo interrupted him sharply. 'She's my daughter now.' After a moment of silence she added, 'I don't expect you to understand. But I couldn't leave her... She's their sister.'

And that was when it hit him.

All this time he'd been thinking about Charles's betrayal and how it would affect Cleo. He'd not thought about how it would affect the boys, to never know their own sister.

'You're a good mother, Cleo.'

'Not always...but I'm trying.'

'You were a good mother to me.'

'Not always.' Cleo's head dropped to his shoulder. 'I owe Maggie an apology.'

'She had no right to tell you.' It was the only thing he could blame her for, and it felt weak even to his own ears.

'And you had no right to keep it from me. But here we are, and believe me, I understand why you did.

Until I saw Charlotte, I didn't want to believe it myself, because then I would have known it was all a lie.'

'Charles did love you...in his way.'

'But he loved himself more. That is the truth of it. I should hate him. But I don't. I am as much to blame. There were so many times when I deliberately looked away from what he was...' She sighed, a deep and exhausted breath. 'At least he gave me my children. I am grateful for that. Poor Archie. He must have hated me for everything we put him through.'

'He didn't.' Hawk gathered the reins in one hand and then reached inside his pocket before handing her the letter. 'This is the last thing I have kept from you. There is nothing else. I swear it. Our finances are now in order, thanks to Archie's foresight, and there are no more secrets.'

Cleo stared at the letter for a moment and then took it. Hawk kept glancing at her face as she read it. There were tears, but they were silent and they slid against a bittersweet smile as she read the final words of her twin brother.

Afterwards, she refolded the letter and handed it back to him. 'Thank you. Keep it safe...they're his last words.'

Hawk nodded, putting the letter back into his pocket, glad that it no longer burned against his heart, and relieved there was nothing left to hide. 'What about William?' he asked curiously. It was the last chasm between them.

Cleo's arm tightened protectively around Charlotte. 'I have five children. Six, including you.'

Hawk tried not to take offence at the inclusion. 'So?'

'He's better off without us.'

Hawk frowned. 'Perhaps you should ask him? Let him decide for himself.'

Cleo gave a derisive snort. 'As you did with Maggie?'

Hawk stiffened; it was a fair point.

Chapter Twenty-Five

Maggie tied on her apron and smiled at her old distillery; she was finally at the magical stage with this batch—the part she enjoyed the most. After malting, mashing and fermenting her grain into a dark liquid called the *wash*, she was now ready to distil it, and would need to distil it three times before she was happy with the final product.

Her grandfather's huge copper still was placed on top of the flat-roofed kiln. Its thin copper spout dropped into her condensing barrel, which was actually more coiled pipework, surrounded by cold loch water where the vapours in the pipe would cool back into liquid, creating *uisge beatha*, the water of life. A much stronger clear liquid than the *wash* that had gone in the kettle originally. This clear liquid would then turn into amber whisky in its maturing process, and she had old sherry barrels waiting to be filled at the side of the room.

She knelt down beside the little hatch of the kiln

and began to build the fire. It was easier in her brother's old breeches and shirt, and no one ever saw her here so it made sense to wear something comfortable and practical. Her hair was also tied up away from her face with a Mackenzie cloth.

Maggie breathed in deeply before blowing gently on the flames that were flickering amongst the tinder. It was good to be back in Scotland, enjoying her hobby. This London season had felt like one disaster after another, and it was a relief to return to the quiet safety of her grandparents' glen.

'You all right, lass?' called a voice from the yard, and she looked over to smile at William as he entered the distillery.

'Thought I'd try another "aged" batch… I'm wondering if different types of sherry or port barrels might change the flavour.'

'I'm sure it will,' said William, sitting on a nearby stool and looking down at her as he scratched his hairy knees, which were just visible beneath his long kilt. 'Yer mother's worried.'

Maggie shrugged. 'She's always worried about something.'

'And yer father's worried, too.'

Maggie sat back on her heels and glared at William. 'I'm sure they're both *worried* about you, too. That's why you came to bother me about it—you're avoiding them, just like I am.'

William chuckled lightly. 'I'll not deny it. But…you living alone in the old croft here… Well, it seems a little extreme… Why not come back when yer work is done?'

Maggie wasn't amused. 'I won't do it.'

William tilted his head curiously. 'Do what?'

'Pretend everything's well and that I'm happy. Because I'm not. And I won't do it anymore. They want me to join them at dinners and parties, help with the grandchildren and be *Miss Sunshine*, and I won't do it! I want to be miserable and alone, and just…well… be by myself for a bit. If that means I stay out here all alone, wallowing in self-pity at my romantic disappointment, then so be it. The main house is less than half a mile away, and I'm perfectly safe here.'

Sadness spread across his face, and he nodded in agreement. 'I understand, lass. Come home when yer ready.'

If anyone else had said that to her, she would have screamed at them out of frustration. But William was the only member of her family who *did* understand.

After a moment of silence, William slapped his thighs decisively and stood up to leave. 'Well, we've spoken. My duty is done. I can go home now, back to Edinburgh.'

Maggie couldn't help but chuckle; her poor uncle had been dragged out of his Edinburgh home to spend less than five minutes *speaking* with her. It was typical of her family to get someone else to do their dirty work. 'You can take one of the bottles from the side if you want.' She gestured to her first ever two-year-old batch, which sat in a crate beside the aging barrels.

'Ahh, thank you, lass. I think I will.' William grabbed a bottle and walked back towards the door, pausing before he left. 'You can always come live with me…if you don't want to return to the big house.'

Maggie was touched by his offer. 'And ruin your life as a bachelor for all twelve months of the year? I couldn't do that to you, William.'

William gave a cheerful shrug. 'Perhaps we can be two miserable old bachelors together? You're certainly dressed the part.'

Maggie grinned and then turned back to her kiln, ignoring the offer. 'Goodbye, William!'

William gave a grunt of acceptance and headed back to his horse tied up by her cottage water trough. He yelled another goodbye before riding away, and Maggie spent the rest of the day working on her whisky or doing chores.

At dusk she left her work and returned to her small whitewashed crofters' cottage. Forested mountains surrounded her cottage on both sides. The landscape was wildly beautiful and rugged; unlike London, which changed every season she visited, this land had never changed and hopefully never would.

It gave her a sense of peace to gaze upon it, despite

the melancholy she felt. She stared up at the sky with its splashes of pink settling across the horizon, and then squinted at the dark shape of a horse and rider galloping across the glen towards her.

Surely, William hadn't come back? Perhaps when he had failed to bring her home, her father had been ordered to come and speak with her instead? With a sigh she entered her cottage, lit the fire and prepared herself for a conversation similar to the one she had had with William. She put out two glasses and a bottle of whisky, as well as a simple supper of bread, cheese and smoked ham.

But when the horse trotted into her yard, and she went out to greet her father, she discovered the rider to be the last man on earth she'd ever imagined to see here.

'Hawk?' she gasped, not quite believing her own eyes as she stared up at him.

He was tying his horse up beside the water trough. Sweat beaded his brow, and his greatcoat billowed in the mountain breeze as he turned to face her.

'May I speak with you?' he asked, his voice gruff, a dark shadow of stubble on his jaw suggesting he'd been on the road for some time.

Why had he come?

Panic immediately rushed in after her initial shock had worn off. 'Is everyone well? Cleo? The boys? Please tell me nothing terrible has happened.'

Hawk's gaze softened. 'They are perfectly well. Cleo has even added a new member to the family—Charlotte.'

Maggie blinked in surprise at the news. 'Then...you best come in.' She opened the door, letting him inside. The crofters' cottage was a tiny single-room dwelling, with a cosy fire, a couple of rickety rocking chairs, a kitchen table and a screened-off sleeping area.

She sat down and poured them both a whisky. She wasn't sure about Hawk, but she definitely needed a stiff drink. Hawk had to stoop as he followed her in, and quickly took one of the chairs opposite her.

'Why are you here?' she asked after she'd taken a sip of courage.

'To see you.'

She rolled her eyes at that. 'Well, you've seen me. How did you find me anyway? There's no way my family would have sent you here alone.'

'I met William on the road. He told me where to find you.'

'Ahh,' she said, taking another sip. She was racking her brain trying to comprehend what had happened. Not only had he found out where her family's estate was—she was sure she'd never mentioned its exact location—but he had journeyed here alone, on horseback for hundreds of miles...just to speak with her. It didn't make any sense...

Surely, he hated her? Or was indifferent at the very least.

'I still don't understand why you want to see me. If Cleo's taken in Charlotte, that means…well, the truth really is out…'

Was there scandal? Had he come to blame her for her part in it?

'Partly. She's decided to adopt Charlotte. But anyone with half a brain will understand who she is—at least in Castleton.'

'How is she? Is the scandal very bad?' She hoped it wasn't for Cleo's sake.

Hawk smiled. 'She's very well, actually.'

'So…are you returning to London, then? I suppose fewer people will know the truth there…' Again, her mind was stumbling ahead. Was this some weird warning for her not to return to London?

Hawk shook his head. 'Cleo doesn't care about that.'

Maggie raised an eyebrow at that. 'Do *you* care?'

'I used to…when I worried about how it would affect Cleo…and us.'

A spark of understanding flared in her head. Did he think she would judge them? Let the ton know the truth about Charlotte? She noticed that he hadn't touched his own whisky and she set hers down with a bad-tempered huff. 'I don't like to drink alone.' Then she fixed him with a hard look. 'And I don't like to blame or shame children for things beyond their control.'

'I know.' He sucked in a deep breath. 'I was afraid.'

'Of drinking?' she joked, although her nails were biting into the flesh of her palms. She was clenching her hand so tightly as she waited for him to explain.

'Of letting you down. I know you think I'm some kind of hero, but I'm not. I am not a joyful man to be around. I think too much and say too little. I was worried...'

'Because of the debts or the scandal? I told you neither of those matter to me. I cared only about Cleo's happiness.' She bit her bottom lip to stop herself from confessing more, from admitting that she loved him.

'I know... But it mattered to me. If I couldn't look after you, protect you...then what good was I to you?'

His words confused her; they were genuine and spoken from the heart. Finally, she decided to be brave and take a chance on finding out the truth...no matter how much it might hurt. 'To be clear... Did you... want to court me?'

'Yes!' he declared firmly and then sighed miserably. 'But what could I offer you?'

'Do you think me so shallow?' She laughed bitterly, gesturing around at the cottage. 'Believe me, I would happily live anywhere, as long as I was happy.'

'I know, and, in fact, we're actually quite wealthy now, thanks to Archie's investments.'

Maggie frowned. 'So now that you are no longer broke, or care about ruin... I am suddenly worthy of your attention?'

'I wish to marry you, Maggie.' He seemed sincere; his brow was furrowed with worry as he spoke and he leaned across the table to hold her hand. 'I'm not a hero. But if you're willing to still have me?'

'Are you...*mocking me*?' she snarled, snatching her hand away. 'You have told me that you saw no future for us, but now you have changed your mind? Why? Because the future no longer seems so bleak? That you think you now deserve me because you are rich and titled? Or because Cleo might now forgive me for speaking the truth? Which reason is it? For I have heard none that would give me a reason to accept you.'

There was only one reason she wanted to hear, and he had not mentioned it once.

Hawk grabbed the whisky and threw it back in one gulp, hissing out a wincing breath before answering, 'Because my future will always be bleak without you in it!' He took a deep breath, his hands fisting on the table between them. 'I have always prided myself on seeing problems before they arise. But the truth is... I have spent my entire life running away from the pain of loss—because I cannot bear it. Even when it is inevitable, as it was with Archie. And with Cleo I couldn't even risk the possibility that the truth would somehow break us apart. I am afraid of losing the people that I love. So much so that I push them away and lose sight of the point of loving them in the first place! That without grief there is no love. Without joy there is no life. Without truth there can be no love… and without you…' He grabbed her hands, squeezing them tightly as he struggled to find the words, his eyes brimming with tears. 'Without you, I cannot take a single easy breath. There is no hope, no future…there is *nothing*. You are everything to me… You are my *uisge beatha*…you are the *maddening miss* I cannot live without. I love you, Maggie, with all my heart and soul.'

'That's all I needed to hear,' she said with a sob, running around the table and jumping into his arms, even as he pulled her to him in a passionate and relieved kiss.

'All? I thought it was quite a lot,' he grumbled, and she couldn't help but laugh before she once again fell into his kiss. Before things became too heated, he broke apart to ask in a genuinely worried tone, 'Did I say the Gaelic bit right?'

Maggie chuckled but gave an emphatic nod, sniffing back her tears, horribly aware that she must look awful, blubbering uncontrollably in his lap… But also not caring, because she knew that he did *really* love her. Without conditions or compromise, he loved her, and it was all she could have wished for and more.

'I love you! Desperately, wantonly, madly, obsessively and always.' She cupped his face in her hands and began to kiss him thoroughly before hopping off his lap and tugging him over to the sleeping area. She pulled back the curtain to reveal a tiny bed. 'Will you join me tonight?'

Hawk chuckled, trying his best not to hit his head on the low beams. 'Yes, and every night after if you'll have me.'

'Good, and I want to experience *all* of it. I don't care if there are repercussions. We can get married tomorrow for all I care!' Maggie giggled and leaned up to kiss him again before kicking off her boots and clambering on top of the bed.

Hawk winced as he bumped his head on the curtain rail. 'It's lucky you decided to come and live at your croft in a way. Otherwise, I doubt your family would allow this, no matter what promises I made. Really, Maggie, I didn't think you'd become a recluse like me—what on earth are you doing out here?'

Maggie shrugged. 'I was tired of being everyone's *Miss Sunshine*, and I just wanted to be miserable in peace.'

'You will be Lady Hawksmere from now on, and you can do whatever you damn please.' He sat down on the bed with a sigh. 'I'm sorry…for making you miserable, for being a—'

'Mutton-heided clod pate?' she suggested, and he chuckled with a nod of his head before shrugging out of his coat and jacket, letting both tumble down the side of the bed.

'Is that what I am?' he asked in a sultry voice, even as he grabbed the artfully tied cravat at his neck and tore it off, tossing it behind him.

Maggie swallowed the knot in her throat and gave a little nod as she stared back at him.

'I like your breeches,' he said with a grin, and she blushed.

'It's more practical out here than silk and fiddly buttons.'

'I see. Where's the Mackenzie tartan? I know you always wear some,' he murmured.

She reached up and pulled off the cloth tying back her hair and shook out her curls. 'Here!'

He smiled, placing it in his pocket. 'I'll keep it safe…but I can't guarantee the rest of your clothes.' Smoothing a hand down her thigh to reach her knee and the ribbon that kept her breeches and stockings in place, he tugged on the bow, and it untied smoothly. He then reached around, cupping the back of her knee in a sensual caress, before peeling off her stocking in one smooth motion.

Maggie bit her lip, desperate to throw off all her clothes, but enjoying his teasing too much to do so. Instead, she shifted a little to offer him her second leg. His hooded eyes peeked up at her from thick, dark lashes with a knowing smile, and obediently he removed the other stocking with the same erotic caress.

Tossing aside the fabric with a smile before unbuttoning his waistcoat and shirt, he said, 'I have dreamt of this, over and over, until it has nearly driven me mad with longing.'

Maggie held her breath as he peeled off his clothes to reveal a broad and solid chest, dusted thickly with dark hair. Heat rushed through her body and pooled expectantly between her legs. She had never seen him naked before, only tantalising slithers of skin, or the feel of him beneath his shirt. She couldn't wait to see all of him.

He prowled towards her, his body eclipsing the light of the softly crackling fire, but compensating for the loss of sight with the warmth of his body. Wantonly, she smoothed her hands up his chest to arch up over his broad shoulders and pull him down to her for a lingering kiss.

She whispered against his lips, 'You don't want to know how many days and nights I have dreamt of having you on top of me…just like this…'

Hawk closed his eyes with a groan, his self-control seeming to snap, because the kiss he gave her was no longer slow and sensual, but filled with carnal passion and longing. Deep and possessive, his hands roamed every inch of her that he could reach. From the red curls on her head, to the back of her now naked knees.

'God, woman! I have imagined taking you in so many places and ways that I fear I have become obsessed.'

Maggie giggled, a little shocked by his confession, but curious all the same. 'Where? Tell me.'

Hawk groaned again, trailing kisses down her face and neck as his eager hands began to unbutton the front of her breeches and shirt. 'I wanted to take you against the bookcase in the study, your arms and legs wrapped around me, your mouth open and panting against mine. I imagined taking you against my desk, bending you forward over the leather top, lifting up your skirts and ploughing into you from behind. Even when I saw you squeezing through that tiny gap in the fence… I wanted to have you. I wanted to slip my fingers between your legs and watch you climax against the climbing flowers…' His hands had worked their magic, and he was now able to slip his hand down beneath her breeches.

She gasped as his fingers began to stroke her intimately; her already wet and eager flesh seemed to throb in answer to his every wicked desire. Something about his confession made her desperately aroused and she longed to hear more. 'I… I wanted you, too. That day when you fell on top of me in the garden. Afterwards, I imagined you lifting up my skirts and…' One of his fingers slipped between her folds and thrust into her. 'Taking me!' she cried out, her back arching, desperate for more.

Hawk hissed a soft curse. 'I can't wait any longer.' His hand slipped from her body and he began to yank at his own breeches, pulling off his clothes in such a rush, she was sure she heard a seam rip.

Not that she cared. She was already tugging off her own shirt and breeches. Not caring that he saw her naked, or if he might not like what he saw…because after his confession, she was more than confident he *did* like her in every single way.

When he rejoined her, he settled between her legs, and with a hot gasp managed to warn her, 'It may hurt a little.'

'I don't care.'

'We can always wait.'

'I don't want to wait.'

Hawk chuckled and began to kiss her deeply until she was begging for him to take her. His manhood was long and thick and it slipped inside her as if it were perfectly made to fit only her. Even the small shock of pain at the loss of her virginity didn't dull her pleasure. She found herself gripping his shoulders and buttocks, urging him to thrust into her with harder and faster strokes, until the tightening she had felt before began to build into such a crescendo that her heels were digging into the mattress and she was crying out his name as waves of pleasure flooded through her.

Hawk followed shortly after, groaning her name into her neck as his own release overwhelmed him.

'I'm going to take you in all of those ways...and more...' he grunted, and it was the sweetest promise she had ever heard.

Later that night, as they lay entangled in the tiny bed of the cottage, Maggie asked softly, 'Do you think there is any hope for Cleo and William?'

Hawk chuckled, and she swatted him on the arm.

'I was only asking!'

'No, that's not it!' He laughed again, pulling her close to kiss her softly before saying with a mischievous smile, 'When I saw him on the road, I told him that if he had any sense, he would travel straight to Castleton and tell my obstinate sister that he loved her, and all her many children, too. Cleo is terrified of being hurt again...that's the real thing holding her back. We're very alike...unfortunately.'

'Do you think he will go?'

Hawk chuckled, the sound deep and rich beneath her ear. 'I should think so. He took the southern road.'

'Och, that's grand! Thank you. I'm so glad to hear there's hope for them.' Maggie leaned up on her elbow to kiss him on the nose. 'And I don't care what you say, or if you think me a dim-witted, hopeless romantic for saying it, but...you *are* my hero.'

Hawk smiled. 'I am afraid you are indeed a hopeless romantic... But it does not matter, because I am hopelessly in love with you.'

Epilogue

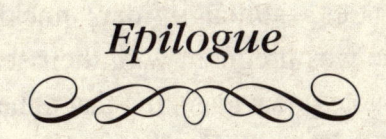

London,
July 1823

'Bloody hell, there's enough children here to fill a school!' said Adam with a laugh as he and his wife, Gwen, joined them on the blankets spread out on the ground. Their son Phillip was with them, too, but he'd been pulled away almost immediately by the others to go and play.

The children all flew around the townhouse garden like an excited swarm of bees, some of them running through the new stone archway that connected the two gardens. After their marriage Cleo had moved into William's house with the boys, allowing more room for Maggie and Hawk to raise their own family.

'There's plenty of room for them to run around. William and Cleo will be back in a minute. They said they needed to go and fetch something,' said Maggie cheerfully as she patted the small space beside her. 'I saved you a spot and some shortbread, Gwen!'

Adam helped Gwen sit down on the ground beside her. Once settled, she gave a relieved sigh and began to rub her ankles—although Adam quickly took over the task. She was pregnant with their second child, her red-and-gold gown matching that of her husband's extravagant waistcoat. 'Thank you. Sorry we're a little late. I had so many shipments to deal with and Adam's been so busy at court with a tricky case, and well, there's just not enough hours in the day!'

Gwen and Adam were now happily married after their initial bumpy start, proof that a marriage of convenience could lead to long-lasting happiness. Their busy lives at Gwen's furniture store and Adam's new career in law only adding to their joy.

'I know what you mean! Oh, were you able to save me a couple of pairs of those matching armchairs—the ones that are designed for both the gentleman and lady of the house?' asked Maggie hopefully.

Gwen laughed. 'Of course! You're one of my best customers. One pair for London and one for your cottage in Scotland, both mahogany and upholstered in Mackenzie tartan. Correct?'

'Wonderful!' Maggie clapped her hands with delight and then impulsively gave her friend a tight squeeze.

Gwen leaned into the embrace, her dark eyes fluttering closed for a moment before opening again, the copper flecks within sparkling in the sunlight. 'Whatever you need, just ask.'

'You're a treasure! Thank you!'

Maggie knew Gwen hadn't had many friends when they'd first met, but now she had plenty and Maggie adored her. She was caring and fun, as well as the owner of the hugely successful Trym's, a magnificent furniture store in the heart of Piccadilly that was doing exceedingly well.

It seemed that with each of their happy marriages, the four brothers in arms had quadrupled their social circle in one season less than seven years ago.

Seraphine leaned forward, juggling her third child, baby Olivia, in her arms while she reached for a pastry. 'How's the extension coming along?'

'I think we're almost done. Thanks for advising on the wall colours—I'm terrible at decor! I'd be lost without you and Gwen helping me!'

Seraphine smiled. 'I'm used to it. I have to make Artington look different every year for the benefit.' She and Ezra had set up the Hart Foundation, and each year there was a benefit ball at Artington that raised money for French emigres who were struggling to find their place in the world.

'And you do a spectacular job, my dearest,' said Ezra, stealing a kiss from her cheek before running off to chase his boys Robert and Marc around the garden.

'Indeed, you do,' agreed Maggie, adding, 'We took

your advice and extended the croft up and towards the back to fit our growing brood. But it still looks as pretty as it did before… Just a little larger. Like me!' She patted her large pregnant belly cheerfully. 'I'm hoping to take the baby there before the first snow fall. I loved spending time there after Mackenzie was born.' She glanced over at her eldest daughter, who, with Charlotte's aid, was currently beating her cousins back with a stick after they'd tried to invade her fort. 'Perhaps…living out there has made her a little too wild…'

'Not at all! In fact, I think she's not wild enough!' declared Hawk, making Maggie chuckle. Hawk could never find fault with their daughter or Maggie for that matter, and kissed her cheek softly in a loving caress.

'I don't know why you have to live so far away! It's damn inconvenient, and has ruined Wednesday Whist at White's,' grumbled Adam.

Hawk laughed. 'Maggie needs to be near our new distillery, and besides, we're always in London for most of the season anyway.'

'It's still not same,' sighed Adam dramatically.

Of course, Adam's expression quickly turned to one of pleasure when his wife suggested, 'Perhaps we could take the children up for our annual holiday?'

'Wonderful idea, darling!'

'Amelia, when you get a moment, I need your advice!' called Hawk, grabbing Ash's wife's attention as she tried and failed to stop one of her twins from jumping off a tree branch. Edward didn't seem bothered by the heavy landing, and immediately sprang up and began chasing his twin sister, Evelyn, while their eldest, Sophie, joined Mackenzie and Charlotte in protecting the fort.

Amelia rolled her eyes at her children's antics and headed back to the picnic blankets. Ash was feeding their youngest, Katherine, some berries, and Amelia sighed good-naturedly at the mess they were making before she sat down. 'I'd welcome the distraction. Ask me anything!'

Hawk shifted closer. 'I want to be sure Maggie's whisky business is well invested. So I might need to sell some stocks. I'd welcome your advice.'

Amelia's smile widened. 'No problem. I'll take a look at your ledgers later.'

'Thank you—as always!'

Amelia had turned out to be the Lord Mortram that Archie had followed to get his family out of debt. After learning the truth, Hawk had done more than shake Amelia's hand; he continued to follow every piece of investment advice she gave, and had even donated one of the Brighton homes to her in thanks.

'But...' said Amelia with a cheeky smile before reaching for a piece of cake. 'I think I should be thanking you this time...for the recent Excise Act? The

Scottish whisky industry is going to go from strength to strength now that's been passed.'

'Let us hope so!' Maggie agreed, raising her lemonade as a toast. *'Slàinte mhath!'*

'Cheers!' chorused everyone else as they also raised their glasses.

'Don't celebrate without us! You haven't got the good stuff yet!' shouted William from the stone archway as he and Cleo entered the garden.

William was carrying a large wooden crate filled with straw, and Cleo lifted up the first batch of Crofter's Glen whisky with its first official and legitimate label.

'I'm also proud to say that our babies are ready!' declared William loudly, lifting up the crate a little.

'What this?' asked Ash, confused as to what they could possibly be bringing them. 'If it's another child, I think we have enough. I've already got four!'

Amelia laughed and smacked his arm playfully.

'It's a bumper crop this year,' William said proudly as he and Cleo joined them. It was clear that his *babies* had done very well.

'How many?' laughed Maggie as she raised herself up onto her knees, trying to peek inside the crate.

'There's one for each family.'

Cleo wrapped her hand around William's arm, which was the only encouragement he needed to give his wife a quick kiss on the cheek. 'You did so well looking after them, Cleo. I was worried the little one was going to perish…but you rallied him through it!'

Maggie beamed happily at them. It had been a slow and sweet courtship, but they had gotten there in the end. Best of all, the boys and Charlotte adored him.

Their guests who didn't know about William's *babies* all leaned forward curiously as he set down the crate.

Laid out on silk embroidered cushions and surrounded by fresh straw were five beautifully ripe…if small…pineapples.

* * * * *

*If you enjoyed this story,
make sure to read the previous books in the
A Season to Wed miniseries*

Only an Heiress Will Do *by Virginia Heath*
The Viscount's Forbidden Flirtation *by Sarah Rodi*
Their Second Chance Season *by Ella Matthews*

*And why not read Lucy Morris's
previous captivating historical romances?*

Snowed In with the Viking
"Her Bought Viking Husband"
in Convenient Vows with a Viking
How the Wallflower Wins a Duke

MILLS & BOON®

Coming next month

HASTILY WED TO THE DUKE
Sadie King

Book 3 in the Regency Secrets & Lies series

'Is that what you want, Miss Pearson—to remain with your mother and aunt here, in Kelda?'

Charlotte shook her head vigorously. 'It does not matter what I want.'

'Of course it matters.' The Duke stepped closer to her. 'What do you want?'

'I want to escape!'

No sooner had the words fallen from her lips than Charlotte wished she could take them back. Wished she could tick back the minutes so that this conversation might never have happened. But it was too late—the words were spoken now. She'd given voice to them, breathed life into them. She felt them hang heavily in the air between her and the Duke as his eyes searched hers and found that they were the truth.

'Forgive me, Your Grace,' she began, shaking her head at herself. 'My mother can be difficult to live with at times, and I think my spirits are just a little low tonight, so I...'

'Marry me.'

The Duke said the words so quickly that for a moment Charlotte believed she must have misheard him. Indeed, what other possible explanation could there be? There was no conceivable way that Edward Scott, the Duke of Falstone, had just asked for her hand in marriage...

'Marry me, Miss Pearson,' he said again, taking a tentative step towards her.

Charlotte felt her mouth fall open. This time there was no denying what she had heard. 'But...why?' she stuttered.

The Duke shrugged. 'You need to escape, and I need a wife,' he replied simply, as though it was the most logical idea in the world.

Continue reading

HASTILY WED TO THE DUKE
Sadie King

Available next month
millsandboon.co.uk

Copyright © 2025 Sarah Louise King

COMING SOON!

We really hope you enjoyed reading this book. If you're looking for more romance be sure to head to the shops when new books are available on

Thursday 19th June

To see which titles are coming soon, please visit
millsandboon.co.uk/nextmonth

MILLS & BOON

FOUR BRAND NEW BOOKS FROM
MILLS & BOON MODERN

The same great stories you love, a stylish new look!

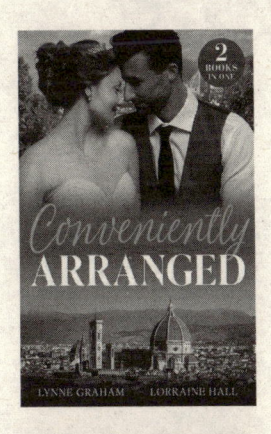

Conveniently ARRANGED — LYNNE GRAHAM & LORRAINE HALL

WANTED: HIS HEIR — MAYA BLAKE & DANI COLLINS

DEFIANT Brides — Tara Pammi & Michelle Smart

THE BILLIONAIRE'S LEGACY — ABBY GREEN & NATALIE ANDERSON

OUT NOW

Eight Modern stories published every month, find them all at:

millsandboon.co.uk

LET'S TALK
Romance

For exclusive extracts, competitions and special offers, find us online:

- **f** MillsandBoon
- **X** @MillsandBoon
- **O** @MillsandBoonUK
- **d** @MillsandBoonUK

Get in touch on 01413 063 232

> For all the latest titles coming soon, visit
> millsandboon.co.uk/nextmonth